EXIT BLACK

BOOKS BY JOE PITKIN

Exit Black

Stranger Bird

The Year's Best Science Fiction:
Thirty-Third Annual Collection
(contributing author)

The Year's Best Science Fiction & Fantasy 2013
(contributing author)

Ergosphere: Astounding New Tales from M-Brane SF
(contributing author)

EXIT BLACK

JOE PITKIN

BLACK STONE
PUBLISHING

Copyright © 2024 by Tower Way
Based on a concept by Scott Veltri and Brendan Deneen
Published in 2024 by Blackstone Publishing
Cover and book design by Luis Alejandro Cruz Castillo
Map illustrated by Joe Garcia

The characters and events in this book are fictitious.
Any similarity to real persons, living or dead, is coincidental
and not intended by the author.

Printed in the United States of America

First edition: 2024
ISBN 979-8-212-63102-0
Fiction / Science Fiction / General

Version 1

Blackstone Publishing
31 Mistletoe Rd.
Ashland, OR 97520

www.BlackstonePublishing.com

For Carlyn

IMPERIUM

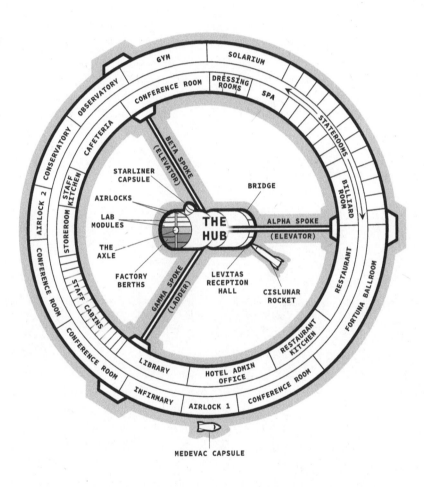

GYM

SOLARIUM

OBSERVATORY

CONFERENCE ROOM

DRESSING ROOMS

SPA

CONSERVATORY

CAFETERIA

STATEROOMS

AIRLOCK 2

STAFF KITCHEN

STOREROOM

BETA SPOKE (ELEVATOR)

STARLINER CAPSULE

BRIDGE

BILLIARD ROOM

AIRLOCKS

THE HUB

ALPHA SPOKE (ELEVATOR)

LAB MODULES

CONFERENCE ROOM

THE AXLE

STAFF CABINS

FACTORY BERTHS

GAMMA SPOKE (LADDER)

LEVITAS RECEPTION HALL

CISLUNAR ROCKET

RESTAURANT

FORTUNA BALLROOM

CONFERENCE ROOM

LIBRARY

HOTEL ADMIN OFFICE

RESTAURANT KITCHEN

INFIRMARY

AIRLOCK 1

CONFERENCE ROOM

MEDEVAC CAPSULE

PROLOGUE

Chloe assessed the damage. Her left ear was ringing: even as the sounds around her leaked away to a tinny little whisper, she felt she could still hear the blow to the side of her head. The left side of her chest labored curiously—broken ribs, maybe. But it was her right hand that troubled her, her immovable fingers, the ballooning numbness in the glove of her suit that she knew would sooner or later give way to a miserable aching. "You're okay . . . Breathe," she whispered to herself, in that calm voice that she might use with a child, hollow and distant inside her helmet. Her mind dropped at length into that animal serenity that sits at the heart of all violence.

The lights had gone out. Only a dim glow from far down the corridor bled into the cafeteria. The emergency claxons kept up their distant bleating, as though their warning were for the benefit of someone else. She felt around her for the leg of a chair, pulled herself gingerly, swayingly, to her feet.

She felt her way to the swinging door that connected the cafeteria and the kitchen. She could feel the door's gentle puffing out against her hand as the air within the kitchen was slowly sucked toward whatever new hull breach the claxons were announcing.

She passed through into the pitch black of the kitchen. The lights had probably shorted out here as well—she wasn't about to check. She groped her way toward a hiding place. Above her, she remembered, hung the magnetized rack of knives—she reached for the rack with her good hand. Her glove passed over the slim blade of a boning knife. She took it up and lurched the last few steps to the edge of the stove. She crouched in the space between the stove and the butcher block, holding the knife out before her like a tiny stinger. The noise of the claxons had diminished almost to nothing now—there must be little atmosphere left in this section of the ring, she thought.

She did not hear the swinging door of the kitchen as it opened again. Rather, she registered the man's entry only as a faint infiltration of a distant gray light from beyond the kitchen.

Then the darkness prevailed again. He had had no reason not to try the light switch; Chloe surmised that the lights were shorted out here too. She wished that she had taken a position from which she could fight: crouched on the floor as she was, the best she could do would be to punch out with the knife while he stood above her. She might stick him once before he put a bullet in her head.

She heard, or more likely felt through the floor, his slow, stumbling steps into the kitchen, like the staggering of a drunkard. She prepared herself for one last moment; in her awareness, he stood perhaps two meters away, perhaps less.

With a kind of mindless desperation, like the stinging instinct of a bee, Chloe punched out in front of her with the knife.

CHAPTER ONE

TWENTY-FOUR HOURS EARLIER

Chloe floated within the spinning hub of the great wheel. For an hour she had been floating. She had woken that morning in her cabin at the slender distant rim of *Imperium*, had walked in the rim's simulated gravity along the curve of the central corridor toward gamma spoke.

From there she had climbed the ladder away from the edge of the station, away from the centrifugal force pressing down on her with nearly one g. As she climbed the first hundred rungs, she had felt her weight slipping away like a fog, boiling off to almost nothing. After the hundredth rung, she had become weightless enough to launch herself with her hands farther up the long cylinder of the wheel's spoke. She had risen like a phantom toward the hub.

Here was the inner sanctum: the bridge, the laboratories. Here the factories would be someday. Here was the Axle around which the wheel of *Imperium* rotated.

But even an inner sanctum needs to be vacuumed. Chloe drifted across the maintenance module. She popped in her earbuds, fired up her cleaning playlist. For one with such an omnivorous taste in music, she had spiraled in on a single brief period of musical history during her time in orbit: Nirvana, Soundgarden, Pearl Jam, and their antecedents, all those ragged, jagged sounds of childhood bouncing off the blank white walls of the station with her.

The Pixies came on loud, then quiet, then loud again, the grave, cool equilibrium of Kim Deal's bass punctuated by momentary eruptions of Joey Santiago's open chords. *And if the devil is six, then God is seven, then God is seven, then God is seven. This monkey's gone to heaven . . .* She launched herself up the module as though propelled by the screaming of Black Francis. The bill of her baseball cap clipped the edge of the bulkhead as she sped by; she spun the long-suffering, salt-rimed cap around on her head. The goofy, bucktoothed grin of the old Oregon State University beaver looked out like a pair of eyes from the back of her head.

Chloe was daydreaming: A memory came to her of long-ago fieldwork, the Dark Divide of the Gifford Pinchot, her still, insomniac hours, the nightjars calling about her in the false dawn. She had stared up at the spray of stars in her insomnia when she saw it: a long golden streak of a meteor, hanging silent in the sky longer than she had ever known a shooting star to do.

Chloe was not one, typically, to daydream. The water-recycler filters needed changing, and well before the CisLunar rocket arrived, she would swap them out. It had occurred to her many times before that whatever space station would follow in the generation after *Imperium*, it would maintain every life-support system without human intervention, an inexhaustible ballet of computer scripts and robotic arms, untroubled by daydreams.

But Chloe was not a robotic arm, and the filters of *Imperium* still needed human hands to replace them. Chloe drifted, remembering the golden trail of the shooting star, while she pulled each filter out of its slot.

"Good morning, Professor." Konrad's voice came over her earbuds. "Ready to roll out the red carpet?"

"I guess I could do more to get myself spiritually ready," Chloe replied into her mic. "Where are you?"

"Dion and I just finished vacuuming lab one. It would be nice to get the labs done before guests start arriving."

Chloe was pulled back to that feeling, stitched together from scraps of childhood memory, of being imposed upon to get the house ready for a party. Back when parties were entirely her mother's idea, at an age—Chloe remembered herself as eight years old in this feeling—when a party meant only a house full of drunken guests and strange kids messing around with the stuff in her room.

"Roger that, Konrad. Are any of the hotel staff on this channel?" She realized, as soon as she said it, that in a way everyone on *Imperium* was hotel staff. But she didn't think of Konrad that way, or Dion, either, even though Dion was just as new up here as the hotel staff. Konrad and Dion were like her—the kind of crew that would be here long after the guests had gone home.

"Good question," Konrad responded. "Erik? Tirzah? Any OrbitalVentures folks on channel one?"

"Good morning, Konrad," Tirzah answered back. "Lorenz and I are on this channel."

"Anything you need us to do before the reception?"

"I think we have things pretty well in hand over here. We'll try to keep our guests from wandering off into your labs."

Chloe was able at last to put her finger on her distaste for Tirzah. Chloe wasn't angry, as she had once thought, that Tirzah was a usurper, the suddenly arrived alpha wolf on the station. Nor was it that this woman, with her made-up title,

Vice President of Guest Experience, symbolized that *Imperium* really was, down at the level of profit curves and budgets, just a fancy-ass hotel in the void of low Earth orbit. Rather, Chloe realized that there was a sunny, carefree quality to Tirzah's tone that pretended that they were all equals on *Imperium*, when the very presence of the new company people up here illuminated a social ladder that had Konrad, Dion, maybe even Chloe herself, on the bottom rung.

"Roger that, Tirzah," Konrad said. "We'll see you at fourteen hundred hours in the Levitas Reception Hall."

Chloe had to admit that she had plenty of time to get her chores done before the CisLunar ship docked. Switching out the water-recycler filters, vacuuming the labs, checking in on the germination rates in her growth chambers—she could take care of all of those before Tirzah and her minions expected her to stand at attention in the glorified airlock called Levitas Reception Hall, dressed up like a page in her blue-and-gold OrbitalVentures Corporation jumpsuit.

Chloe swam through her maintenance routines before launching herself back up the access hall to the lab modules and her own work. The other labs had been empty since March, when Kamara and Zhou locked up their anaerobic digesters in lab three and headed home. There would be more someday, Chloe knew. OrbitalVentures would be leasing lab four to a Penn State team again; ESA was sending another team up on a CisLunar rocket in two months; eventually Tsinghua would be sending another nanomaterials group. The lab residencies on *Imperium* had always been two steps forward, one step back, ever since the station had opened. Maybe it was more like one step forward, two steps back.

To Chloe, the empty lab modules felt like the lonely, labyrinthine heart of a mansion, of no concern to anyone except her, as she glided through the darkened corridors like a ghostly housekeeper. That was just a feeling, of course, brought on by the darkness and solitude of the lab wing: she knew that the thoughts of the OrbitalVentures people must return to the hub many times a day. The Starliner capsule that had brought the last of them was docked to the hub, off lab module two. It would be hard for them not to think about their only ride home (excepting the medevac capsule, which the hotel types might not want to contemplate having to use). For now, though, nobody moved through the labs besides Chloe. She glided into the long hall of her dim lab space without bringing up the lights—there was enough streaming out of the windows of the growth chambers to see by. Within, the BRIC-X planter units were lined up under the artificial sunlight, each rank an iteration of Chloe's work, her attempt to emulate a gravitropic response in radicles that had germinated in the absence of gravity. She could just make out a few of the beans within, pale as strange little thumbs behind the plexiglass of their BRIC-X and the porthole of the growth chamber.

On the lab console, Chloe pulled up the spreadsheet where she kept her data on germination rates, angles of gravitropic emulation, the diameter of each radicle. She pecked at the keyboard to drop new data points into each cell. It was the kind of clerical work that would have gone to some poor, overworked undergrad if this had been a phytology lab back at Oregon State. Not that Chloe had ever felt that this kind of work—or any kind of work, really—was beneath her. Rather, she reflected fleetingly, as she had on hundreds of mornings before, that she was at this moment the most expensive bureaucrat in the history of humanity.

Tirzah's voice came in over Chloe's earbuds. "Are you ready to join us in the reception hall, Doctor?"

Chloe let out a weary exhalation, inaudible over the communicators. At least she hoped it was inaudible. "Just finishing up some data entry, Ms. Fowler. I'll get dressed and be over there at fourteen hundred." Actually, Chloe had finished up the day's data entry a half hour ago. Since then she had been sifting through data points with a kind of improvisational joy, like a session musician noodling out explorations on a guitar, as she sorted data in the columns, contemplating the outliers, double-checking her entries, imagining the dimensions by which the numerals mapped onto the tiny living things she measured.

She closed up the spreadsheet, closed up the station system apps on her laptop, closed up her laptop. As she launched herself out of the lab and toward the spoke that led to her cabin, she tried once again to empathize with Vice President of Guest Experience Tirzah Fowler. They were, after all, just two women trying to get their jobs done. Chloe didn't think that babysitting a passel of space glampers was much of a job. Then again, maybe observing the behavior of bean roots in zero gravity didn't seem like much of a job to Tirzah. *Be friendly*, Chloe imagined her mother scolding her, as though Chloe were once again a shy little girl.

She dove along the Axle, the corridor that ran the length of the hub of *Imperium*, the cylindrical heart of the station that connected zero-g lab modules, spaceship docks, the bridge, the planned factory bays. The three slender spindles of the wheel of *Imperium*, like bicycle spokes of fabulous strength, formed three long passages from the center of the Axle where Chloe glided, connecting the hub with the glittering chambers on the rim of the station: the staterooms of the guests, the Fortuna Ballroom, the solarium, the glittering observation cupola.

She made her way down gamma spoke toward the rim, toward its slow carousel simulation of gravity. As she descended

the rungs of the ladder, floating past one of the brief discon-
tinuities in the rungs where a circular hatch could close like a
sphincter in case of a decompression event, the perception of
weight grew bit by bit upon her, as though she were a phantom
taking solid form. Chloe had been assigned a cabin not far from
where gamma spoke opened out onto the rim, next to Konrad's
and Dion's cabins, in the same section as the galley and store-
rooms. She dropped down the last two rungs of the ladder to
the floor of the rim with the whispered thump of a footpad.

The sliding door of her cabin didn't open. It took Chloe a
couple of seconds to comprehend that once again she had forgotten to clip her key fob to her jumpsuit this morning. The
introduction of the key fobs to *Imperium* was, she realized, one
of the reasons she so disliked Tirzah Fowler. Before the hotel
staff had arrived, earlier in the year, when the station housed
only a few researchers and crew, nobody had locked anything.
That had been the golden age, Chloe understood only in retrospect. Now everyone had key permissions and fobs and swipes,
just like at any Marriott.

She wasn't about to embarrass herself, admitting again over
the communicators that she had forgotten her key fob. She
walked up the main ring corridor a little way to the hotel administration office.

The door to the administration office, she couldn't help no-
ticing, was wide open. More accurately, the security hatch to
the office was open, hotel administration being, like the bridge,
a space that could be sealed off completely during decompression, just like sections of the spokes, sections of the main rim
corridor, the hub itself. Chloe walked in, hoping that she wasn't
going to have to explain herself to Tirzah Fowler.

The only one behind the desk was Maryam, that eternally
chipper songbird of a person who had come with the last launch

of hotel crew. Chloe gave her an uncharacteristically warm smile, as much from relief as anything. "Maryam, love, I'm afraid I've forgotten my key fob again."

Maryam had the look of an eager, earnest college intern, though Chloe suspected she was older than she looked. "No worries, Chloe—I've got you."

Maryam led her back to Chloe's cabin, swiped her in with whatever universal fob had been given to hotel employees. "I wish I could say this is the last time I'll forget," Chloe said.

"Come back anytime, Chloe. Old habits die hard."

Chloe's cabin was as narrow as a freshman's dorm room, and nearly as spartan. At least she had the luxury of a double bed. There were palatial staterooms for the high rollers, the paying guests. But, Chloe reminded herself, every window on *Imperium* looked out over the Earth the same number of times every hour.

She shucked herself out of her work jumpsuit, splashed through a quick shower, zipped herself into the dress uniform. She had to admit that the uniforms looked smart: they had a kind of retro space-age charm, as though she worked aboard a rocket of swooping curves designed by Eero Saarinen. Her suit was a sleek-fitting high-end spandex, the blue of the western sky at nautical twilight, with the insignia of the OrbitalVentures Corporation on her left breast. The insignia itself took the shape of a teardrop, or an aerodynamic golden fender of a 1937 Talbot-Lago.

Chloe slipped on her soft-soled blue slippers, attached her access fob—also a teardrop—to her waist, gave one last check to the tightness of her braids under her cap. The thick black ropes of her hair would have been worn the same way by her grandmother or, for that matter, by an ancestor of two thousand years ago.

The quickest way back to the hub and the Levitas Reception

Hall would have been the way she had come. But—whether to satisfy some truant urge or because she wanted a final moment of luxury in the absence of the coming guests—Chloe strolled nearly two-thirds of the circumference of the rim, over four hundred meters, clockwise past the gym and observation decks, the spa, the billiard room, the conservatory, the grand staterooms, to alpha spoke.

Alpha and beta spokes housed the elevators. Chloe preferred the ladder of gamma spoke, liked the tactile reality of the rungs on her hands and feet offering differing amounts of pressure as she climbed and descended. Alpha spoke stood in the middle of the rim's main corridor like a stout pillar. Then the doors parted for her, and all around Chloe saw the vision of Olivia Fauré, the reclusive designer that OrbitalVentures had paid a million dollars to design the sections of *Imperium* that guests would see. The walls of the elevator car were upholstered in luminous blue satin, padded as though to suggest some genre of biological tissue, as though Chloe were ascending through the esophagus of a sleeping arctic dragon. The handholds, which she grasped as she ascended into weightlessness, were the slender outlines of teardrops, the insignia of OrbitalVentures Corporation always visible, worked in aluminum and upholstered in gold leather. A soft light bathed the elevator from many angles, reflected everywhere.

Chloe glided into the Levitas Reception Hall at 1354. She could see as soon as she entered that she was the last of the crew to arrive. "Ah, Professor," announced Tirzah with a kind of manic brightness. She was tall and pale and lithe, her red hair upswept with an architectural precision and a great deal of hair spray. Her black jumpsuit opened at the top to reveal what looked like a linen oxford shirt and an OrbitalVentures blue silk necktie. "I think we're all here. Let's have you over here with

Captain Whittaker and Commander Stubblefield. The hotel
team will form up on this side."

The hotel team seemed to refer to the fourteen underlings
who had arrived on three Starliner flights over the last several weeks. Erik, Assistant Vice President of Guest Experience;
Lorenz, Administrative Assistant to the Vice President of Guest
Experience; Nina, Administrative Assistant to the Assistant Vice
President of Guest Experience; Maryam . . . Chloe had no idea
what Maryam did. For that matter, she was unclear what the
other ten did as well, or even their names. She supposed they
were cooks and housekeepers.

During the hour that Chloe had been in the lab, Konrad and
Dion had taken up their posts on the bridge of *Imperium*, walking through the rendezvous protocol with the CisLunar rocket
that ferried their guests. Now that the ship had docked and the
air pressures of ship and station had been equalized, they could
stand at attention, to the extent that anyone stands in zero gravity, anchoring themselves by the gracefully curved handholds.

"Oh, and Chloe?" Tirzah added. "Please lose the hat."

Chloe had to admit that this was probably sound fashion
advice. That sun-bleached cap had never left her head during
field season; Hellmund had bought it for her back when she
took the OSU job. Four years of sweat and dust had stiffened
it so that it folded up almost like a wallet, which she slipped
into the slim hip pocket of her jumpsuit.

Chloe had a fleeting impulse to make a joke about getting
to stand by the two hotties, an urge she abandoned as soon as
she was aware of it. Too many ways for such a remark to land
badly. Konrad and Dion wouldn't care, of course, and neither
of them would get the wrong idea, but still—this moment in
the Levitas Reception Hall seemed an uncommonly humorless
time and place.

"Are we . . . supposed to bow when they come in?" Chloe whispered.

Dion snorted quietly, perhaps taking for a joke what had been a serious question. He leaned over and whispered back: "It might make them feel more at home if we were to bow." He gave her a conspiratorial nod that made her wonder if he was flirting with her: "But bowing isn't really our style, is it?"

Nina touched some button on the screen of the tablet she held, and the foyer filled with a curious sequence of ringing tones, what Chloe imagined she might hear in some heavenly orthodontist's office. It was Brian Eno's *Music for Airports*. Chloe was reminded of the discussion that had occurred months before, back when Tirzah Fowler was still in California, about the music that would be played during the guests' arrival in the Levitas Reception Hall. She couldn't remember who at OrbitalVentures had been so adamant about having a live string quartet aboard during the arrival—someone Tirzah was carrying water for. She remembered Dion's patient explanation of the challenges presented by four musicians playing stringed instruments in zero gravity, drifting around like four priceless wooden billiard balls. Olivia Fauré, patched into the call from France, had suggested a recording of Brian Eno.

The hatch opened. Chloe could see the leather upholstery of the rocket cabin beyond. Just behind the hatch stood a man from the CisLunar Spaceways crew in what looked like a pleather jumpsuit the color of raw beef. Anchoring himself to a handhold on the other side of the hatch, with his free arm he guided the first of the guests along with the same fluid swinging motion he might use to push a child around a merry-go-round.

The first guest glided in wearing the heavy CisLunar flight suit. He was a wiry, handsome man with angular features, the face of a weary forty-year-old or a well-conserved sixty-year-old.

Like a butler of an ancient hall, Nina announced him in a sonorous Oxbridge accent: "Mr. Zhiming Li."

Chloe discovered that Li was both shorter and more handsome than she had been led to believe from the many photographs she had seen. In most news photos, the founder, CEO, and principal stockholder of Xia Enterprises bore a kind of disdainful grimace, as though he couldn't believe the stupidity of the people he was dealing with. Now that she could compare the pictures with the man in the flesh, it occurred to Chloe that these photos might have been intended to communicate something about Xia Enterprises to the public. Li's face as he entered *Imperium* betrayed an unguarded joy unlike any of the photos Chloe had seen of the man: he looked around the Levitas Reception Hall like a bookish child inspecting the Rosetta Stone at the British Museum.

Now came the dreariness of the introductions, the nodded greetings and floating bows. Yet Chloe had to admit to herself that Tirzah Fowler was quite skillful at shepherding Li in weightlessness around the hall. Tirzah introduced Li to Chloe with an eager chirp: "And here we have *Imperium*'s resident scientist, Dr. Bonilla."

"No formalities," Chloe said, nodding decorously. "Please call me Chloe."

Li nodded a smart bow but did not attempt Chloe's name. Chloe couldn't remember how much English Li spoke—she thought she had read that one of the guests spoke a little. Li seemed to attend to Tirzah's ministrations with a steely intensity.

And at any rate, Tirzah quickly handed Li off to Maryam, before Chloe could have asked even an empty question about Li's flight. Maryam guided the man through the circular portal toward the Axle, and from there, Chloe assumed, to the gleaming elevator of alpha spoke.

As Chloe watched him recede up the access corridor to the Axle, Nina announced the entry of the next guests: "Nicholas and Samir Winters-Qureshi."

The pair of angel investors floated in, shining with that apollonian beauty common to Californians at the apex of their earnings curve. Chloe searched out Samir's lamb eyes as though she might receive some oracular insight there. But his smile right now, like his husband's, seemed surprised more than anything, as though being among the first tourists to spend two weeks in low Earth orbit were a sweepstakes they had just won. If an OrbitalVentures publicist was nearby (which, for all Chloe knew, Maryam or one of the others might be), the childlike looks on Nicholas's and Samir's faces would serve as a fitting advertisement for *Imperium* among the hotel's target demographic. Of course, the target demographic for *Imperium* needed no advertisements at all.

Again the introductions. Chloe opened her mouth to ask them how their flight had been, but Nicholas jumped in before she could inhale. "How long did it take you to get used to weightlessness?"

The honest answer was that one never fully gets used to it, that humans are not evolved for weightlessness. But the tone of Nicholas's question was so bright and sunny, as though they were all sitting poolside in Palm Springs and he was asking her what she was drinking, that she said instead, "It gets a lot easier after a couple of days." This was also true, somewhat.

The one she really wanted to talk with was exquisitely beautiful Samir. She wasn't sure exactly what she wanted to ask him: something about his feelings, his loves—what had he felt when he had almost single-handedly financed the eradication of African sleeping sickness? But all that she could think of when faced with him was, "I hope that you love it here," the banal standing in for every meaningful thing she wanted to ask.

And before either man could open his mouth again, Tirzah spirited them away toward Maryam, who had just reappeared in the circular hatchway. Like a clock chime set in motion by a spring, Nina announced the entry of the next guest: "Sir Alexander Dunne."

Chloe had studied even more photos of Sir Alexander Dunne than she had of Li. The laugh lines around his eyes, the creases across his forehead, made him seem perpetually on the verge of guffawing. His hair had taken to weightlessness by doing what it always seemed to be doing in photos, only more so: flying out like a child's homemade mane on a Halloween costume of a lion. There was no gray in his hair, which seemed so garishly ginger that it couldn't possibly have been dyed that way on purpose.

Sir Alexander shook everyone's hand in the old, pre-COVID style, with the kind of gentle, searching eye contact that one would expect him to display on a visit to a children's hospital or a nursing home. He leaned in, as though sharing a confidence, with Tirzah, then with Erik, then with Konrad.

Once again it fell to Chloe to insist that Sir Alexander needn't call her Dr. Bonilla. "And what are you a doctor of?" Sir Alexander asked, arching a wisp of eyebrow.

Plant phenology. Applied genetics. Ecological stoichiometry. For audiences of a certain type, she had at the ready a stock of such terms for what she did. But Sir Alexander Dunne—and indeed everyone else on *Imperium*—was not the type. "I'm a botanist," she said. Sir Alexander gave an appreciative little gasp that seemed to Chloe both a little flirtatious and a bit lazy—he would have gasped the same way if he'd just learned she was an insurance adjuster or a pipe fitter.

"How did you enjoy your second trip into orbit?" Chloe asked.

"Ah, you remember the first one," Sir Alexander chuckled.

Just about anyone who had watched YouTube in the last four years—which is to say just about everyone on Earth—remembered Sir Alexander Dunne's first space journey. While riding in orbit on one of the space planes of his own spaceflight start-up, Hesperus, he had given the world an object lesson in the consequences of drinking champagne in zero gravity. Carbon dioxide precipitates out of fizzy drinks differently in space: *wet burps*, NASA people had called them back in the day. The video of Sir Alexander's orbital puking was still the sixth-most-viewed clip in the history of YouTube.

"I admire your grit for coming back into orbit," Chloe said.

"I suppose I am quite gritty," he responded in a strangely high voice that might have been an affectation. But whatever else he had hoped to say just then was interrupted by Nina's announcement of the next guest, a name Chloe didn't hear.

As Maryam (who had just returned to the Levitas Reception Hall) whisked the sandblasted Sir Alexander toward the elevator and the staterooms, Chloe whispered to Dion: "Wait— who just arrived?"

"Seriously, Chloe? That's Viv Volterra."

The woman looked as though she were meeting a date at a wine bar. Of all the guests, Volterra was the first (and, Chloe would realize later, the only one) to have found some way to accessorize her raw-meat-colored flight suit: at some point during the long wait of airlock pressurization, she had produced an old-fashioned white silk aviator's scarf, which she wore with a nonchalance complemented by the effect of zero gravity on the shimmering fabric. Volterra was more odd looking than what Chloe would have called pretty: she had a long, almost imperceptibly lopsided face that gave the impression of a mountain whose layers had undergone a slow geological deformation. Yet the scarf accomplished something that the flawless beauty of the Winters-Qureshis had failed to: Volterra looked interesting.

Chloe knew that *Imperium* would be full of guests who had gamed the system, or who had caught a fantastically lucky break, people who had dropped out of Harvard or Stanford to strike it rich selling genomic testing, or nanotech snake oil, or simply gossamer images of themselves on social media. But even in this parade of hucksters, Viv Volterra had the look of a woman on the make: a sphinx's smile, impossible to stare down, concealing more than it revealed. On second thought, Chloe realized when they greeted one another, Volterra was indeed very pretty. She was a creature whose terrible beauty would outlast that of the others; she would still be beautiful when *Imperium* grew old and stale and OrbitalVentures dropped it from orbit and cast it into the sea.

"I've read a lot about you," Volterra said. There was gravel in her voice that Chloe hadn't expected.

"I find that hard to believe," Chloe answered. She regretted her sass as soon as it came out of her mouth. But she was sure that Volterra was bullshitting her: not many people follow the lives of plant physiologists specializing in gravitropism.

If Volterra was offended, though, she masked it. "So this is *Imperium*," she said with a sage nod. "Looks like a real shithole."

A long, mortifying moment passed before Chloe realized that Volterra was joking. In a giddy panic, Chloe followed up from her impoverished store of stock questions: "How was your flight?"

"What can one say about the g's at the end?" Volterra said.

Chloe commiserated with the well-rehearsed story of her own liftoff, which chased off the questions she really wanted to ask: *Are you running from the feds? Are you planning on staying up here somehow? Is this trip a last hurrah before you are indicted?*

Out of the corner of her eye, Chloe noticed Tirzah take Volterra's arm gently, as she had with Li and Sir Alexander and the Winters-Qureshis, on their slow, drifting circuit around the reception hall. It dawned on Chloe as she told her story that Tirzah was playing for time with these introductions. Maryam needed time, Chloe supposed, to accompany Sir Alexander down the alpha spoke elevator to his stateroom on the rim. That elevator could hold at least ten people at once. But the guests hadn't paid so much money to be crammed into an elevator with one another.

But soon enough, Maryam had returned from ensconcing Sir Alexander in his stateroom, and she reappeared to lead Volterra down the silken sapphire-lit corridor.

As though she were a clock chiming the hour, Nina intoned the names of the next guests: "Mr. and Mrs. Roger and Jessica Van Cleave."

The next guests floated into the Levitas Reception Hall as serenely as angels. The couple seemed even younger now, or more ageless, than they had seemed in the *Vanity Fair* photo spread that had chronicled their $10 million *Star Trek*–themed wedding on Kwajalein Atoll. They had accomplished through tanning of one kind or another an imagined median skin tone for the human race, a gold of freshly baked bread. Their smiles suggested—or so Chloe imagined—their beatific satisfaction with all the arrangements on Earth and in heaven. It had cost the two of them $164 million for two weeks on *Imperium*. They were on their honeymoon.

"This is awesome," Roger exclaimed as they were introduced to Chloe. Chloe wondered whether his pronouncement referred to *Imperium*, to the couple's first spaceflight, to the weird mélange of formality and farce in a zero-gravity receiving line. Perhaps he was speaking about the universe in general.

Chloe decided to leave that question a mystery. Instead

she followed her safest line of questioning: she asked how their flight had gone.

"Just like sitting in an airplane," Roger replied.

This was not the way that Chloe would have described her own experiences with spaceflight. Still, she wasn't especially interested in the ways that Roger Van Cleave's experience differed from hers. She turned instead to Jessica Van Cleave: "And how did you like the flight?"

Jessica Van Cleave took in the question as though she were watching an iridescent hummingbird that hovered in front of her. She opened her mouth to answer, but just then Maryam reentered the Levitas Reception Hall and Nina announced the last of the guests.

"Ms. Kassandra Ng."

Jessica Van Cleave nodded a smiling acknowledgment that the conversation was over, and Maryam drew them off toward the elevator as Chloe tugged on her handhold to turn her attention to the new arrival.

Chloe had watched a handful of Kassie Ng's YouTube videos in anticipation of her visit. She seemed somewhat less perky in person, a short, skinny twenty-six-year-old in an ill-fitting Cis-Lunar flight suit. Her skin looked a little gray; her waxy smile reminded Chloe of a person coming out of anesthesia. Kassie hadn't paid her own way, Chloe knew: Konrad and Dion had joked that the girl's flight suit would be plastered with sponsors' decals as though she were a NASCAR driver. Following Kassie Ng's Instagram feed of fashion tips and pet hedgehogs and makeup tutorials had confirmed for Chloe her suspicion that Instagram was a waste of time. "Twelve million Instagram followers can't be wrong," Konrad had said, to which Chloe had replied that of course they could, that all kinds of horrible people had twelve million followers.

"Does your head feel full of snot the whole time you're up here?" Kassie said as they were introduced.

"Yep—so long as you are in zero g."

"Do you ever get used to it?"

The correct answer was *not really*. However, Chloe had received some training from the OrbitalVentures people on responding to such questions diplomatically. "It takes a while, but you'll get the hang of it."

"Your head will feel a lot more normal after you move out to the rim," she continued. "Centrifugal force gives us the equivalent of .85 g out there."

Kassie asked whether Chloe had met Olivia Fauré. Then she asked about the air pressure inside *Imperium*.

Chloe was still explaining the oxygen cycling of the station when Maryam reentered. Kassie seemed to notice the arrival before Chloe did.

"In some ways I'm more curious about the rim g's," Kassie said as Tirzah drew her away.

"About what?"

"The .85 g. That actually sounds more interesting than zero g."

Chloe wasn't sure what to make of such a remark—she suspected that nobody in the history of space travel had come in hopes of experiencing .85 g.

"I look forward to asking you about your research," Kassie called out as she left the Levitas Reception Hall.

Oh, my research isn't worth talking about, Chloe felt like answering. But she kept that to herself.

CHAPTER TWO

"There are some ways that a party is lonelier than working by yourself in the lab," Hellmund said from her laptop screen.

As had often happened over the course of their relationship, he seemed to express exactly the feeling Chloe had been trying to articulate, even as the longer arc of the conversation suggested that he was missing her point entirely.

It was true that while watching her beans grow over the last months, reading new papers, sometimes reading old papers from botanists long dead, shooting off emails to living colleagues, holding imagined conversations with long-dead ancestors of her discipline—Mayr and Dobzhansky, Morgan and Mendel, Darwin and Wallace, all the way back to John Ray and those parson-naturalists tending flowers outside their rectories—Chloe had never felt alone with her growth chambers and seedlings. But that had not been the real matter she was trying to express to Hellmund.

She stared at the image of herself in the square next to his, her long hair pulled back under that weather-beaten ball cap. "I guess I always assumed you'd be at the first guest party," Chloe finally, after all her many indirections, managed to say. She understood then, at last, that she had nursed a hope, right up until the CisLunar rocket docked with the station and disgorged the guests, that Hellmund would step off that rocket into the Levitas Reception Hall as a romantic surprise.

"Oh, Chlo," he sighed, as though her name weighed a great deal in his mind. "You know that I would be there. I would." She couldn't tell from the angle of Hellmund's webcam whether he was in one of the OrbitalVentures offices; it looked almost as though he was connecting from one of the white stuccoed rooms of his basement.

"What came up down here I would much rather have avoided," he said. It was the fourth or fifth time he had had this conversation with her; Chloe was familiar enough with the explanation that she didn't labor over his convoluted wording or even attend to it. "I can't hand off this negotiation to anyone else; I need to be down here."

"Anyway, the opening gala's not really my kind of scene," he added.

"Ron, what other kind of scene would it be? You sent Tirzah up here, but you can't show up to your own opening gala?"

"Look, as much as I want to be with you right now, this gala isn't just some party. It's the company's meal ticket. Your meal ticket, too: all those tech bros up there are subsidizing the station's labs. Tirzah's the right person for the gala job. She has hosting skills I don't have."

He had a point, Chloe knew. Ron was one of those people who could inhabit, fully, a conversation with her, listen to her, draw her out, offer an attention that fell on her like a spotlight beam. Yet in a group, as people around him laughed and loosened up, he would withdraw within himself as though into an invisible carapace. It was that hermetic quality that had drawn her to him in the first place, back in graduate school.

"So we're not going to be seeing you up here for a while, then."

"You just get in there and be your beautiful self," Hellmund responded. "I'll say a few words remotely to kick things off. I promise I'll make it up to you when you get back."

"You promise, huh?" Chloe smirked. "It might take a lot to make it up to me."

"I miss you, love," he said.

"I miss you, Ron," she said, and the screen went dark before she could identify what it was that she hadn't said, what she had really wanted to say.

Idly, and without a perfect awareness of what she was doing, she slipped a ring from the fourth finger of her right hand to the fourth finger of her left. It was no ring that Ronald Hellmund had given her. And yet, on her wedding finger, she felt the ring take on a protective, almost totemic quality, as though she anticipated some danger that another man would hit on her here in space when her boyfriend wasn't around. The ring she placed on that finger predated Hellmund, had actually come from her father: it was the tiny Sacramento PD lapel badge he had been wearing when he was killed. Chloe's mother had had it made into a ring, set it with a tiny stone in the center. It had passed to Chloe during her second year of community college.

It was time for the glampers' space walk anyway. Chloe climbed from the rim toward the weightless heart of the hub. She disliked having them crowd through the Kamara-Zhou lab to get to the airlock they would be using. Of course, it hadn't been Kamara's or Zhou's lab for months—now it was just lab module three. It wasn't like they'd be poking around in *her* lab.

Samir and Nicholas were already in the airlock by the time Chloe arrived. Dion was explaining to them how the custom space suits of *Imperium* offered a slightly different range of motion in a vacuum than the suits the guests had trained on during their weeks preparing for the trip. They took in his low, gentle voice like sunflowers tracking the sun.

The others arrived in ones and twos. They suited up in silence or in laughter; Chloe took a guilty enjoyment in what she perceived to be their contained terror. "This feels a little like lifeguarding," Chloe murmured to Dion.

"Did you go to the public pool when you were a kid?"

She said that she had.

"Did you pay attention to the lifeguard?"

"I did, mostly. I was a rule follower when I was little."

"Not the kids I ran with. Let's hope that this is better than lifeguarding."

Kassie, the most petite of the guests by far, seemed to have been issued a space suit for a large doll. Chloe had to help her squeeze into it; if the suit had been made to measure, it certainly didn't seem to have been made to *Kassie's* measure.

Like an instructor for the most ridiculous aerobics class imaginable, Chloe led the guests through the in-suit light exercise protocol that would help ward off the bends after their space walk. She anchored the guests as they suited up, set them to work pumping their legs, their arms, undulating like thick-limbed sea anemones and starfish. Chloe undulated with them. Dion pulsed his legs with a burly precision that reminded her of an NFL player doing warm-ups in full pads.

Dion had made half a dozen space walks in his NASA days and another two back when he worked for CisLunar. He'd logged over forty-five hours total, according to a kid in Scotland who maintained a website listing the record holders for space walks—extravehicular activities, as the kid (and NASA) called them. Dion was in the top twenty worldwide.

Chloe had made a single EVA two months into her time on

Imperium, when she and Kamara and Zhou had assisted Konrad with the repair of a Vernier thruster. She neither dreaded space walks, as Kamara had, nor was as giddy as Sir Alexander Dunne or Roger and Jessica Van Cleave seemed to be as they mugged and giggled through the long depressurization protocol. Rather, for Chloe a space walk was merely another of the chores of *Imperium*, one she found unpleasant but not beyond her powers. "Let somebody know if you're feeling sick," Dion announced over their radios just as the airlock door began to retract.

Then came the vision of the stars beyond them. They hung before the spacewalkers like a parliament of distant gods, more stars than any of them would ever have seen from Earth. One by one the guests checked their umbilical cables; they followed Dion out toward the stars, or more properly, into the nothing that surrounded *Imperium*.

From the bridge, Maryam was directing a robot camera far beyond the guests, beyond Chloe, taking pictures. Chloe turned from her charges for a moment to watch the robot photographing the scene. She imagined what Maryam was seeing: the dark wheel of *Imperium*, the light flooding out of the open airlock like a streetlight of incomparable loneliness, the last streetlight in the solar system, the eight guests drifting out on their umbilical cables like newly hatched spiders on silken leads. The dim nightside of Earth was invisible to them on the other side of the station; far out beyond their feet, they could see a scabrous slice of bright moon. They would bob and float in this suspension until the sunrise, reel out until they could see the glittering jewel of Earth.

Chloe returned to the task at hand, such as it was. She and Dion played lifeguard, moving untethered around the group using their personal maneuvering units, those compact back-pack-like carapaces derived from NASA's old armchair-size MMUs.

The guests floated and gasped to one another over their communicators. There was a girlish giggling, maybe Kassie's—like the laughter of a child playing in new snow. One of the guests blurted, "Oh my God this is better than sex," in a breathless, headlong utterance. Chloe thought the voice might have belonged to Nicholas.

"I have been one acquainted with the night," declaimed Sir Alexander amid the laughter, as though he were calling out from the proscenium of a vast stage. "I have walked out in—"

Just then Sir Alexander's voice cut out; so did the gasps and giggling of the rest. The light from the airlock went dark. The station diminished to nothing but a silent inky shadow spread under the light of the moon.

"Come in, Bonilla," came Dion's voice over her radio.

"What the hell just happened?" Chloe asked.

Dion lit up the headlamp on his suit; he had fired the thrusters on his maneuvering unit and was moving fast toward the guests. "Some kind of power outage, it looks like," he said. "We have to get the guests back to *Imperium*."

Of the ten of them on the space walk, only Chloe and Dion were not tethered; their oxygen tanks were integrated into their massive backpacks. The rest had everything—communications, propulsion, air—piped in through their umbilicals. Chloe turned on her headlamp as well, propelled herself toward the guests. By the time she reached the one nearest her—maybe Samir Winters-Qureshi, to judge by the figure's height—she noticed Dion had scooped up another of the guests in a full nelson hold and was propelling himself and his charge toward the dark hole of the airlock.

Chloe grasped the guest she had reached under the arms and began to propel herself and him in the direction of *Imperium*. She saw around her that it had occurred to some of the guests to begin hauling themselves hand over hand up their umbilical cables toward the airlock. She knew there was a manual override for the airlock door; she raced through her memory for an image of the crank that she or Dion would need to find and turn.

They reached the airlock. Then, just as she was turning to retrieve another of the guests, the lights flickered to life again. Chloe heard gasping and screaming over her communicator from the guests. Dion was trying to bark over them—"Let's get everybody back on *Imperium*."

A few of the guests seemed to have experienced the thirty seconds of airlessness and silence and darkness in a panic that they could not dispel now. The one Chloe had brought back—Nicholas, actually, she was sure now—grasped one of the handholds in the airlock. Dion had carried another in; four others had hauled themselves in on their own tethers, or they had had the presence of mind to use their rocket packs when the nitrogen propellant began flowing again.

The last two screamed and gasped, suspended still on their tethers. Once they could get handholds and footholds, Chloe and Dion began pulling the last two in. They were a man and a woman, Chloe could tell by their voices—Sir Alexander, she thought, and maybe Kassie. The two drifted in slowly from the darkness. The voice of the man gibbered as though his moment in the utter airless dark had changed his vision forever.

The larger of the two was the one whose tether Chloe had hauled on; the figure landed as gracelessly as a sack of meal, crashing gently into her as she grasped the figure with her free hand. Dion had retrieved the other; the airlock doors crept shut.

The airlock repressurized within two minutes. The ten of them opened their visors. The last panicked figure Chloe had brought in was in fact Roger Van Cleave, ashen faced. The other who had panicked was Kassie Ng: "I'm so sorry," she said to the group, or to the world in general. "I thought I was suffocating."

"What happened?" Chloe whispered to Dion. Dion returned only a tight-lipped glance that Chloe interpreted as consternation or stoic befuddlement. Perhaps, though, his face showed simple irritation.

Just then Sir Alexander Dunne ejected a burgeoning cloud of vomit that floated before him in the airlock.

Tirzah held an emergency meeting two hours later in one of the OrbitalVentures conference rooms at the rim of the station.

There had been some kind of electrical overload near the airlock, Konrad reported. Thankfully, each of the airlocks was on its own circuit in the event of a power failure on the larger station; thus, the bridge was wired on a different circuit and had been unaffected by whatever brief failure had occurred. Nina and Vitaly were troubleshooting the event. Until they could report, Konrad wouldn't have many answers to give.

Konrad's pronouncement didn't stop Tirzah and the rest from peppering him with questions. Yes, he said, the overload had shut down all power in the airlock, as well as one of the lab modules, for thirty-two seconds. No, there had never been a power surge on *Imperium* before. Yes, so far as he knew the power had returned spontaneously. No, there were no lightning strikes in space.

The opening gala would continue, had to continue, as planned. It was the first time Chloe had seen Tirzah say something without her flight attendant's smile winched up: "We have to do the gala." Chloe sat at the table and watched, like a child on a merry-go-round horse, as *Imperium* wheeled away from the Earth. Across the table from her, Dion wore the same unreadable scowl she had seen in the airlock.

Later, as she inputted a new batch of data points on her

radicles, Chloe knew—despite her deep impulse to call bull-shit on the whole evening—that she would be going to the gala. She listened to the chatter over her earbuds while she worked: Maryam and the housekeeping staff were being run ragged; Lorenz and Nina (and for a little while even Erik, Assistant Vice President of Guest Experience) were deputized as impromptu dressers and factotums. Perhaps Chloe didn't sit on the bottom of the social ladder after all.

The Fortuna Ballroom sat on the rim of *Imperium* at the antipode of Chloe's cabin. That evening Chloe walked the long corridor that ran along the rim as though along the inside of a gigantic bicycle tire, rising before and behind her as she walked, like the eternally rising floor a hamster would perceive in an exercise wheel. All along her approach she could hear a roiling underbeat of music pumping toward her like a pheromone, some genre of electronica that she imagined guests might find danceable.

She walked in as the gala was beginning. The light in the Fortuna Ballroom was a lower twilit blue than the azure of the corridor; Nina stood at the archway entrance, surveying the perimeter like a humorless guard. She left off this real or imagined responsibility for a moment to nod at Chloe as she entered. The gesture seemed so expressionless that Chloe wondered whether Nina was nodding at the recognition of their shared livery more than anything else.

Along the walls, airy mottos materialized and faded away on massive screens: HEAVEN. EARTH. HOLD INFINITY IN THE PALM OF YOUR HAND. BEAUTY IS YOU. For a space that the company had billed as a ballroom, the hall seemed dark and blank except for the wall-length screens and their ephemeral words. At the end of the room stretched a black counter as featureless as the walls, behind which another OrbitalVentures employee—Vitaly,

Chloe thought his name was—seemed to be filling a tray of drinks for Maryam to carry.

Chloe took in the fifteen or so attendees: guests, Orbital-Ventures administrators, CisLunar flight crew. She wandered about the room, eavesdropping on the discussions. But whatever feelings the guests harbored about their recent scare outside the airlock, they were keeping quiet about them now, or at least quieter than the pounding of the music. "A bunch of damn clowns," someone with a man's voice and an American accent shouted in one of the little groups over the pounding, but those were the only words Chloe could make out in her whole tour of the ballroom.

The guests did seem to be drinking with some enthusiasm, however. Maryam and another young woman attended them like bees working an orchard. The guests and crew and administrators had mixed and remixed with one another; they all seemed to be laughing and shouting, well-lubricated.

Roger and Jessica Van Cleave then appeared in the entryway of the ballroom. As soon as they came in, Chloe spied Nina saying something into her mouthpiece. The music faded out then; the words on the screens—*PEACE. SUCH STUFF AS DREAMS ARE MADE ON. WE ARE ALL MADE OF STARS*—evaporated.

Then the diffuse light of the Fortuna Ballroom began to gather, took shape in a tight circle on the floor in the center of the crowd. Everyone turned to regard the new bright spot in the darkness: it was a hologram of Hellmund, standing among them large as life. Larger, actually—Chloe knew that he was five foot nine on Earth, while his image before her towered at least six and a half feet tall. The image disoriented her, as though it were a promotional poster hung above them all, his tailored blue suit both exactly what he would wear and nothing she had ever seen him wear before. His luminous gold silk tie bore a diamond OrbitalVentures pin that glittered as though reflecting an invisible light source.

Hellmund's voice rang out over the group, his plosives and fricatives finely synchronized with the movements of the hologram's mouth. "Ladies and gentlemen," the hologram said, "I am Dr. Ronald Hellmund, founder and chief executive officer of OrbitalVentures Corporation. On behalf of our entire family of engineers, technicians, scientists, and hospitality specialists, I welcome you to *Imperium*. You are the honored—"

From the group a burst of hooting, triumphal and simian, interrupted the hologram's address, as though nothing odd or unpleasant had happened to them six hours before. The hologram paused for the interruption. The image continued: "You are the honored guests of humanity's first extraterrestrial hotel. If you'll indulge my speaking poetically, I declare that you are pioneers in a new land, harbingers of a new age in the history of our species."

Hellmund's recording, or the algorithm representing Hellmund's speech, paused for the guests to emit a more decorous, self-regarding round of applause. Chloe watched, rapt, as the image of the man she so closely knew enumerated the virtues of *Homo sapiens*, especially those fortunate *Homo sapiens* who worked for, or contracted with, the OrbitalVentures Corporation. There was a quote from Shakespeare: . . . *in action how like an angel, in apprehension how like a god*, something something something.

Chloe's dismay grew deeper as the hologram went on speaking. The voice was Ron's, she knew. The sentiments were his, too, in a way—how could her boyfriend have so irrevocably thrown himself into OrbitalVentures without believing something along the lines of what the image was saying? But the real Ron Hellmund would not have spoken any of the things his simulacrum was speaking now: this sounded like a TED Talk written by a marketing major for a convention of Carl Sagan impersonators.

"I bring you"—the hologram finally drove to its conclusion—"to the threshold of all human existence; I reveal before you the cradle of humanity. My friends, I give you—the Earth." Hellmund's hushed tone seemed for a moment at odds with the hologram's expansive salute, his arm sweeping as though he were a sorcerer casting a spell.

At the figure's gesture, the color of the wall opposite the entryway, as well as the floor and the ceiling, seemed gradually to brighten. The guests gasped, then cheered, discovering that the blank walls were no longer opaque, no longer walls, that they were made of some kind of polarized material. In front of the gathering, beneath them, an expanse of windows let out now onto a view of the great curve of the Earth, as though *Imperium* were the highest rooftop casino in history.

The phantom of Hellmund had disappeared; the dance-club pounding of the electronica began to wash once more into the ballroom. Maryam and the other waiter—her name tag read *Meredith*—whisked their trays of tumblers back and forth from the bar to the celebrants.

Sir Alexander Dunne whirled across the Fortuna Ballroom in a florid purple wizard's robe and pointy hat. The stars that spangled his outfit seemed to be moving across the fabric by themselves, their color deepening into a redshift as though he were shooting across the hall at near light speed. During a pause in the music, Chloe could hear him giggling a throaty chuckle that edged into hysteria.

She heard a young woman's voice emerge from the music and laughter. "Dr. Chloe, can I interview you?"

Kassie Ng scampered toward Chloe in a skintight white jumpsuit with red racing stripes, her hair bound in a shimmering crimson scarf. She was looking vaguely in Chloe's direction as she approached, her eye on the phone she held out toward her.

"Please, call me Chloe," she said. Kassie nuzzled in so that they were both facing her phone. Kassie's extended arm above her called up in Chloe the sense of taking a selfie in a stadium; she submitted to a Pavlovian urge to smile.

But it took her only a moment to realize that Kassie was recording and that she was standing for an interview. "So, guys," Kassie blurted in the breathless tone Chloe had gotten familiar with on those YouTube videos, "I'm here with my friend Chloe. Dr. Chloe. She's the main scientist on *Imperium*."

"Right now I'm the *only* scientist."

"I've heard she's brilliant. What are you working on out here in space?"

"I'm part of a project that studies gravitropism in plants."

"So! In twenty seconds, will you explain gravitropism to us?"

Chloe found that she could in fact explain gravitropism in twenty seconds. Many interviewers gave her thirty seconds or even a minute, but it turned out twenty seconds was enough.

Yet even from the periphery of her vision, Chloe recognized the face that Kassie was making. A thousand young students she'd met, slow students or students only pretending to be slow, had offered up the same theatrical glazed stare for material they wished not to contend with for some reason, whether it was factoring polynomials in eighth grade or integrating predator-prey equations in an upper-division ecology class.

"That's fascinating, Doctor. So, guys, there you have it: gravitropism on *Imperium*. Dr. Chloe, maybe we can talk more as the evening goes on. Right now, I want to see if we can catch up with a real knight of the British Empire, Sir Alexander Dunne. He's dancing across the hall right now, but maybe we can get him to talk to us for a minute. Thank you, Dr. Chloe!" Kassie gave Chloe a socialite's peck on the cheek and launched herself on an interception course with Sir Alexander in his robe of wandering stars.

The celebration was far too small, too intimate, to have been called a gala anywhere on Earth. For that matter, Chloe suspected that most of the guests had living rooms larger than the aspirationally named Fortuna Ballroom. But the opening gala was the largest party that had ever occurred in space—in fact, it was the largest orbital gathering of humans in history. Twenty-four people floated around, between the hotel staff of *Imperium*, the visitors and management from OrbitalVentures headquarters, the CisLunar rocket crew, a social media influencer, and seven of the wealthiest people in the world.

Not far from where Chloe watched the South Atlantic rolling beneath them as *Imperium* rotated away from Earth, Maryam was handing one of the gracefully curved tumblers to Li. His jumpsuit fit slender in the waist and slim in the legs, simple and featureless as a black silk scabbard. He nodded at Maryam as they passed one another like dancers at a ball, then nodded in Chloe's direction as he strolled over. He raised the cup toward her.

"*Gānbēi*," Chloe shouted over the music.

Li lifted his eyebrows in mock or real surprise, or perhaps playfully. He responded in a way she didn't understand.

"I'm sorry," she said, "the only Mandarin I know is *gānbēi*."

Li raised his cup to salute her again and sipped from the gold mouthpiece, which drew the cup's contents along a winding path of capillary straws embedded within the walls of the tumbler, as though he were drinking from a sippy cup in the form of the OrbitalVentures teardrop. "This is a fascinating vessel," he said in an accent that Chloe found flawless.

"The company wanted a cup that would work all over

Imperium. You can take it to the hub; it works even in zero g. What are you drinking?"

"Asombroso Añejo."

Chloe admitted that she didn't really care for tequila.

Li scrutinized his tumbler again as though he were reconsidering the virtues of his drink. "I find it one of the world's perfectly designed beverages." His voice was like a river pebble that had had every edge ground down to a curve.

"I'm crazy, I know. I'd rather have a good hoppy IPA." But beer was one of the drinks they would not find on *Imperium*— too much could go wrong if someone had to hustle to the hub after drinking a beer. There had been enough wet burps already without adding fizzy drinks to the menu.

The two of them occupied one corner of the Fortuna Ballroom, surrounded by observation windows. The rotation of *Imperium* brought the Earth into view again, a dusting of lights illuminating the Brazilian coast, strings of glowing pinpricks edging into broad lightless swaths in the interior of South America. On the opposite wall, the word *INSIGHT* formed in great blue letters as though emerging from a dark fog.

"Have you gotten to know the other guests?" Chloe asked.

Li's face resolved into a meditative cast, as though her question were a calculus problem that he was trying to set up. "We trained with one another a long time before our trip."

Li's tone was such that Chloe couldn't tell whether he had gotten to know the other guests more closely than he had wished to during the training or whether he was simply not interested in gossiping about them with her. Come to think of it, she wasn't crazy about talking with Li either, except that her job right now, as she understood it, was to make small talk with this man. "What do you think of the gala so far?" she asked.

"The revealing of Earth was quite effective," Li said. "The

hologram's speech was perhaps a little . . . poetic . . . for my tastes."

"Hellmund doesn't really talk like that, I can assure you."

"Does anyone really talk like that? It seemed an odd humil-iation for the man who had founded OrbitalVentures."

"What do you mean?"

"Forgive me," he said, "I didn't intend to speak ill of the company's founder." He began scrutinizing his mysterious tum-bler of tequila once more. "I think I'll freshen my drink." He nodded a courtly goodbye at Chloe and retreated to another part of the ballroom.

Nearly everyone was dancing. Tireless Maryam and Mere-dith shuttled from one shimmying person to another, passing out bourbon and tequila in the cups that OrbitalVentures had designed and iterated and 3D printed over a period of eighteen months. Nicholas Winters-Qureshi spun Jessica Van Cleave around the center of the hall while Samir Winters-Qureshi and Roger Van Cleave danced with Tirzah Fowler between them. She was drinking as well—a prerogative of her role as host, Chloe supposed. INSIGHT receded from the viewscreens and BLISS emerged, like creatures sinking and rising in dark water.

The music felt to Chloe as though she were standing at the bottom of a deep canyon, listening to a geological sequence of auditory strata, deposited one after another by synthesizers and algorithms over a distant pulse of beats carving its way along at the basement rock of the sound. She ventured to dance a little—it occurred to her that she felt less uncomfortable dancing here, perhaps because Sir Alexander Dunne moved so prepos-terously. Even Konrad and Dion, ostensibly there with Chloe to babysit, danced a little. Sir Alexander in his wizard robes of Doppler-shifted stars shared a passing, tongue-lashing kiss with Viv Volterra, then another at the other end of the hall with

Samir Winters-Qureshi. The word BLISS disappeared, and the screen went dark.

"I hear you are the Dr. Spock of *Imperium*," a man said to Chloe during a break in the wall of sound.

Chloe turned to look at who had addressed her. The captain of the CisLunar rocket stood nearby. He was lean and tall as an elite marathoner, his face weathered with laugh lines and crow's-feet in a way that even the older guests' faces were not, like a man whose time on starvation rations had prematurely aged him. His smile, though, was open and unguarded in a way Chloe hadn't seen in many months on *Imperium*. "Dr. Spock was a pediatrician," Chloe answered. "Are you talking about Mr. Spock? The Vulcan?"

"Uh, yeah—*Star Trek* Spock, I mean. I guess I assumed that he had gotten his PhD."

"He never did. I think he must have had a pretty rough dissertation committee." The music had begun again, and she enjoyed leaning into him to shout into his ear.

"Another example of a brilliant scientist being hounded out of academe," the captain shouted back. The CisLunar crew had changed out of their raw-meat-colored flight suits; he was dressed in a charcoal-gray CisLunar jumpsuit that didn't look like it had cost $100,000 to design. His name tag read *Pasquale*.

"How do you like the opening gala?"

"OrbitalVentures throws a good party. This place is swanky."

"*Swanky* is one word for it, I guess," Chloe said. She had attended a couple of parties more her speed on *Imperium*: a handful of scientists floating in one of the labs, passing around a bottle of vodka and playing reggae. Dull parties, she supposed others might call them. "Does CisLunar have you working while the glampers are up here?" she added.

He smiled warily before leaning in to shout: "I'm on the clock, if that's what you're asking. I don't exactly have much to

do besides cool my heels and not embarrass myself at the gala."
At the center of a circle of the grandees, Sir Alexander Dunne
had hiked his wizard robes a long way up his thighs in order to
twerk. The tightness of the fabric around his butt suggested to
Chloe that he was wearing either very abbreviated underwear
or nothing at all underneath.

"Sounds like a nice job."

Pasquale shrugged. "I guess so. I'm still curious how many
of these camping trips OrbitalVentures will be able to sell. Especially with the changes coming for the company, this might
be a very short-lived route for me."

Chloe wasn't sure what changes he was referring to, or even
whether the company he referred to was CisLunar or Orbital-
Ventures. But the idea that the OrbitalVentures Corporation
might not succeed at offering a service that people would pay
for, at a price that the market would bear, had never seriously
occurred to her. Like any adult with a mortgage and a car payment, Chloe was aware of money and its uses. But she regarded
economic planning as a distraction from the real issues of life,
which for her were the energy and nutrient flows within eco-
systems. At some level of abstraction, money might be said to
represent those flows, though only sloppily and irrationally.
Unlike Hellmund's knack for bird-dogging backers and funds,
Chloe's mind did not follow the tracks of human currency.

"And what about you?" Pasquale continued. "How long are
you going to be up here?"

"Another forty-one days, fourteen hours, and . . . thirty-two
minutes, if CisLunar is on time with resupply."

"So you're having a great time, then?"

Chloe realized when the question was put to her so directly, so sarcastically, that she was in fact having the time of her
life, her separation from Hellmund, Tirzah Fowler's presence,

and *Imperium*'s self-involved guests notwithstanding. Watching them dance and drink hadn't been so different from watching the pale radicles emerge from her beans: she was watching the two experiments unfold in parallel, cataloging the ways that life could be teased into normality in the absence of that mighty independent variable, the Earth's gravity. Even what seemed like gravity here in the Fortuna Ballroom was mere imitation, the centrifugal force of a colossal Tilt-A-Whirl. *Imperium* felt like an ordeal only because life in space was an ordeal, a hope chest of stopgaps and work-arounds and provisional answers to profound technical challenges. Chloe loved it the way Darwin had loved the *Beagle*.

The sun had risen, set, risen again, set again. *Imperium* hurtled in silence over their home at twenty-seven thousand kilometers per hour. The glampers nuzzled and cackled drunkenly. Kassie's phone was perpetually pointed at something or someone, usually herself as she narrated her inner state. The others alternately mugged with Kassie for her videos and mocked her uptalking and vocal fry.

"Are you expecting an indictment?" Kassie asked Viv Volterra during a lull in the music. The other guests all turned to look, and the question hung above the abashed group like a great predatory bird.

But Viv Volterra, still wearing her silk aviator's scarf, now with a furred suit that looked like Max's wolf costume from *Where the Wild Things Are*, offered up the serene half-smile of a bodhisattva. "We'll have to see what the DOJ has in store for me," she said. "I only know what I read in the *Wall Street Journal*."

"What does the *Wall Street Journal* say?"

"You'll have to read that for yourself, sweetheart. I'm not going to do your homework for you."

Her rejoinder conjured a flutter of laughter from the others as the music picked up again and Kassie protested ever louder and gigglingly that she actually subscribed to the *Wall Street Journal*, had the *WSJ* app on her phone.

Over the course of the next revolution around the Earth, the guests retired in ones and twos to their staterooms. "I wish you all a peaceful night," intoned Sir Alexander Dunne with all the tenderness of Saint Francis, waving his hands like doves' wings in every direction. Pasquale leaned in to hug Chloe, and she had a fleeting, scandalous thought about a good-night kiss with him. Their hug was chaste, however, and she couldn't read his look.

Only after the last of the guests had departed did Tirzah Fowler permit herself one weary sigh. Then she nodded smartly to her underlings: "Right. Nina, let's put you on first concierge shift. You'll switch off at zero four hundred with Lorenz. Lorenz, if I'm not up by zero six hundred, give me a call. Let's all of us meet back in the conference room at zero six thirty to go over the day's script."

Chloe came out into the silk upholstery and omnidirectional blue light of the central corridor. She returned to her cabin and lay down, watching the stars drift by from her bed.

She imagined, or dreamed, as she drifted off that *Imperium* was being rocked like a massive ship of the line over a deep oceanic wave. She had been coupling stout links of an anchor chain from her tiny workspace in the forecastle, bending the thick rods into rings as easily as if the iron were bread dough. The anchor took up one entire wall of her workspace, glittering like a star. The word INSIGHT was inscribed on one fluke; DURO was inscribed on the other.

She woke in the dark. She checked the time—0330 Juliet. She had to look up on her phone what time it was on the West Coast. Maybe she could check in with Ron, dish him a little gossip about the gala. Of course, she had signed the nondisclosure agreement about what she saw on *Imperium* during camp days. But her boyfriend didn't count—Hellmund would certainly find out from Tirzah if Chloe kept quiet.

The internet seemed to be down, however. Maybe there was a problem with the router, or maybe the laser transmitter—it was hard to tell from what she saw, a tiny icon of a lighthouse sweeping the corner of her phone screen.

She had the rueful insight that if she had brought her laptop from her lab to her cabin at the end of the day, she could do a little more troubleshooting of the internet now. But it was her insomnia that had kept her from bringing her laptop back to her room in the first place: she had learned over hard nights of graduate school that her body's capricious wakefulness at three or four in the morning had to be managed with care. When she woke in the middle of the night, the thing she most wanted to do, and the thing that most undid her sleep, was to get on the computer.

But Chloe knew that she would not be getting back to sleep soon. She wondered whether anyone else on the station was aware of the internet outage. She dropped her phone on the bedside table and picked up the radio communicator, pulled her earbuds out of their storage pouch. No one on channel one. She scrolled through the channels.

On channel seven, she heard something: ". . . not responding. Trying auxiliary. Konrad, what's your ETA?" The voice was Pasquale's. There was a clipped quality to his voice, a blunt affect that had not been there when they flirted at the gala.

"I'm making my way over the starboard delta wing," Konrad answered. His voice, too, sounded oddly clipped. Something wasn't right, Chloe knew. She realized then with a creeping dread that both men were speaking through space suit transmitters. "I'm heading for the starboard hatch now," Konrad announced.

Where's the alarm? Chloe wondered. *Imperium* had an emergency protocol: if anything had happened that would have required an emergency EVA—meteorite, hull breach, electrical failure—a warning claxon should have gone off. Why then had she heard nothing? A chill that she hadn't felt in many years, not even during the blackout in the airlock the day before, descended on her.

Quickly, so quickly that she was not conscious of her calculus, she weighed the data before her, everything she could see and hear, and much she could not. Someone had overridden the station's alarm, had wanted *Imperium*'s sleepers not to wake up. She chose silence.

She muted her transmitter, slipped out of her bed and into the hallway. She was still wearing the OrbitalVentures dress jumpsuit—she had been too exhausted at the end of the gala to do anything but unclip her key fob and flop into bed—and padded down the corridor to the hotel administration office. Empty.

She walked back up the hall, peered up the darkened gamma spoke leading to the hub. The ventilation fans were laboring at a pitch that was strange to her.

"Entering starboard hatch," Konrad said over channel seven. "Yeah, there wouldn't have been enough clearance to get a PMU in here."

Chloe began to climb the gamma spoke ladder toward the hub, toward weightlessness, in silence and darkness. The blue lights of the hotel corridor below glowed with a nocturnal, bioluminescent chill.

Floating now, she topped the ladder and peeked into the Axle. Empty. Chloe wondered where Nina's concierge post was intended to be. It wasn't as though *Imperium* had a reception desk like some orbital DoubleTree. Maybe she was still down in the Fortuna Ballroom.

Chloe glided up the Axle toward the bridge and the Levitas Reception Hall. The hall was also empty. But she saw something else there: the bulkhead connecting *Imperium* with the CisLunar rocket had been closed. Had there been some kind of decompression event on the rocket? A meteorite strike, a shipboard explosion? But a meteorite strike would have awakened everyone. And why was *Imperium* so silent now? The absence of the emergency claxon chilled her far more than if it had been blaring.

Chloe made her way back down the access corridor to the Axle, crossed over into the access corridor for the bridge. Dion's voice came over channel seven. "Konrad? Ensio? Noelle? Are you all aboard? What's your assessment?" The timbre of Dion's voice suggested to Chloe that he was unsuited. On the bridge, probably.

"Konrad's on board," Noelle, the CisLunar copilot, replied. "Holy shit, this thing's a mess. The instrument panel's melted—two, three, four, at least five connectors totally fused, including attitude thruster control, main thruster control—" She broke off.

"I don't understand how this didn't trip the fire alarm," Konrad added. "Why would Nina close the bulkhead without sounding the alarm?"

Chloe drifted slowly toward the glare of the lights coming from the bridge at the end of the corridor. From her spot up the hall, she could see the flicker of the security camera monitors on the bridge computer, shuffling slowly through each dim room of the public areas on *Imperium*. She saw her own lab on the screen, viewed from above, the windows of the growth chambers hinting at the light within shining on the beans, the light of a June day at high latitude.

"Any word on where she is, Dion?" asked Pasquale.

"No sighting yet," Dion answered. Chloe heard his voice coming from the bridge as well as from her earbuds.

"Find her if you can," Konrad said. "She didn't just walk off."

Something about Dion's voice—or maybe it was simply the commitment Chloe had already made to secrecy—kept her from entering the bridge right then. Beneath her conscious powers of deduction, some part of her had concluded that the claxons had failed to sound for a reason, that the bulkhead to the CisLunar rocket had been shut for a reason. She took in the access corridor outside the bridge. Above her head, a single surveillance camera stared in silence. She felt a small, consoling relief that wherever Dion was on the bridge, he didn't seem to be sitting in front of the security monitors. Chloe pushed off one wall to put herself behind the camera. She wished for something she might improvise as a lens cap—a wad of chewing gum, a ball of tape. She held the back of the camera as though she held a cottonmouth behind its head.

Konrad's voice broke in over channel seven. "Shit, Dion—what just happened?"

Dion was silent.

"The rocket's been uncoupled," Konrad nearly shouted. "It looks like one of the port Verniers has fired. Ensio, did you get a connection from one of the controls?"

Pasquale's voice came back over the channel: "There's no voltage in any of these controls. One of the computers must be malfunctioning."

"Dion, come in. We're pulling away from *Imperium*. We're accelerating—the retros are firing. Our controls are totally dead over here. Dion, come—"

Then it was silent. Chloe craned her neck to peek around the bulkhead into the bridge. Dion sat with his back to the bulkhead, strapped into one of the control chairs, watching the massive CisLunar rocket pull slowly away from *Imperium* on one of the exterior monitors. The narrow side hatch of the rocket gaped open. The disconnected or cut umbilical cables of the three people aboard now trailed behind like three spindly fingers snatching at thin air.

Chloe hung suspended between heaven and Earth. More than she had ever felt it in her last 238 days on *Imperium*, she now knew the rootlessness of her condition. She wished that her feet had never left the ground.

But her instinct called her out of this reverie. "The rocket is launched," she heard Dion say to someone she couldn't see on the bridge. If he was saying it into his transmitter, Chloe heard nothing on her earbuds. She realized that he must have switched channels. "Take your position and wait for my signal."

Chloe probed at the security camera's mount. It wasn't mounted on a swivel—the whole field of view in this corridor was maybe fifteen degrees—and it seemed doubtful that she'd be able to twist the camera's view elsewhere without making a sound. Dion sat five meters away. Four monitors glared before him, above the instrument panel and to the right of the windows of the bridge. The views on three of the monitors seemed to cycle from one room to the next every few seconds, while the fourth remained trained from the outside on the airlock where the CisLunar rocket had been docked. Now that monitor was fixed on empty space; the rocket had tumbled and receded to the size of a toy on the screen.

She watched Dion remove the bridge headphones, spool in the cord, and hang them up. He pulled out a small pouch from his jumpsuit. Probably his earbuds—she had to move.

She had spent the last thirty seconds calculating the route she would need to take to avoid showing up on the bridge security monitors. She knew it was not a complicated problem. It was the kind of brainteaser that she would have found entertaining if she were sitting at her desk on a rainy afternoon in Corvallis: she needed only to know how many camera feeds there were and how many seconds each feed appeared on a screen. Now, though, she balked at modeling in her head the cycles of the monitors. She abandoned the problem half-done when Dion slipped his earbuds on; she could hear him unbuckle the belts that strapped him in at the captain's chair.

Chloe pushed off from the wall, leaped as ungainly and silent as a bat through the bridge access corridor back to the Axle, then down the length of the Axle to the access corridor for the lab wing. She knew that the PMUs she and Dion had used the day before were still stowed in the airlock that the company had used for the guests' space walk. In the time it would take her to get suited, the CisLunar rocket might be a kilometer away, maybe a little farther. If its retros didn't fire again, the ship wouldn't be moving fast. If she could reach them using the PMU, she might have enough propellant to bring one of them back before they suffocated.

Chloe rushed through the many *if*s and *might*s as she bounded from wall to hatch to corridor to hatch. She imagined the cameras' lenses upon her like a prickle she sensed on her skin. She glided like a shadow through lab module three.

Then she stopped herself. Through the window at the other end of the lab, Chloe could see that the airlock beyond was lit. She floated up to the window. She saw Nina and Vitaly moving about in there. They wore space suits and PMUs, perhaps the same PMUs that she and Dion had worn the day before.

For one moment, Chloe's mind filled in a flurry of details to confect a prosocial narrative out of what she was seeing: Nina and Vitaly must be mounting a rescue effort for the three people drifting away in the rocket. Never mind that neither Nina nor

Vitaly was an astronaut; never mind that there had been no emergency claxon.

And, Chloe noticed after a few seconds, Nina and Vitaly were in no hurry to leave *Imperium*. Neither did they seem to be going through depressurization protocol: their visors were open; they were not doing an oxygen prebreathe.

At last Chloe understood. They had already been outside the station; now they were back.

In that moment she saw the trap that she and all the guests were in. She felt a visceral urge to get out of sight—it was dark enough in the Kamara-Zhou lab that she might not show up on the bridge monitors, but sooner or later Nina and Vitaly would come through that hatch.

She considered returning to her own cabin, pretending to have seen and heard nothing. And, she understood, if Dion or Nina or Vitaly meant her any harm, they would find her exactly where they expected to find her.

There was a path in Chloe's mind that she had not used, had nearly forgotten about, in the years since her lonely fieldwork in the Dark Divide. Bears and cougars moved there, even a few reintroduced wolves. But humans were the only ones that had ever scared her: a long way from cell service, a long way from a road, she had had to run one season, had had to hide. Now her mind dropped once more into that mental furrow, that trail of fright and muscle memory that had once been necessary for her survival.

She slipped out of the Kamara-Zhou lab and pushed herself into her own lab space. In the dim light, she snatched from pouches and cabinets anything her instinct told her she could make use of: a Phillips-head screwdriver, a plastic scraper she used to wrangle potting soil, a roll of masking tape, a ball of twine she used to make moisture wicks for her seedlings, a permanent marker. If she'd had the foresight to change back into her regular work jumpsuit after the gala, she would have had half a dozen zippered pockets to slip her cargo into. As it was, she stuffed it all as best she could into the two slender hip pockets.

She darted from her lab back into the main lab corridor and from there pushed off into lab module four. Penn State was supposed to be renting this module again in a couple of months. For now, though, it had been dark and empty since January.

The layout here was nearly the same as in her lab. Chloe felt around in the dark for the seams of the closeout panels. She found the door to the instrument locker that would have housed the ion trap mass spectrometer in her lab and that, she confirmed with an almost silent rapping with her knuckle, seemed to be empty in this module, awaiting whatever machinery Penn State was planning to bring up.

She opened the latch, then taped the mechanism down so that she would not be shut in. Then she shimmied in feetfirst. She pulled the door shut behind her.

Breathe, she told herself. She slowed her breath willfully, mindfully, down into her solar plexus, granted herself the refuge of three wakeful inhalations, in which she imagined every planet of the solar system traveling in its eonic ellipse whether she lived or died, whether *Imperium* kept to its tiny nested course or fell out of orbit and burned up into dust.

She contemplated the disaster she had awoken to. Pasquale, Noelle, and Konrad would be dead as soon as the rocket tumbled into Earth's atmosphere, if they hadn't suffocated already. They might still be punching every unresponsive button and toggle on the rocket even now, not knowing how dead they were.

Was she any less dead? Trapped in the strange, faraway manor house of *Imperium* with three killers? At least three. And why?

A working hypothesis wasn't hard to come by. The guests were among the world's wealthiest people, and they were more remote than the most secluded Amazonian tribe on Earth, harder to rescue than any castaway in the Pacific Ocean. It seemed odd to her that Li and Dunne and Volterra and the Van Cleaves and Winters-Qureshis would be taken hostage here— they hadn't exactly brought briefcases of currency with them. But a wealthy hostage could prove valuable for many purposes.

The compartment she had shut herself in felt something like she imagined a coffin would, close and pitch black. Chloe yearned to say one last thing to the three people tumbling away in the rocket—not to call them back or say goodbye, but to say some wise thing that would justify all that had happened and that would happen. But if they were even conscious now to listen, their communication had been lost when their umbilical cables had been cut or disconnected. And anyway, whatever she wished to say would have been for her own comfort more than for theirs.

She scrolled through each channel on her communicator. There were ten channels on *Imperium*'s radios, and for all she knew Dion, Vitaly, and Nina might have brought other walkie-talkies with a totally different set of frequencies.

But she heard them on channel eight. ". . . as soon as Vitaly is out of his suit." That was Nina, she thought—last night's butler. Now her voice sounded clipped and quiet, with none of the lethargic self-importance that it had when she had announced the guests' arrivals on *Imperium*. She sounded in her own way a little like Konrad and Pasquale had in the last minutes Chloe had heard them: like a person facing a crisis.

"Let's get everyone formed up," Dion said.

"Copy that. Proceeding with plan."

Chloe closed her eyes in her shortened coffin.

CHAPTER THREE

Kassie Ng and the rest of the hostages sat in a sorry herd on the floor of the Fortuna Ballroom. The giant screens beside them had no blithe or breathy slogans to declare. Before them, in front of the wide view of Earth, the three hostage takers kept watch. Nina and Vitaly stood on either side of the entryway arch and held their guns as though they were the handles of invisible leashes connecting them to the prisoners.

Dion stood before the center of the bank of windows, the final vertex of the deadly triangle. Though he wore the same blue OrbitalVentures jumpsuit he'd worn the day before, he had also put on sunglasses; even if she had been able to get close enough to look, Kassie would have seen nothing from looking into his eyes except a fun-house reflection of her own condition in the mirror of the lenses. Dion also had a gun, holstered at his rib cage; his left hand, meanwhile, held a curious device, curved and tapered, that looked to Kassie like a large, ungainly cell phone. All the hostages regarded this other object with a vague dread, which stood in for their dread of the man. The object itself, however, would have seemed simply odd if it had appeared in one of the many cabinets of *Imperium*: it looked more than anything like a miniature steely coffin with a pistol grip.

"Okay, people," he said in a soft voice, even a gentle one, though Kassie had no difficulty hearing him, "time for instructions. If you behave wisely, you're going to find this whole process quite painless. We'll conduct our business together like civilized people, and you'll go home to live the rest of your lives. Good?"

The flock of prisoners was silent, except for a barely audible groan from one of them. The groaner sounded like Sir Alexander Dunne.

Dion pursed his lips and regarded them with an expression that Kassie couldn't divine. He might have been a chess player taking in a field of pawns and knights and bishops. "Let's operationalize what *behaving wisely* means. Here's the definition I propose: in your case, wise behavior means that when I or someone on my team tells you to do something, you do it. It's that simple."

With his right hand, Dion drew from his breast pocket a tiny remote, which he used to turn on the large viewscreen beside the hostages. "Now, viewer discretion is advised, but I want to make sure that you fully understand your situation." The screen filled up with what looked like washed-out security camera footage of the exterior of *Imperium*. The CisLunar rocket was visible on the screen, docked at the airlock leading to the Levitas Reception Hall. The side hatch was open; three filaments snaked out of the rocket. Kassie recognized the same umbilicals that had failed her the day before on the space walk.

Then there was a silent, languid blast of the retrothrusters: the rocket uncoupled with the station. A few moments later, the umbilicals went taut, then snapped. That brief tension was enough to drag the rocket into a lazy spiral as it drifted off like the slow-motion pass of a football, receding in the field of view until it had diminished to a gray point on the monitor.

"Ensio Pasquale, Noelle Johns, and Konrad Whittaker were on that rocket," Dion announced. "They've burned up over the Indian Ocean by now. Is that clear?"

There was a flush of gasps; at least one person began a stifled sobbing. Kassie Ng clapped her hand over her mouth, as though there were something for her to say that she had to stop herself from saying.

"To put it another way, you'll have to stay up here with us until you can provide what we are asking for. If you help us with what we require, my team and I will go home in the Starliner capsule. Then you can reestablish communications with OrbitalVentures, or NASA, or whoever you like." He seemed to turn his attention toward Sir Alexander Dunne when he said this. "Surely someone will send up another rocket for you."

The hostages took in his speech where they sat. They looked faded; the brand-new jumpsuits and gala costumes that some of them wore seemed now grubby and wrinkled, far cheaper than they actually were. Nicholas and Samir wore matching jammies, like grade-school friends on a sleepover. Most of the staff still wore their employee uniforms.

When one of the hostages spoke, his voice seemed to startle the others. "How much do you want?" It was Roger Van Cleave.

"I'm glad we understand each other, Roger. I knew that you would catch on right away." Kassie couldn't tell whether Dion was mocking him. He didn't seem to be, in spite of what he was actually saying: Dion's voice seemed deep and generous as a monarch's. "All human activity really can be reduced to economic relations, don't you think? Here's how much we want you all to contribute: eight billion dollars. Once you deposit eight billion dollars' worth of cryptocurrency into the digital wallet I provide you, you'll be free to go."

There was a general groan. "You think I have eight billion fucking dollars?" Roger asked.

"Not eight billion *each*, Roger. Do you think Maryam has eight billion dollars lying around?" Dion strolled from his spot in front of the Earth toward them. "Also, Roger, I think it's important that I make my preferences clear." He pointed his odd device directly at Roger. There was no flash of light, no report. But Roger began to howl and writhe in pain. Dion pushed a button on the device again and again, once for each word of his next softly spoken sentence, like four pitiless punctuation marks: "I. Dislike. Foul. Language."

Dion lowered the wand and walked back toward his original spot. Roger's wailing subsided after a few moments to a whimper as his wife held him and he rocked in her arms. A raking of dark, jagged weals had begun to appear across his face and throat.

"As I was explaining before Mr. Van Cleave's outburst, I'm not asking for eight billion dollars from each of you. That would be unreasonable. However, we have done a little research into your finances, and we are optimistic that between you all, you'll be able to put your hands on that much money."

Kassie pondered his words: *We have done a little research.* It seemed hard to believe that *we* referred to just Dion, Nina, and Vitaly. Just how would three of them have gotten through OrbitalVentures' background checks independently? How would they have stowed away guns and that torture wand?

The hostages each looked in a different direction. As best they could, they kept the people with the guns in view, without looking directly at the guns or the faces of the people holding them. Some took in the view of the Earth below, that heedless, rolling mass of theft and exploitation. Kassie had the sudden thought that the Earth was not so very far beneath them.

"Excuse me," Kassie said. She felt, as she sometimes did in

stressful situations, embarrassed at the smallness of her voice. Dion turned his mirrored sunglasses toward her. "Do we all have to give the same amount?"

Out of the corner of her eye, she noticed Vitaly smirking. But Dion remained aloof behind his sunglasses. "No, Ms. Ng," he said at last. "We're demanding eight billion dollars because we know that's what all of you are able to pay *together*. Some will pay a larger share of it, obviously. What was it the Russians used to say, Vitaly? *From each according to his ability?*"

Vitaly smiled again.

"Did you change the Wi-Fi password?"

Even in his sunglasses, Dion seemed flummoxed by her question. "Um—yes, we did. We thought about leaving it as it was, but we decided that your having internet access might interfere with the hostage taking."

"Of course," he continued, "we'll need to give you an opportunity to talk with financial advisers and banks back home. You'll each have a little supervised internet time. Even you, Ms. Ng."

Like the others, Kassie Ng considered the view of Earth. She found it curious how all her viewers, all her fans, were living their lives down there, casually unaware of her fate. If that was Australia beneath her—it looked like Australia, anyway—she had something like a hundred thousand fans just in that one spot. She could take in the view of all of them in a few minutes. She had far more fans in Australia than in Vietnam, a vagary of her fandom that had always seemed strange to her (though, since she never posted content with more than a word or two of Vietnamese, it wasn't really that strange, once she thought about it). The thought of giving up whatever quantity Dion demanded so that she could live, so that she could return to Earth, gave her almost no ill feeling at all. She had worked hard for the money, sure. Especially at first. But there was a kind of *easy come, easy go* feeling to the prospect.

But she also felt a chill near to panic as she wondered how she would come up with whatever her part of the ransom was. Were they expecting her to sell her car? Her house? How long would that take, while she floated up there at gunpoint and Skyped . . . who? Her brother? Who would be able to liquidate all that for her? She estimated that she had no more than $50,000 sitting in bank accounts and lines of credit right now, stuff she could put her hands on quickly. As New South Wales rolled past beneath her, Kassie Ng silently calculated that her ready cash made up only about six ten thousandths of one percent of $8 billion.

"All right," Dion addressed the group. "We need to begin soon if we plan to finish on time. You're each going to be put in touch with your financial advisers to figure out what you can liquidate." Kassie wondered what kind of asset manager a person like Maryam might have. For that matter, how much did someone like Maryam even make working for OrbitalVentures? Her wealth might be far greater, or far less, than Kassie imagined.

Vitaly pointed at Li. "You first—come with me." He waved with his gun in the direction of the corridor.

Li stood up with what seemed a preternatural grace, like a ballet dancer emerging on stage. Vitaly kept his pistol trained on him as Li walked into the corridor. The sleeves of Vitaly's jumpsuit were rolled up to reveal the corded muscles of his forearms, which looked as though they had been ratcheted into high-tension ropes on a windlass. He followed close behind the slight billionaire.

Dion slipped the strange device into his pocket and drew his pistol from the shoulder holster. He stood before them, between their miserable circle and their view of the Earth, in the way that armed men have exercised the monopoly of force since the dawn of civilization: his body ready to spring, under a kind of wary focus that seemed to lens great diffuse clouds of sensory data into a single intense light by which he could see what his hostages couldn't. Dion neither smiled nor frowned. He seemed a man meditating deeply upon the powers of the cosmos.

"Why are you doing this to us?" Samir Qureshi asked. The sound of his voice struck Kassie strangely: his tone wasn't remonstrating; rather, his trim British public-school accent seemed to communicate nothing but a fearless curiosity.

A bemused smile crept across Dion's face. "I thought our motives would be obvious. We want money."

"Yes, you've made that clear," Samir said. "But for what? Even if you manage to steal that much, eight billion is more than you'll ever be able to spend."

"Is eight billion dollars more than *you're* able to spend? With all due respect, Mr. Qureshi, you have no idea how much we're capable of spending. But I'll give you a hint: The Reckoners are not common thieves. If you all cooperate and return to Earth in one piece, you'll see soon enough how we put the money to use." Dion's voice sounded benign, even avuncular.

"The Reckoners?"

"Yes, the group that just took you hostage. I invite you to contemplate why we've targeted you."

Then the oppressive silence returned. Kassie had expected, or perhaps hoped, that Dion would explain himself a little more plainly. She had her own guess, which had the benefit of simplicity: a group that calls itself the Reckoners is there to make some kind of reckoning. But honestly she wouldn't have to guess if he would just explain what the name meant.

She could hear two people whispering with one another, maybe Roger and Jessica. Dion turned his attention toward them, or seemed to—it was hard to tell which way his eyes looked beneath his sunglasses. But Roger and Jessica must also have concluded that he was staring at them, because they went silent.

Eventually Vitaly brought Li back from wherever he had been taken. Kassie searched his face for any sign of what might have happened. But the man bore himself with an unreadable poise: his eyes expressed nothing, his face as still as a card sharp's. Even his hair looked as perfectly in place as if Vitaly had just taken him out of the crowd for a trim.

"And how was Mr. Li's visit?" Dion asked Vitaly as the large man, larger even than Dion, took up his position again.

"We made only first contacts," Vitaly replied. "Mr. Li's asset managers have begun making preliminary inquiries. The word is out now." Kassie was surprised at Vitaly's voice, high and lilting, incongruous with the size of the man, offering barely a hint that English was not his first language. She realized only then that she had imagined Vitaly to be a communicator of grunted, Slavic-inflected monosyllables.

But Dion gave no response to Vitaly's accounting. The silence was enough to entice Kassie to sneak a look at Dion and the pistol in his hand. He was holding his other hand up to the receiver in his ear. Even close by, his reply was too low for her to hear. ". . . not that big," she thought she heard him say. Then, "Take care of it." Dion's mouth was an implacable, grim line that emitted those quiet words with all the self-possession of a concert cellist beginning a cadenza.

Something was up. Vitaly shot Dion a glance with a raised, quizzical eyebrow. Kassie looked away again, afraid of her own voyeurism of these quiet predators. She took in Australia once more as it drifted beneath her.

"Very well," Dion announced after a long, terrible moment of silence. "Messrs. Winters-Qureshi, you're next."

Kassie wondered how she felt about the married couples

being taken together. She was in no position to protest it, and at any rate she wasn't sure that it was even unfair that they should go together. She knew it would be less terrifying for her to go with another person. However, Li seemed to have come out of his lonely interview none the worse for wear.

Again the silence. From time to time, she could hear Dion murmur something into the transmitter of his headset. Now he covered his mouth when he transmitted—Kassie could make out nothing that he was saying. Anyway, he seemed to say very little. For the dozenth time, she wished that her phone hadn't been confiscated, wished she could pull it out of her pocket and start recording.

Kassie turned away from the Earth to search out the faces of the others. Most did not meet her gaze; they seemed to be meditating in silence like wretched socialites in a Quaker meeting. Roger Van Cleave stared at an imaginary point in the middle distance, or perhaps at a real point on Earth, with a smoldering malice. Purple welts raked garishly across his face. Jessica Van Cleave seemed to be staring into her own lap, her face made invisible by the disheveled mass of her hair. Only Sir Alexander Dunne sought out Kassie's eyes with a world-weary smirk that seemed to say, *Can you believe how stupid all of this is?* He had flirted so shamelessly and creepily with her the night before, when he was dancing across the Fortuna Ballroom in that wizard's robe. She had believed at the time that it was highly unlikely she would ever sleep with him, but not strictly impossible. She had found it excited her last night, in a way that she had not anticipated, to be wanted by one of the world's wealthiest men. The fact that he was forty years older than she, that he reminded her of some kind of pale, unblinking lizard, did not totally outweigh the strange energy that had seemed to constellate about him, as though he were in fact a wizard of great power. Now, though, he looked seasick and bleary eyed, his robe slovenly. Perhaps it was chagrin that he was communicating. However, he seemed to Kassie to be beyond chagrin.

The saddest, most chagrined of all was Tirzah Fowler. She sat hugging her knees in the crowd of prisoners, her collar open and her necktie slack, as though she were a stock trader of another era, beaten down by a rough day on the trading floor. She met no one's gaze.

Then a pop punctuated the air, and another a second later, Dion stiffened. "Team, report," he said into his transmitter, no longer bothering to cover his mouth, the three crisp syllables of his order audible to everyone in the Fortuna Ballroom. Kassie realized, after a moment's wondering, that a gun had gone off.

That was when Kassie noticed something else that had escaped her up to this point. The scientist, Chloe or Dr. Chloe or whoever she was, wasn't among the prisoners.

CHAPTER FOUR

TWENTY-FOUR MINUTES EARLIER

Chloe waited in the hollow where she had planted herself. She didn't trouble herself with the question of what she was waiting for; whatever danger was coming, there was no sense inviting it early.

A memory intruded on her even now of a game of hide-and-seek she had played once as a little girl. She had hidden herself then, a crouching, wide-eyed mammal, behind a hedge of mock orange in the stifling heat of a July twilight. It had occurred to her for the first time in that moment that the real playing field for hide-and-seek is the whole world. Why not take a bus to Sacramento and hide there? Why not fly to India?

There was no bus to Sacramento now. A new wash of adrenaline coursed through her body every few minutes, whenever she heard Dion or Vitaly or another voice come in over channel eight. That spike of hormones, which she both expected and found unpredictable, honed her attention such that it ground away many biological deficits and annoyances: the short night of horrible sleep, the months of her body's corrections when she moved from the zero g of the hub to the centrifugal force of the rim, a whole summer without once feeling the grass under her bare feet.

There was another voice on channel eight, another male. "I'm back in Bonilla's stateroom," the voice said. "Chloe left her key fob on her desk."

Chloe felt an awareness of having made a fatal mistake. Yet she also felt an inexplicable gratitude that the hatches of the labs had remained unlocked. She never locked them—who else would have?

"Then check the labs. *Imperium* is not that big." The voice was Dion's. "Take care of it."

Chloe wished for some vision of the lab outside her locker. She could, if she wanted, push the panel door open a crack; however, anyone who entered the lab would notice that the door was unsealed and ajar. She kept still then, and her mind retreated into its ancestral line of thinking, that unreasoning sequence of wordless images that moves through the neurons of any cornered bobcat, any wolf held at bay by hunting dogs.

A minute passed, two minutes—Chloe could not count the time of the excruciating wait—before she heard someone click the light switch in lab four. Even with the earbuds in, she heard that click; she was aware, or perhaps only imagined she was aware, of a tiny buzz in the LEDs outside the black box where she waited.

She had never known the LEDs in the labs to buzz; perhaps they had been damaged in the electrical short the day before. Her feet were braced against the back of her hiding place; her palms rested against the inside of the panel door, like Atlas anticipating the weight of the world on his shoulders for the rest of time.

She heard, or felt, the working of a hand on the latch of the panel door, felt it almost before the hand knew what it was to do with the latch. Like a cat she sprang, pushed off the back wall, drove all her explosive force against the inside of the door. The door flew open a few inches before it slammed against some meaty obstacle—what? The arm of the man? His shoulder? Whatever Chloe hit, his grunt of surprise and the crisp, nauseating crack that sounded when the door struck him released in her a follow-on flush of adrenaline, poured over the waterline of hormones already coursing through her body. Had she a moment to reflect on what was happening inside her, she would have remarked that this was a perfect example of a positive feedback loop in a biological system, such a good example that she could have incorporated it into her lecture on the subject in the undergraduate biology-majors class. But she had left off reflection; her mind had contracted to a pinpoint of aggression that flared out in the tiny blazing seed of her hypothalamus.

The door of the case stood open now, and the lights of the lab module flooded in, dazzling her eyes. The man grunted in shock, though he appeared as only a hazy bundle to her eye, floating across the lab module. From her pocket she drew the screwdriver; like someone launching off a diving platform into a deep pool, she pushed against the back of the cabinet where she had hidden.

Just as she sprang out, a human projectile, she heard the crack of a firearm. In that moment, time slowed down: she expected the bullet with an equanimity that surprised her. But she felt nothing. She did not have the time to remark that even from less than three meters away, the man had failed to hit her. Notwithstanding the time dilation of her awareness, it did not occur to her that the man was an object in motion, remaining in motion, across the lab module. He moving, she moving, the bullet a tiny spinning third dancer in the lethal galliard—Chloe was harder to hit than she might have guessed, if she had had time to guess it. And he, whoever he was, had not considered Newton's verdict over his behavior when he had pulled the trigger: Chloe watched the man pushed backward, head over heels, in reaction to the firing of his pistol, until he landed with another meaty thud against the opposite wall of the lab after a full somersault. He fired again, wildly.

But Chloe took no time to reflect on that either: she was flying across the lab at him, whoever he was. She punched upward with the screwdriver, connected. She felt the warmth of his blood gush over her hand. The man grunted once more and was still. He floated, derelict; Chloe reached out for a handhold to steady herself.

Her eyes at last adjusted. The man was one of the Orbital-Ventures support staff. Chloe vaguely remembered him from the opening gala, dispensing drinks and running errands like a gofer. His name tag said *Angel*. She had driven the screwdriver in at the base of his chin, just above his Adam's apple, all the way to the handle. The shank had penetrated, Chloe guessed, through the man's soft palate, perhaps all the way into his cerebellum. Angel's blood clouded about the lab module in a mist.

Then Chloe did something that she had never once resorted to in twenty dissections when she was an undergraduate biology major, not once in her summers working at the cadaver lab back at Santa Rosa Junior College: she threw up.

Chloe had acquired her sense of detachment early in life, like an inoculation. Her childhood had been solitary, clouded by the emotional distance of her parents—her mother's narcissism, her father's leaden silence—and all her years studying the processes of life in their nutrient flows and biochemical feedback loops and hormonal semiosis had only deepened her far-off sense of the world. Unaware of what she had been about, Chloe had, through all her thirty-three years, cultivated a talent for seeing life as nothing more than a curiosity, neither sacred nor profane, and death as a thoroughly natural consequence of entropy unbinding every ordered process sooner or later. But she had never killed another human being.

She knew that she had to come back to herself, that she had no time to be squeamish. The pistol Angel had used floated nearby; the bullets had possibly penetrated the hull of *Imperium*. And the reports of the shots had certainly been audible throughout the hub, if not through the whole station.

First things first. She swam through the suspended muck of blood and vomit toward the pistol. She recognized the Glock 18, a pistol her father had loved, one that seemed absurdly overpowered for firing in zero gravity. At least the man hadn't switched it to fully automatic. It spun like a fatal top at the other end of the module. She tested the mechanism, found twenty-nine hollow-point bullets still in the magazine. She would have given a lot for a holster right now. But finding none on Angel's corpse, she had to accept the risky indignity of slipping the pistol into the overstuffed pocket of her blood-speckled jumpsuit.

The hull, if it had been breached, would have to wait: at any rate, no alarm sounded to announce a pressure drop in the module. She had to move. If someone hadn't seen her on the security cameras already, she would be seen soon enough. In the man's pocket she found a second magazine, which she slipped into her own. She had the sense of things moving quickly now, a train barreling down a track, the scenery slipping past her before she could notice its passing. She called on a final reserve of scientific dispassion and wrenched the screwdriver from the corpse's throat. She wiped the tool off on her cuff and stowed it in her other hip pocket.

She left the slowly spreading cloud of gore and glided across the lab module access corridor to her own lab. She could access the bridge's command and data-handling system through her laptop, make a radio call for help that way.

She was surprised for only a moment to find that her password to enter command and data handling no longer worked. She clapped her computer closed, pulled herself out into the lab module corridor, made for the Axle. That hallway was silent all along the length of the hub; compared to the abattoir she had just left, the place seemed preternaturally clean. Security cameras stared at each end of the corridor like two black-hooded cobra heads.

She would make her way to the bridge at the other end of the corridor. If she could secure the bridge, she could hole up there until rescue. Hauling at one of the handholds, she crept up the Axle. Every two meters of her voyage, she looped her left arm through the next handhold along the hallway, pointing the pistol with her right at the entryway to the access corridor of the bridge. It intruded on her focus briefly that she was leaving smears of the man's blood on each of the handholds' pristine grips.

Just then a figure swung head and arm around the entryway of the bridge access corridor at the other end of the Axle, about forty meters away. Almost before it registered in her brain that the woman's hand held a pistol and that it was firing on her, Chloe had launched herself across the hallway, a darting fish in a long barrel.

The white blank cylinder of the Axle offered her no cover at all, except for the entryways to the three long spokes of *Imperium*. These were arrayed around the midpoint of the cylinder about ten meters from Chloe, each 120 degrees from its neighbor. Both alpha and beta spokes, the spokes with the elevators, were sealed with circular hatches like the automatic lens cap of a massive camera. But gamma spoke, with the ladder, was open.

She zigzagged up the hallway, launching herself off the walls of the corridor like a billiard ball in an improbable bank shot.

The shots rang out one after another. Two shots, three shots—unlike Angel, the woman had the chance or the presence of mind to brace herself, probably by looping an arm through a handhold just inside the bulkhead of the access corridor to the bridge. Chloe felt the parting of the air around her ear as a bullet passed close by. She dropped into the shaft of gamma spoke. She hauled on the first rung of the ladder to vault herself over and feetfirst down the spoke toward the rim. Like a child getting a merry-go-round up to speed, she pulled against another rung as she floated farther down, then another a couple of meters farther, until she was descending quickly enough that she wondered whether she would be able to slow herself on the rungs of the ladder when she began to reach the bottom.

Like someone who had jumped deep into the ocean, Chloe craned her neck upward as she dropped, looking back toward the aperture of the spoke that she had entered for any sign of the woman. She drew the pistol from her hip pocket and held it above her head. The posture felt both like and unlike firing from a prone position, the way her father had taught her one summer half a lifetime ago. Yet she was lying on nothing, dropping toward the rim like a driven spike—it was just as easy to think of the pistol she held up as a tiny engine. If she fired, she would be pushed even faster toward the rim. She wondered whether firing would get her speed up enough to kill her when she hit. It would have been an interesting physics problem for someone else, at another time.

Still, she kept the gun trained on the opening as she dropped. By her estimate, she had dropped about a third of the length of gamma spoke.

But the shadow of the woman and her weapon never appeared at the aperture to fire on Chloe. And she would have to begin slowing herself down if she wanted to land easily on the rim. She reached out and felt one of the rungs slap against her open palm as she sped by. Then another. The third rung slapped into her palm like a baseball she had caught bare handed. A female voice was coming over her earbuds, saying something she couldn't attend to, something about her, about a weapon.

The third rung slowed her enough that she could grasp the next rung without wrenching her arm. She pocketed the pistol once more and allowed herself to slide down the ladder into the corridor, brightly lit, hushed and empty.

She heard Dion's voice coming over her earbuds: "Copy that. Stand by."

Chloe saw a security camera above her head, out of reach, in the form of a glossy black dome rather than the long-bodied, fixed cameras in the hub. She couldn't remember at what intervals the security cameras were placed on the long, lonely ring of the passageway. As she looked beyond, she saw nothing but the sky-blue curve of the hall rising before her and behind her.

She had not chosen to drop through gamma spoke with any strategy in mind. She wondered for a moment whether taking one of the elevators on one of the other spokes, if she had been able to, would have provided her a better escape route. Without knowing where Dion was, she couldn't say. And in any event, all spokes connected to the same silent, eerie ring.

Chloe raced through a mental map of defensible spaces she could go from here. She uttered a single nearly silent curse for having forgotten her key fob again in her cabin. Then she cursed under her breath a moment later when she realized what she had just left behind: Angel's corpse must have had a key fob on it. She had been so intent on the second magazine, and on finding Angel's apparently nonexistent holster, that it hadn't occurred to her to hunt for Angel's fob.

She had to get better, and quickly, at having things occur to her. She considered a moment—if the hostages were being kept in one place, there weren't many places on the rim to put all of them together: the Fortuna Ballroom, maybe the gym, possibly the restaurant or the solarium. The ballroom was close by, between alpha and gamma spokes on the wheel; the other spaces were farther away, between alpha and beta spokes.

The medevac was nearby, docked to the airlock adjacent to the infirmary. If she could get to it, she could be gone in a minute, splashing down in the Pacific within an hour.

She took a single step before she heard the voice of the woman again over the channel—not Nina but the other, a high-nasal-voiced American with a whiff of a plains accent: "I've got a visual on her: she's on the main corridor, moving from gamma toward alpha."

"Copy that," came a man's voice, Vitaly's. Chloe realized with a new flush of focus that his voice traveled not only through her earbuds but also through the corridor itself. Vitaly was near, perhaps as close as the infirmary or the library.

Chloe turned around and ran up the corridor, away from the voice she had heard. She heard the Midwesterner's voice— Meredith's voice, Chloe thought—over her earbuds, announcing Chloe's movements—"She's doubled back! Running past gamma and toward beta"—as though Chloe were a competitor in an obstacle course.

"I've got hostages here," Vitaly replied.

"Copy that. I'm on my way." This voice over channel eight was Nina's.

On Earth, Chloe had always considered herself more of a diligent, tireless jogger than a sprinter. But now, under the insatiable adrenaline bloom released through her limbs, and moving in the equivalent of .85 g, she sprinted like a rabbit.

As she ran, her mind raced through a sorry catalog of unacceptable hiding places. The next security camera in the corridor loomed before her as she approached. She paused a bare moment: from three meters away, she took aim at the camera, shot it out. A spray of plastic shards spangled the carpet where they fell.

"I've lost visual," Meredith announced over the radio.

Without a key fob, there were few places Chloe could enter: the conservatory, the library, perhaps the fitness center. She scanned the doors within view on this stretch of the hallway. On one side, there were two doors leading to conference rooms. *Imperium* harbored an aspirational number of conference rooms. On the other side, the door to the galley, and adjacent to that, the open alcove of the diner where she had eaten most of her meals for the last eight months.

The door to the kitchen was locked. She dashed into the alcove of the diner. The ghostly shadows of low cafeteria tables and chairs spread around the empty room. The blue-washed light of the corridor filtered in through the broad main entrance to the diner, wide as the alcove of an airport bar. The overhead lights came up then in response to her entry. She scanned about for a security camera. There was none that she could see: she supposed that the cafeteria was visible from the security camera she had just shot out in the corridor.

She glanced at her regular seat, the utilitarian bench where she had spent many of the hours she wasn't in the lab or in her cabin, the place where she read papers and emailed colleagues and ate her microwave meals, where she had once thrilled herself sexting with Ron. It had seemed a lonely, dreamlike space even when she wasn't the only person sitting there—rarely had there been more than four or five people in the whole cafeteria at one time, even back when the Kamara-Zhou lab was fully staffed. Now, as its empty darkness disappeared in the glare of the overhead lights, with Nina somewhere close by in the corridor, there was only nightmarish solitude and dread about the place.

The cafeteria connected to the kitchen through an interior swinging door. Chloe was struck by the foolishness of the design: a kitchen with one locking door and one door that couldn't be locked. Perhaps the wide entry to the cafeteria could be closed off with a mesh gate like a restaurant in the food court of a mall. She had never seen it closed, though, and had never in her time on *Imperium* thought to look for a gate.

She slipped through the swinging door, reached over as she entered to hit the light switch, disabling the motion sensor. Yet she heard Meredith's voice again. "She's gone into the galley off the employee diner."

Chloe would have cursed if she had heard Meredith say that an hour before, as though she had suffered a reversal in a game of hide-and-seek. But her minutes in terror had slowly dropped her into a kind of flow state; her fear had settled over her like a caul of so much sensory data, information no more or less remarkable than an itch or a stomachache. She would hide, would run, not on the strength of any deep reflection but rather because that was what she was made to do, as though she had transformed into some articulate prey animal, like a talking rabbit.

Meredith must have seen the door swing open on a security camera in the kitchen. Surely there was a camera here, though in eight months of microwaving meals she had not noticed it.

Nina's voice, more tightly strung than it had been before, came over channel eight: "I have her holed up in there. Chief, could I get Vitaly over here to back me up?"

"Vitaly's still chaperoning." There was a pause. Then, "Vitaly, bring back Nicholas and Samir—we'll continue their calls later." Dion's voice was unreadable to Chloe now, if she had ever been able to read it in the past.

"Copy that," Vitaly said. "Nina, give me two minutes, babe."

Chloe crouched and crept back into the cafeteria. She got the best angle she could looking out on the corridor. She saw no one. Nina would not be so foolish as to just stand in front of the kitchen door. Yet the main corridor offered no real secure vantages: Olivia Fauré's design had dispensed even with the garbage cans and tall planters of an Earthside hotel. Her look was sleek and minimal, punctuated by nothing more than low-slung chairs and tables at long intervals, a decorative ribbing of false buttresses every few meters. But even these small touches would have been too small for Nina to hide behind. Except for the columns of the spokes, which came down into the center of the hallway at three points on the rim, there was nothing for a person to hide behind in all 628-odd meters of the ring corridor.

Chloe did not see anyone from her vantage. Perhaps Nina had taken a prone firing position farther down the hall, or perhaps she had opened up one of the conference rooms opposite the diner and hid in the darkness of an open doorway.

Chloe considered the factors she knew and the ones she didn't know. Meredith was watching the security cameras: known. Others were tracking her besides the voices she had heard on the communicator: unknown. Nina was nearby: known. How she was armed, whether with a handgun and hollow points or with a long gun with rounds that could punch through the hull or with some other weapon entirely: unknown. Vitaly was coming: known. She had less than two minutes: known.

She slunk back into the dark of the kitchen. Even in the dark, she knew this place as though it had been the kitchen in her house, which in one sense it was. She felt around for the storage cabinet against the back wall, her fingers brushing over the tops of bottles and containers until she found the slick plastic of the jug she was hunting for.

She groped around for the other end of the room, stumbling once, to find the galley's sad liquor cabinet. Anything would do here. She reached in, and her fingers closed around some kind of stout, angular bottle. She had the fleeting, irrelevant realization that it would be a shame if out of the entire liquor cabinet she had happened to grab the bottle of Jefferson's Reserve Kentucky bourbon.

As silently as she could, Chloe sneaked back into the cafeteria. Near the door, she set down the plastic container, a nearly full three-liter jug of sunflower oil. Holding the other bottle, she moved as close as she could to the entryway without being visible from the corridor. She got a look at the bottle as she opened it, and she regarded it as a good omen that it was not the Jefferson's Reserve but rather some kind of nearly undrinkable lime-flavored vodka that one of the Penn State team had left behind. She poured the vodka out in a broad puddle over the tile; at the edge, some began to soak into Olivia Fauré's sky-blue carpet.

Chloe moved quickly now. She ran back to the kitchen, cast about in the dark for some kind of fabric. There was a laundry hamper near the exterior door for rags and dirty napkins. She pulled the whole bag off its rack, went to the stove, lit one of the burners.

"I've got a visual on her," Meredith said. "It looks like she's lighting up the stove."

"Come again?"

"I'm serious," Meredith answered. "I'm watching her now. She's lit the stove."

But by that point Chloe had managed to light one of the dirty kitchen towels—thankfully a bit greasy—and dashed out to her puddle of spilled vodka. She threw the ignited towel into the puddle, which went up at once into a tiny lake of cool-blue flame.

People were chattering over channel eight. Chloe's focus was elsewhere, though: she threw the rest of the towels and dirty napkins in a pile and proceeded to soak them with the oil from the plastic jug. Ten seconds later, she was tossing the oily cloths into the alcohol fire, as the blue flame by degrees turned to the yellow of a grease fire. A black noisome smoke began to billow out into the corridor.

The smoke alarm started blaring. Behind that sound, she could just make out in her earbuds some kind of frantic chattering between the people hunting her. She couldn't hear what they said; probably, Chloe realized with some satisfaction, they couldn't hear one another over the smoke alarm either.

She pulled out the pistol again and assessed the depth of the smoke in the corridor. The sprinklers hadn't kicked in yet, and the carpet of the hallway was beginning to smolder. She couldn't see Nina; she couldn't see five meters up the corridor. It was time.

Just before she dashed, her eye fell on the fire extinguisher hanging on the wall of the galley. Years of observation into the evolutionary processes of living things had given her the intuition that the fire extinguisher would be useful in ways she could not anticipate, that it was preadapted for many functions, as a biologist might say. With the pistol in her right hand and the fire extinguisher in her left, she sprinted down the corridor, away from the cloud of smoke, away from the sprinklers, which had just engaged, away from Nina on the other side.

Chloe ran toward beta spoke. She might be running toward

Vitaly, she knew, if he had decided to take the long way around the rim to cut her off. Meredith announced her movements over channel eight as she ran up the corridor. When she passed the next security camera, she coated the little black dome with a spray from the fire extinguisher.

She disliked her own plan. Taking the beta spoke elevator back to the hub struck her as reckless: the elevator could be controlled from the bridge, she was sure. If Meredith shut the elevator down, Chloe would have to climb out of the car and climb the emergency ladder in the shaft of beta spoke—it would be a simple thing for Meredith to fire on her from the elevator landing.

An insight dawned on Chloe, a dismal understanding, but without recrimination or self-hatred, that she should never have come to the rim in the first place. She would have been better off staying put in lab module four, clouded by the haze of Angel's blood. But so long as Meredith occupied the bridge—Chloe hoped, at least, that Meredith was the only one up there—there was nowhere on the rim to go that she couldn't be seen.

She ran the last of the distance, spraying another security camera with foam on her way. The landing for the beta spoke elevator, a thick, tapering pillar like the central column of a towering bank, took up the center of the rim corridor here. The car was at the bottom, awaiting her.

Chloe climbed in the car and punched the button for the hub. She could see Nina up the hall, taking up a firing position with a pistol as the doors shut and the car glided into its ascent. Chloe flattened herself against one side of the cylinder of the car, presenting as narrow a profile to the doors as she could. Yet she heard only the *plink, plink* of two bullets striking at what she imagined were the exterior doors of the elevator. She would have expected even a hollow-point bullet to penetrate both exterior and interior doors on an elevator—neither door seemed especially thick. Perhaps Nina was using safety slugs to minimize overpenetration in the pressure vessel that was the space station. Or perhaps the doors were better reinforced than Chloe realized.

"She's on the elevator," a breathless Nina called out over channel eight.

"Copy that—I have her," Meredith replied.

Chloe waited for the car to stall in response to a shutdown order from the bridge, prepared herself to climb out when the moment arrived.

The elevators of *Imperium* were unlike any that had ever been made. The car bore a display above the curved doors to announce to passengers what percentage of Earth's gravity (or, more properly, the centrifugal force that mimicked gravity) the car was currently subjected to. The car glided quickly on its cables; the display already read *18% of Earth's Gravity—Please Grasp a Handhold*. The handholds around the circumference of the car were the same leather-bound teardrop loops that beautified the public areas of the hub of *Imperium*.

But the greatest difference in the car was in its doors. Each car had two sets: the central opening telescopic doors, which would have been at home on any terrestrial elevator, and the circular hatch that took up the ceiling of the car. One entered the car on the rim the same way one would enter an elevator on Earth; the landing at the hub, however, occurred between the hatch atop the car and another circular hatch on the cylindrical wall of the Axle.

Chloe wondered why Meredith had not arrested the car's ascent. The car continued to rise until it seemed that it was going to dock with the hatch of the Axle. Perhaps Meredith had not been quick enough to shut down the elevator; perhaps shutting it down had not occurred to her.

Chloe put those musings out of her mind. She anchored herself with one of the car's handholds and trained her weapon on the hatch that would open onto the Axle. The panels of the circular hatches slid open.

No one waited just outside the door.

Chloe could not see far down the Axle in either direction. But she imagined that Meredith had set herself up at one end or the other, hiding in the mouth of one of the access corridors. In all likelihood, she had taken up the same position she had taken when she had last fired on Chloe: just inside the bulkhead of the bridge access corridor, anchored to one of the handholds near the hatch.

It was a gamble to assume that Meredith was where Chloe had last seen her. However, it seemed unlikely that Meredith would have traversed the entire length of the Axle to post herself at one of the access corridors on the other end. Chloe knew that she had to get out of the elevator at some point.

Chloe pocketed her pistol and took up the fire extinguisher in both hands. Braced against the floor of the car, she shot a swath of foam into the Axle, a great marshmallow curtain hanging in the weightlessness like a thick, flocky nebula between the entrance to the elevator and the bridge. She hoped she had guessed correctly where Meredith was.

"She's filling up the Axle with foam," she heard Meredith complaining over channel eight in a tone that reminded Chloe of a petulant college freshman. Chloe took her chance then. She pushed herself off from the floor of the elevator car and into the Axle just as the circular hatches shut behind her. She darted one glance toward the access corridor to the lab modules, saw a clear way for herself, and fired the extinguisher in the direction of the cloud she had made.

She hugged one edge of the cylindrical wall of the Axle.

She could hear a pistol shot ringing out through the Axle, another shot, a third. Whether in reaction to the sound of the extinguisher or just some intuition that Chloe was making her move, Meredith was apparently firing into the cloud of foam from the other end of the corridor. Chloe did not consider her chances of being hit by a stray shot or the relatively high probability of being hit by a bullet ricocheting off the concave end of the Axle that she was speeding toward.

Two seconds of fire extinguisher exhaust was enough to accelerate her more quickly than she was comfortable with. She sped toward the opening of the access corridor to the lab modules until she slammed into the bulkhead separating the Axle from the access corridor. Chloe shook off the pain of the impact that shot through her back; she shot one more squib of exhaust to the side of her. She glided out of the Axle and into the access corridor as a fourth and fifth shot rang against the wall where she had just been.

Chloe grabbed one of the handholds in the corridor to arrest her flight. She hitched the trigger of the fire extinguisher into one of her stuffed hip pockets, drew her pistol again. She looked about her for the corridor's security camera. She pulled the roll of tape from her pocket, pulled a strip long enough to wad into a ball, and stuffed the ball in the lens socket.

She floated through the access corridor and into the lab modules, closed the security hatch between the modules and the access corridor, listened for any signs of Meredith.

But the next thing she heard, a long minute later, was Dion's voice, coming over her radio on channel eight.

"Let's talk, Chloe."

CHAPTER
FIVE

Dion surveyed the circle of hostages in the Fortuna Ballroom while he waited for Chloe to answer.

The asymmetry of information flow between captive and captor seemed curious to him. The Reckoners had studied these hostages—the billionaires, anyway—from the moment they had been accepted as the first guests of *Imperium*. He knew their real estate holdings, their stock portfolios, their divorce settlements, the price-to-earnings ratios of their various companies. What did they know about him?

Whatever they thought they knew about him—his NASA celebrity, the interviews, the up-from-poverty story about his childhood in Saint Louis—all of that was worse than false. Rather, that whole constellation of journalistically true events from his life, confected by press secretaries and marketers into inspiring narrative, functioned only to tell a certain self-satisfied population of Americans what they wanted to believe about themselves. What did these hostages know about him, indeed?

When his parents and his older sisters moved up to Saint Louis before he was born, every one of them probably already carried the tumors in their bones, their brains, barming like flecks of yeast as they slept and ate and worked. Dion had been nine years old when his father fell ill. His parents took in that news with a resignation that had struck Dion even then: their acceptance that this was the lot of people who had lived where they had lived, who had worked where they had worked, hung over Dion from that time on like a fatal dark star.

His parents had fought back, of course, pushing as best they could against the companies of the place downriver, the great false ecosystem of refineries and factories, its exhalations of vinyl chloride, benzene, chloroprene. They joined lawsuits, filed the ever-renewing sheaf of paperwork that seemed designed to never be completed, consulted lawyers, coughed up stories and their own flesh for a legion of toxicologists, oncologists, occupational epidemiologists. But how does one fight against an ecosystem? By the time Dion's mother died, the year before the first of his sisters got sick, ten years after his father had wasted away, the settlement check arrived: $40,000. Dion used his share to repair the roof of the family house and pay down his car loan.

Dion brought his attention back to the Fortuna Ballroom. He appraised the hostages in front of him: They had a rumpled, almost shabby air, both the hungover wealthy ones and the OrbitalVentures people who had worked far into the evening and then awakened to being taken hostage before they could get four hours of sleep. They kept their eyes on the floor, most of them, most of the time, though every so often one of them would sneak a glance at him, as though trying to find his eyes behind his sunglasses.

Dion disliked the necessity of lumping them all together, the rich and the poor; the act seemed inimical somehow to the Reckoners' mission. For example, Maryam—she hardly deserved the kind of trouble she was in now. Even Tirzah and Erik were just working stiffs of a sort. To be sure, they had cast their lot with some true social parasites, and Tirzah and Erik made more than they deserved for the parasitic work that they did, but they were no closer to being billionaires than he was.

However, he was not about to drift away from the work at hand with his philosophizing.

Vitaly and Nina had come into the ballroom together when he called them back a few minutes ago. Vitaly appeared a bit more amped up than Dion liked, all the more reason for the team to reassess its position, slow down, apply pressure more mindfully.

Vitaly seemed to be enjoying the power dynamics of standing over the hostages, scowling at them, corralling them with his pacing like some terrifying bipedal sheepdog. For all Dion knew, maybe Nina was enjoying herself as well, standing like a gaunt receptionist at the door. However, Nina was at least a bit more circumspect.

Dion had to admit to himself some enjoyment at what he was seeing. But the pleasurable sensation Dion felt in his chest had little to do with seeing a bunch of wealthy folks brought low before him. He considered *that* satisfaction, fleeting as a sugar rush, not worth indulging for more than a moment. Rather, his quieter, steadier sense of fulfillment was the consequence of an operation carried out like clockwork, a plan with a myriad of decision points and contingencies refined into a single course of action that had so far (within broad tolerances) minimized danger and loss of life. The sabotage of the CisLunar rocket, the rerouting of control of the rocket's thrusters to the station's bridge, the luring of the three pilots aboard—in retrospect, what now seemed fated had in fact been a long series of careful gambles, each of which had required a cool head to order the tossing of the dice.

It was time for a new plan now, surely, but he admired how far the original plan had taken them. Much that could have gone wrong had gone well. The overloaded circuit in the lab module airlock, for example, could have killed all the hostages during their space walk. That, too, would have been poetic justice of a kind, the deaths of some of the wealthiest people on Earth because they had placed their trust in the blandishments and self-assured press releases of a breathtakingly rickety company. But Dion was glad that the Reckoners' operation hadn't been aborted by wiring problems on the station.

Of all the many things that might have gone wrong, he would not have predicted that Chloe would slip the dragnet. Of course, he disliked losing Angel as well: he wondered how an unarmed woman Chloe's size had managed to overpower him. Once the danger was past, he intended to study the security camera footage to see how she had done it.

But six months of planning and training had yielded at least a partial, provisional victory so far. If Chloe could be neutralized—and there were several ways to do that—Tsadok could get the money siphoned into a Reckoners' account Earthside and Dion and his team could get themselves off *Imperium* quickly.

Had she been any other person on the station, the most straightforward method for counteracting Chloe would have been to seal off the lab wing from the bridge and open the airlock, flushing the air out of her redoubt. But leaving out any other consideration, he had dismissed that strategy as promising a low likelihood of success: she had a pressure suit and oxygen tanks available to her in that wing, and she had trained to suit up quickly in a decompression event. If she was unlucky, she might lose consciousness before she could get her suit on. But if she remembered her training, she'd very likely survive the decompression, and she'd be motivated then to discharge all kinds of mischief.

In any event, he was obliged to use a lighter touch, regardless of how much he disliked her armed presence on the station. The Reckoners had not trained for this peculiar contingency; however, in the absence of further instructions, Dion would have to deal with her somehow. He couldn't have her shooting his people.

The least distasteful way of neutralizing her would be to appeal to her rhetorically. Who was it that had said diplomacy was the pursuit of war by other means? Dion turned away again from the hostages, walked to the other end of the ballroom to look over the Earth out of earshot. He spoke again into the silence of channel eight. "Chloe, I know you are on this channel. Let's talk."

Was she in fact on this channel? If she wasn't, neither she nor the hostages would hear him embarrass himself. And if his hunch was right? There was no reason to begin a negotiation if he couldn't transmit confidence. It wasn't too much to imagine that Chloe had awakened in the middle of the night—she complained of insomnia all the time, now that he thought about it—and that she might for some reason have listened in on the communicators. It was one of the more parsimonious explanations for her hiding herself in the lab modules before the rest were rounded up.

"Chloe, listen," he said, not pleading, not wheedling, but rather like a classroom teacher offering a student one more chance to straighten up. "I have no intention of hurting you. If Angel wasn't clear about that, that's his mistake. This can all end peacefully if you'll just let us carry out our business here."

Dion waited over the dead air for a response. He began to walk back toward the circle of hostages.

"What the hell are you doing, Dion?" Chloe's voice came subdued and small over channel eight.

Dion permitted himself a smile, not that anyone could see it, for interpreting her behavior so well. "We're engaged in political action. You don't have to be involved in any unpleasantness, Chloe. You stand aside, we all go home. It's that simple."

"What about Konrad and the CisLunar people?" she asked. Her affect seemed flat and gray, as though it were metal plated. "Did you kill them for not standing aside?"

Of course she would have heard the dialogue with Konrad if she had been searching the bands last night. "That had to be done," Dion said. He didn't owe her any more explanation than that. That Konrad had known the station's systems better than anyone, that he had had as much combat training as any of the Reckoners—and more zero-g combat training—that the Cis-Lunar pilots had been only unfortunate collateral damage when Konrad was removed: Dion wasn't going to lose even more initiative by explaining all his reasons.

"What do you want, then?"

"From you? Just that you don't act foolishly. We won't have to trouble you at all if you'll stay out of our way while we conduct our business."

There was a long pause. Dion imagined her barricaded in her lab, pondering the broad chessboard of *Imperium* between them.

"I suppose your definition of not acting foolish includes my not sabotaging the Starliner capsule."

Well played, Chloe Bonilla, Dion thought. Whether by design or dumb luck, she had ensconced herself between his team and their ride back to Earth. Meredith had already informed him that Chloe had disabled all the security cameras in the laboratory wing, including the airlock where the Starliner was docked. He disliked having such an important part of the station blacked out to his forces.

"I'm not sure why you would want to sabotage the Starliner," Dion mused. "That would just keep us all up here shooting at each other longer."

She didn't know how to fly the Starliner herself—he was sure of that. She wouldn't have made the threat she had if she knew how to fly it. But the thought that she might be able to get aboard, mangle the Starliner's controls the way Nina had done to the controls of the CisLunar rocket, gave him some misgivings.

The only other way down was the medevac capsule. That was under Reckoners' control, of course, docked to one of the two emergency airlocks on the rim. But the medevac would hold only two, and it couldn't make a powered landing—it was just a tin can loaded with parachutes, as helpless as an old Gemini capsule on the way down. Dion wouldn't be escaping that way, even if things went south. He wasn't about to plop down in the Pacific Ocean or Siberia if there were still Reckoners aboard *Imperium*—he would either complete this mission or die with them, but he wouldn't abandon them.

The thought of the medevac capsule did give Dion pause, however. In a flash of improvisational insight, he saw a method by which the team might retake the initiative and oblige Chloe to react to the Reckoners' decision loops rather than the reverse. It would involve some unpleasantness, but what manner of un-pleasantness had they not prepared for? *This struggle may be a moral one; or it may be a physical one; or it may be both moral and physical; but it must be a struggle.*

Dion crossed the ballroom. With Nina first, then with Vitaly, he explained the two tracks of his plan, the carrot of the medevac and the stick of killing the hostages one by one. A wolfish smile crossed Vitaly's face when he heard the new plan. Dion didn't like that, and he gave the broad man a look. This wasn't an operation where bloodlust was a virtue.

Dion walked back to the position he had taken when he guarded the prisoners. He transmitted again to Chloe, in a voice neither theatrical nor passionate, but loudly enough that all in the circle could hear him.

"Chloe, listen," he said, "I'm going to tell you this once: I don't want to kill any of the people we're guarding here. It works against our goals. If you will come out and give yourself up in the next ten minutes, everybody lives, and we all get to go home safe. If you don't surrender in ten minutes, though, we're going to start killing people. I know you don't want that on your conscience."

Dion remarked to himself how traumatized the hostages seemed now: almost all of them took his pronouncement in complete downcast silence. Only one—he thought it was the humiliated Tirzah Fowler—let out a high, choked sob that she could not stifle immediately.

On channel eight, there was no sound for a long moment. Finally, Chloe was able to muster a flaccid assessment: "You are sick, Dion."

"I assure you, I'm one of the only healthy ones on *Imperium*. Are you going to risk your life and the lives of others to keep a handful of billionaires from losing a small fraction of their wealth? You're an observant person, Chloe, so please take me at my word: you will come, unarmed, down the alpha spoke elevator in the next ten minutes, or I will begin killing hostages. Dion out."

It was then that he realized that he had said twice what he had promised to say only once.

But Dion had discovered over long years that embarrassment was an unproductive emotion. He redirected himself by addressing the hostages: "I want to concentrate your attention on the task at hand. If Chloe Bonilla doesn't give herself up, we have a few minutes before I need to choose who will be leaving us. You guests have lived your lives as though there were no such thing as a common good, as though all good things on Earth are privately held—that belief is, after all, why the Reckoners picked you in the first place. Perhaps a visible sign of the suffering of others will awaken your empathy. However, in the likely event that even the death of someone sitting in this room right now cannot awaken your moral imagination"—he looked around at his charges to assure himself that they were following the offer he was about to make—"what you may remember from your Earthside training is that there is a medevac capsule quite nearby. The capsule can carry two of you. If any two of you are ready to pay, you may head for home and safety as soon as you have made your payment." Dion looked over the downcast group, the sullen eye contact that peeked out from them every few moments like a flash of baleful firefly light.

"Of course, if more than two of you are ready to pay, we can auction the seats to the highest bidders. I start the bidding at one billion US dollars."

There was a general groaning and rolling of eyes from those who did not have a billion dollars. Dion remarked to himself that none of the billionaires looked particularly sanguine either. Roger seemed to be whispering something petty or perhaps venomous to his wife; Li scowled and muttered with Sir Alexander. Viv regarded the news with what looked like stoic resignation, staring out at the Earth like a deposed monarch.

At length, Samir Winters-Qureshi spoke up: "I think that several of us would pay that kind of money. But it's not that simple to move a billion dollars into Bitcoin. You say you have researched our finances, so you must know already that we don't have a billion dollars cash on hand. At least I don't have that much cash—practically all of Nick's and my money is tied up in equities and real estate. It would take us weeks to liquidate a billion dollars."

Dion listened to Samir's excuse impassively. The Reckoners had talked about that challenge at length during the months of planning. For his part, Dion had anticipated that lack of liquidity would be the biggest stumbling block. But during the strategy meetings, Tsadok's representative had argued for the strategy: "Some of the guests are worth a lot more than a billion dollars. Li is worth at least twelve by himself. A motivated seller can gin up liquidity very quickly; all one needs is a phone and a willingness to discount assets."

Now they were going to find out whether Tsadok's man had been right. They had a few hours to work, maybe more than a few. Somebody, NASA probably, would mount a rescue operation as soon as they knew what was going on up here. Surely the word had gotten out by now, an hour after Vitaly had taken Li to make his first call to his financial people. But a rescue mission would still take a while: NASA was not the kind of place that could approve a new cafeteria menu in a few hours, much less put together a rescue operation on such short notice. CisLunar, or maybe Hesperus, might work faster, but neither company had security teams trained for boarding operations, for counterterrorism, for hostage negotiations—the Hesperus people barely seemed to have active-shooter training for their facilities on Earth. The Reckoners had to work fast, but they didn't have to work *that* fast. Dion felt gratified at the way both carrot and stick had presented themselves in the new circumstances.

Dion, impassive behind his aviator sunglasses, loomed above the hostages while he eavesdropped on their low talking.

"We don't have much time," Samir was murmuring, "but I

wonder whether we could each make a good-faith estimate of how much we could come up with on short notice."

"How short a notice?" Roger asked. "Ten minutes?"

"Not *that* short. They must know we don't have a billion dollars hidden in our mattresses. Hold on—I'll ask."

And then came the tenor schoolboy voice again: "Pardon me, Commander Stubblefield? If we can make you a *commit-ment* of the money, will you commit to not killing any of us?"

Dion affected a look of contemplation, as though consid-ering an offer that was not exactly to his liking. "Very well. If you make the commitment of the money, you'll be given the chance to move it into cryptocurrency and transfer it to us."

"But," he continued, "the ten-minute deadline—excuse me, eight-and-a-half-minute deadline—applies to Chloe Bonilla's course of action, not yours."

"But if, hypothetically, we could agree to the eight-bil-lion-dollar commitment in the next eight and a half minutes? Can the top two bidders go home and the rest of us live?"

Samir was beginning to annoy him. Still, Dion admired the man's ability to confront his situation head-on. And, Dion had to remind himself, influencing Chloe's course of action, and how quickly she took that course, was really means to an end and not the end itself. There were many other methods of handling Chloe if she didn't give herself up.

But a thought intruded on him then: Would the hostages still respect him if he went back on his threat? It took him a moment to articulate this anxiety to himself. He did, how-ever, have the presence of mind, or emotional maturity, to recognize the thought for what it was: an unseemly preoccu-pation with what other people thought of him. Of course the Reckoners should take yes for an answer; he didn't want any killing of hostages just for kicks. He didn't want to be that guy.

"I think we're beginning to understand one another, Samir. We'll accept your offer if some combination of you can make the commitment in the next few minutes."

Sir Alexander spoke up, or croaked up: "Would you accept voting stock in the Hesperus Corporation? Or in OrbitalVentures?"

"Do you think I'm an idiot, Mr. Dunne? No, it's cash or death. You have less than eight minutes."

Tirzah Fowler commented in a leaden voice. "I think we may see some drop-off in OrbitalVentures' stock price over the next couple of days, Sir Alexander."

The hostages turned back to one another. "I would pay the whole eight billion right now if I could," Viv Volterra stage-whispered. "But I'm sure you've seen the stories about my company. Therapis stock has suffered a drop of its own at the moment."

This drew a grim chuckle of commiseration, or perhaps schadenfreude, from a couple of the men in the circle. "Just at the moment?" somebody whispered.

"Everything I have is in real estate," she continued. "But what if one or a small group of us—of you, I mean—put up the whole eight billion? The rest of us could pay our shares plus interest back to you when this is over and we have some time to liquidate assets."

It occurred to Dion that even facing indictment, even as a hostage, Volterra was a very skilled cheerleader.

"Talk is cheap, Viv," answered Roger Van Cleave. "If someone wants to sign a contract to that effect, I'll think about loaning money on reasonable terms. Until then, the only ones who should be speaking are people who are ready to commit."

"Are you saying you're ready to commit?" Li asked.

"Eff yeah, I'm ready." Roger looked directly at Dion for the first time since the rebuke with the active denial device. "I bid one billion two hundred and fifty million dollars. I can liquidate that much in forty-eight hours."

Dion checked his watch. He wished he had set a timer when he made his threat to Chloe—had four minutes passed or five? He transmitted to Meredith on channel eight: "Bridge, this is the ballroom—keep your eye open for activity in the alpha elevator. Chloe may be headed that way. Please apprise us if she does."

"Roger that, ballroom."

Dion watched the guests scooting little by little across the floor as they sat crisscross applesauce and tried to speak to one another. Perhaps they didn't even notice that they were moving, they went by in such small degrees and at such long intervals: leaning far forward to hear someone else in the group talking quietly, then scooting a foot or so forward to hear better. But within a couple of minutes, the guests had formed an inner circle where they could confer and bargain. The OrbitalVentures employees, scooting out of the way of the billionaires little by little, sat more and more in silence at the margins. As usual, they depended on the largesse of others.

It was a shame to submit folks like the station employees to the reckoning, Dion mused. But like Rosencrantz and Guildenstern, they did make love to this employment—they were not near his conscience.

Of the hotel guests, only Kassie Ng sat in the outer circle with the OrbitalVentures suckers. Dion had discounted her as a hostage long before the guests had even begun training for their trip to *Imperium*: Kassie scarcely had two million dollars to her name, much less two billion. Granted, two million dollars for hawking lip products on Instagram seemed like a nice job for a twenty-six-year-old. But her money was small potatoes in this field; it barely added up to a tip for the Reckoners' hazard pay. She was definitely outer circle.

Li and Roger continued conferring. "I must not have expressed myself well," Li was saying. "I'll try to rephrase: I believe that if we begin from a principle of cooperation, we may arrive at the eight-billion-dollar figure more efficiently than if we simply bid against one another for the two seats. I will pay my share, but I don't intend to pay more than my share."

"Cooperation, fine—that's great," Roger blurted. The contortion of his facial muscles accentuated the heat ray's purple weals across his skin like the garish lines of a topographic map. "Somebody's getting killed in the next two minutes, and it won't be me. Or my wife."

Sir Alexander flashed a wry smile. "It won't be you under any circumstances. They want your money, remember?"

Two minutes left? Dion asked himself. Had so much time passed already? He glanced (he hoped surreptitiously) at his watch. Roger had been exaggerating, or panicking: there were still more than three minutes remaining. Dion wished again that he had remembered to set a timer for the stopwatch. It was a remarkable thing to have forgotten, given his training. *Okay, best estimate,* he thought to himself, *the deadline is zero nine twenty-five hours. Zero nine twenty-five. Zero nine twenty-five.* It occurred to him—as good ideas often do, at inopportune moments—that a smartphone assistant could be programmed to listen for phrases from its user and set a timer automatically. *You have ten minutes,* a person might say, and Siri or whatever program replaced Siri would know what they wanted and start the timer without prompting. Of course, you'd have to leave your phone microphone on for that, so it wouldn't work as well for a hostage taking like this, not if you were trying to minimize evidence. But it would be good for making coffee or going down for a nap. Someone like Roger could probably write it into the app over a long weekend.

Nicholas and Samir Winters-Qureshi had been whispering to one another as Li and Roger bickered. Nicholas broke in at last: "I think Mr. Li has a point. Those of us who can raise the money quickly could agree to pay eight billion for the group; we can set up a system where those who paid are made whole by the rest of us when we get back to Earth."

"No offense, but I wouldn't exactly trust a handshake agreement with everybody here," Roger countered. "And anyway, how are we going to figure out who pays what? All these people"—he gestured at the cooks and housekeepers in the outer circle—"do they just pay nothing while the guests pay a billion each?"

Dion held his tongue—it would have brought him great satisfaction to say that yes, this was precisely the idea behind the Reckoners, that these billionaires would, for once in their lives, pay the bill for all. But this was not his conversation to facilitate.

Samir answered instead: "Roger, every one of these employees could give you everything they own, and it wouldn't add up to one percent of a repayment. Let's cover this—people are depending on us."

"Fine. Fine. We're running out of time. I want to get this in writing."

"Roger, you just said yourself that we're running out of time. How are you going to get an agreement in writing? Are we going to type out a contract on our phones?"

"They took all our phones."

"That's my point."

Maryam, who sat at the outer margin but was more and more able to follow the conversation as the volume had risen, called out, "There's a Moleskine journal and pens in every room. Maybe they'd give us the paper to write out a contract."

"And who's going to draw it up?" Roger spit back at her. "Did anybody in housekeeping bring their legal team?"

"I'm not a contract attorney," Nicholas said with a kind of pep-squad earnestness, "but I have passed the California Bar."

Roger turned to face him. "Are you licensed to practice law *in space*, Nick? If you aren't, then what the fudge does it matter which bar exam you passed?"

"There's no time!"

"Then we ask for an extension."

"This isn't a term paper we're turning in."

Dion checked his watch. Zero nine twenty-five and four-teen seconds. Casting one of them out of the airlock right now, when the guests seemed so close to a breakthrough, struck him as singularly counterproductive. But, he reminded himself, the intended audience for his threat had been Chloe Bonilla, not the hostages.

With one slim access of hope, he got back on channel eight. "Bridge, this is ballroom. Any movement on alpha elevator?"

"Bridge here. No movement on the elevator, chief."

Dion could not help heaving a weary sigh. The old line from Orwell's essay about shooting the elephant came to him unbidden: *I often wondered whether any of the others grasped that I had done it solely to avoid looking a fool.*

He had spent part of the last ten minutes contemplating the people before him, weighing each of them in the balance of his discernment. And now, over ten minutes since he had made the threat, he had identified dispositively who should *not* be made a sacrificial victim. None of the guests, of course, could be cast out of the airlock. Not even Kassie Ng, a little fish in *Imperium*'s big pond—it would be foolish for the Reckoners to so carelessly alienate twelve million Instagram fans. As for the OrbitalVentures staff, it seemed ironic, given the Reckoners' philosophy, to kill folks from the kitchens or from housekeeping, even though these were hardly blue-collar Joe Six-Packs: all of the *Imperium* staff had college degrees, stock options with OrbitalVentures, vested retirement plans. Gwen Newhouse, the chef, had won a James Beard Award back in 2022.

That left Tirzah, Erik, Lorenz, Maryam. Now that he was forced to it, he supposed that Tirzah was the obvious choice. This unpleasantness did seem like a responsibility for the ranking manager.

"Okay, Ms. Fowler," Dion said, "please go with Vitaly." Vitaly took one solemn step forward. To Dion's surprise, Tirzah seemed to have composed herself over the last minutes while the guests bickered, and she stood with a kind of cold and unassailable dignity.

"Wait," said Erik, Assistant Vice President of Guest Experience. He stood up next to Tirzah. "Can I go instead?"

I don't have time for this, Dion thought. Erik leaned in to give Tirzah a deep, unprofessional tongue kiss. Dion found the whole display unseemly. He scanned the room, wondering whether the two of them were trying to carry off some kind of distraction.

In the end, he concluded that the kiss was really just a kiss. Maybe there was some kind of traditional-gender-role gallantry afoot, at least in the Assistant Vice President of Guest Experience's imagination. "Fine, Erik. Fine," Dion said wearily. "Just go with Vitaly."

Erik kissed Tirzah's fingers as they parted, and she stood watching him pace out of the room in front of Vitaly toward the second of the airlocks on the rim, the one that didn't have the medevac capsule docked to it.

If he were carrying out the plan again, Dion would have sent Vitaly with Erik or Tirzah or whoever to the airlock in the sixth minute or so of the countdown, so that when they hit the ten-minute mark he could signal and Vitaly could flush the person out into space right then. That would have been far more effective from a behaviorist standpoint than carrying out the threat four minutes late. Instead they all had to wait for the long walk around the rim to the antipode of the Fortuna Ballroom, where the rim's second airlock was. Tirzah had sat back down and shook with her head on her knees; Maryam and Lorenz snaked their arms around her. What a mess.

They heard the report of a pistol from up the corridor, followed by a hoarse, grunting scream like the bawling of a bull. "Vitaly, report," Dion barked into his mouthpiece. He signaled to Nina with a jerk of his head, and she took off up the corridor at a run.

The bellowing continued for what seemed like an interminably long time, though in retrospect Dion realized it must have only been two or three seconds. Then silence.

"Vitaly here," came the voice over channel eight. "The guy tried to roundhouse kick me—a real Walker, Texas Ranger. Maybe he thought to kick the gun out of my hand. I had to shoot him. He's out the airlock now."

In that moment there was a stricken gasp among the hostages, then a cry and a quick turning away, as the guests and employees of *Imperium* caught sight of Erik Rasmussen when the great windows of the Fortuna Ballroom rotated past his discarded rag-doll corpse.

"Let's get you and Nina back to the ballroom," Dion transmitted. "Meredith, any elevator usage?"

"None, chief."

Dion looked over his pitiful charges. "Okay, people, I'd prefer not to have to do that again. If you are going to come to an agreement, now is the time."

Then, into his transmitter, "Nina, take a journal and some pens from one of the staterooms."

CHAPTER
SIX

Kassie Ng listened to Tirzah's weeping as it grew quieter and quieter and eventually dried up into what Kassie imagined was some kind of numbness. She wished she sat closer to Tirzah to squeeze her hand or offer some other gesture of comfort. But Lorenz and Maryam were all over her with the comforting.

Kassie felt a blooming, impudent curiosity about the relationship Tirzah had had with Erik. Had they been having an office affair? Were either of them married? What were the company's policies about workplace relationships? Had Erik been acting out some doomed gallantry? Had he believed he'd be able to escape somehow at the last moment?

Anyway, what did any of that matter now? The money people had returned to their bargaining, sitting on the floor in a tight circle. Their voices had dropped to a murmur as their negotiations grew more concrete. From where she sat, Kassie couldn't make out most of what they were saying. But trying to eavesdrop brought up in her a long-buried, incongruous memory from childhood, when she had watched a pair of kids making out on the bus seat in front of her. Her family had just moved to

Sarasota, Florida, and Kassie had started at her new high school in the middle of her sophomore year, a mostly white school of cliques and covens that she never was able to infiltrate. Her fashion sense had been different then, full of adolescent blunders, avant-garde beyond the abilities of other kids to appreciate. She had been sitting by herself on the bus ride with her AP history class to an exhibition of the treasures of Ramses at the Museum of Fine Arts in Saint Petersburg; two kids sitting in the next seat shocked her with their kissing and groping. Why that memory would return to her now, when what she needed more than anything was to focus on the situation at hand, struck her as foolish, childish. *No wonder I'm a hostage*, she thought.

She had resigned herself to not heading back to Earth in the medevac capsule. Someone much, much wealthier would get that trip. And anyway, even if she were a thousand times richer than she was, Kassie wasn't even sure she would have bid on a ticket in the medevac. After all, she had hated the ride up to *Imperium*, when she had been ferried on a massive, luxurious liner of a rocket. How would she have handled parachuting back to Earth packed into that three-meter-long lipstick tube?

She felt a little like a primatologist, squatting just outside the circle of the billionaires, observing them the way that one woman spent her life observing the chimps in Africa. Roger and Li and Sir Alexander and Samir, especially, seemed to contort their faces in their own ways as they whispered. Roger was the most excitable, jerking his head forward at intervals like a striking cobra when he spit out his objections; his welts looked like some kind of blotchy skin condition. Li had his back to her and seemed to say little, although everyone in the inner circle appeared to watch him in rapt attention when he did open his mouth. Samir had a half-lidded, sorrowful calm when he spoke, which was often. In Kassie's imagination, Samir seemed to be explaining, pleading with the others; frequently as he whispered, he would lift his hand with fingers poised like an image of a lecturing monk. Sir Alexander's face was hardly visible behind his unruly mop of hair. While he whispered no more loudly than the others, for some reason Kassie could make out some of the phrases that he spoke: "fear of public humiliation" and "promissory note" and "why people carry insurance."

Even within the inner circle of guests, a circle within the circle seemed to have formed. Roger and Li and Samir and Sir Alexander conferred together in a tiny knot; Roger's wife and Samir's husband and Viv Volterra all sat just outside that center, watching the four men argue and haggle. Nicholas scribbled in the journal as the other four men spoke. Once, he interrupted the four with something, a question or point of clarification maybe, and three of the four scowled at him as though he had interrupted a string quartet they were rehearsing. Only Sir Alexander smiled back wanly, exactly the way he had smiled right after he had thrown up in the airlock the day before.

Jessica Van Cleave and Viv Volterra both watched the proceedings in silence. Once, the four men at the center turned to address Viv directly. As usual, Kassie had trouble reading her expression; she saw a tiny intimation of something at the corners of Viv's eyes—frustration, anger, dread?—when Viv arched her brow and nodded, dignified as an empress.

Kassie wondered how long they had been speaking. Maybe fifteen minutes, though it also occurred to her that the time was probably shorter than it seemed. She felt a rising, teasing anxiety as the time passed, sitting beneath the silent menace of the Reckoners with their guns. She realized that Dion had given them no deadline. Paradoxically, this thought filled her with as much fear as if the man had announced that the next hostage would die in ten minutes.

From the look of the other three in that innermost circle, it seemed Li was saying something that concerned them. Roger nodded along with an exaggerated rocking forward and back, like an enraptured parishioner listening to a church testimony. Then Roger seemed to speak in alliance with Li, his face contorted into an accusatorial glare at Samir opposite him. He punctuated his whispered oration by pointing straight at Kassie Ng, his finger jabbing at her from across the room without his looking in her direction, as he went on turning his gaze to the other three men, one after the other.

Samir shrugged finally to concede whatever point Roger and Li were making. Sir Alexander gave a slow, resigned nod, and he began scooting through the crowd, from the inner circle to the outer, to approach Kassie.

"Kassie, my dear," he murmured as he leaned in. His breath cast a rancid, anaerobic pall over the distance between them. "Some in our party are unwilling to pay their parts unless all of the guests pay *something*."

Of course that was it. She stole a glance at the other three men who occupied the innermost circle. None were looking in her direction; they seemed to be engrossed in a conversation of their own. "How much?" she said.

"I suggested that you contribute some token amount to indicate your solidarity with our losses. What would you say to one million dollars?"

Her first thought was that one million dollars was close to half of her total worth. She had no idea how she would be able to liquidate so much so quickly; maybe she could secure a loan. It occurred to her, too, that she would gladly pay everything to get off *Imperium*. "That's fine," she said with what she hoped sounded like insouciance. Roger's tantrum, or Li's, seemed an absurd objection to raise over what was 0.0125 percent of the total ransom.

Sir Alexander led her into the circle of paying hostages and related her assent to the terms. Jessica Van Cleave reached out and stroked Kassie's forearm, gave it a single warm squeeze that Kassie interpreted as a sign of welcome, or pity, or some more ancestral primate social bonding. Roger scowled at Kassie as though at some petty criminal who had wronged him. "I'm not sure how I'll raise that kind of money," Kassie said.

Li chuckled ruefully. "We're all concerned about that."

"People on Earth know that we're hostages," Roger put in. "They've known since they took Zhiming to the library an hour ago. Your fans have probably already set up a GoFundMe and raised double your ransom."

This possibility had not occurred to Kassie, though she immediately recognized that Roger was probably correct. She took in the information with what she hoped was the appropriate gravity.

After a moment, though, the reality of her giving up half of her total wealth, or soaking her fans for that much money, evoked in her a curiosity that she had not felt when she was watching the billionaires haggling before. "I don't see how the Reckoners are going to move all that money," she said. "It seems like investigators will be able to track eight billion dollars' worth of Bitcoin."

"If these guys are stupid enough to use Bitcoin, then yes, the ransom will be tracked," Roger muttered almost imperceptibly. "But I bet they're not using Bitcoin."

"There are more cryptocurrencies in heaven and earth, Horatio, than are dreamt of in your philosophy," Sir Alexander whispered to her with a smirk. "Some would be very challenging to trace through the dark web."

"Still," she went on, "if everybody knows that we're hostages, how are the Reckoners going to get back to Earth without being arrested?"

Sir Alexander shrugged. "I suppose that is their problem to solve. But the Earth is a big place: there are many places a Star-liner could land without anybody's knowing, especially if they disable their transponder."

"Let's get a move on," Roger said. "Are you in or not?"

Kassie nodded, and so it was agreed: Samir put his hand over his heart and dipped into a bow, one of the more popular replacements for the old European business handshake in the years since COVID-19. Sir Alexander and Li responded with the alternative crisp, Japanese-style bows; Roger responded with the split-fingered *live long and prosper* salute of the Vulcans. All the others in the billionaires' circle made one gesture or another to show that they agreed without having to touch one another's hands. From the floor, Samir turned to Dion: "I believe we've reached an agreement, Commander Stubblefield. We ask only to have Nicholas read the contract out to us."

Dion gave a slow nod that seemed to Kassie, given the context, oddly benevolent. Nicholas began reading out the agreement with all its ancient adverbs and conjunctions: *Whereas. Whereas. Hereinafter. Whereas. Hereinafter. Now therefore. Hereunder. Aforementioned. In witness whereof.*

So far as Kassie could tell, Roger Van Cleave would pay three billion six hundred and thirty million dollars: one billion to ransom himself, one billion for his wife, nine hundred and thirty million as a loan to Viv Volterra, seven hundred million as a loan for Sir Alexander Dunne. Roger's payment being the highest, he and his wife would return to Earth immediately on the medevac capsule. Sir Alexander and Viv would repay Roger the principal of their respective loans within a year at twenty-five percent interest. Roger's lips pursed like a tiny, aggrieved sphincter at this mention of Viv's name, or maybe at the mention of her pledge to repay. Sir Alexander would pay a further two hundred forty-nine million dollars out of pocket to cover his own share; Viv Volterra would pay one hundred twenty million out of pocket for hers. Zhiming Li would pay one billion dollars. Samir and Nicholas Winters-Qureshi would jointly pay three billion to cover themselves and all other hostages, excepting Kassie Ng, who would pay one million dollars. Eight billion dollars in total.

At last Nicholas passed the journal around the inner circle for each of the guests to sign.

"I'll want a copy of this," Roger said.

The signatories looked uncomfortably at one another, then at the OrbitalVentures staff. "Tirzah, is there a photocopier on *Imperium*?" Nicholas asked.

Tirzah turned a slow, quizzical look to Lorenz, who replied in a mortified hush, "I don't think there's a copier on board."

"Wow," Roger said. "Four conference rooms, no copier."

"We're not exactly a business hotel."

"So do I need to copy this out five more times?" Nicholas asked.

"Wait," Viv said. "If one of us had a phone, we could scan it and email everyone a copy."

The group looked up at Dion, who gave a slow, judgmental shake of his head. "You won't be using our phones."

"You wouldn't need to use your phone, Commander. Just bring one of our phones from wherever you have hidden them. You can hold on to it the whole time if you like—just take the scan and send it to us."

Dion regarded the request with what looked to Kassie like pained irritation. But after a long moment's consideration, he motioned to Nina with a jerk of the head, and Nina went out.

She came back two minutes later with a scuffed-up iPhone SE in a black case. She held it up for the group. "Whose phone is this?" she called out.

There was a long silence, broken at last by Tirzah's flat voice: "That was Erik's."

Nina exhaled an exasperated sigh. But before she could turn back to fetch a different phone, Tirzah spoke up again: "Wait—I know his PIN. It's *007007*."

"Really?" Nina looked askance at the little phone as though expecting it to confirm for her the multilayered idiocy of such a passcode. But *007007* was in fact the PIN. "Okay, you're in," Nina said, handing the phone to Dion.

Vitaly glowered over the group from the other end of the ballroom while Dion and Nina entered the new password for *Imperium*'s Wi-Fi and hunted for the scanning app. The task seemed to require a lot of swiping and pointing. But eventually Dion was able to scan the hard copy of the contract, and then Nina emailed the file to the signatories: Roger, Li, Sir Alexander, Samir, Viv, Nicholas, and Kassie. Kassie had the impression of some momentous business passing her by, as though she were a citizen of a small war-torn country that had, with a spasm of signatures, just been partitioned. Nina dropped Erik's cell phone into the breast pocket of her uniform.

"I'm gratified that you have been able to come to some agreement about your ransom," Dion announced. He leaned over the journal that Nicholas had written in, reading over his shoulder. "Am I to understand that you'll be moving your funds first, Mr. Van Cleave? I don't think the contract is clear on that point."

Roger nodded, staring at Dion with a kind of malevolent obedience.

"Vitaly can accompany you to the library; you'll be able to arrange your transactions there."

Jessica Van Cleave gave her husband a questioning look. Roger answered her in Spanish. Or maybe not, Kassie thought—maybe he was speaking Portuguese. If his wife was Colombian, then why would he speak Portuguese with her? Yet Kassie had taken enough Spanish in high school that she could at least recognize when someone was speaking it. Roger's accent now seemed odd to Kassie, not Spanish. Or maybe his Spanish was just that bad. Roger went alone before Vitaly into the hall.

Over the next hour, Kassie felt an unexpected lightening within her. The money would be paid. The Reckoners would leave. She and the other hostages would have only to wait for rescue. The ransom, an abstraction that seemed to her no more real than numbers on a computer screen, would be exchanged for a reality of Manhattan she could visualize: turning off Houston Street, walking toward Chelsea, in a coat that had come out of her closet for the occasion, making her way to Axiom Coffee to meet one of the young women from her production company. She would never leave the Earth again.

And if Roger was correct about her fandom's devotion to her, she would pay little or nothing of the ransom herself. The realization nagged at her a bit, a tiny gnawing discomfort beneath the undercurrent of her relief, which itself flowed beneath the overcurrent of her dread of these armed people standing over her. Was she feeling survivor's guilt—that she had paid nothing at all for this trip and might pay nothing at all to be ransomed?

Don't be a boob, Kassie. Survive first, she thought. *Then you can feel survivor's guilt.*

And anyway, the least wealthy of the other signatories— probably Viv, Kassie guessed—would still own orders of magnitude more than her even after everything was paid off. Some of them had lost more money than this in their divorce settlements.

The mood in the Fortuna Ballroom grew both more subdued and more casual. Samir and Nicholas had wrapped their arms around one another's shoulders; Jessica Van Cleave and Sir Alexander conferred in a low, funereal Spanish, or whatever language Jessica spoke. Three of the housekeepers, all of them MBA student interns, seemed to be muttering about how their career plans had changed over the last twenty-four hours. Tirzah stared out blankly at the Earth as though at a crushing weight.

Nina surveyed the prisoners with arms crossed, her pistol in its shoulder holster near her hand. And Dion had once again stepped away like a businessman taking a call, cupping his hand over his mouthpiece as though he were lighting a cigarette in a phantom wind.

They sat a couple of hours that way. Eventually a few of the people in the circle couldn't hold it anymore, and Nina had to escort them one by one to the restroom. Kassie wondered how long, in a functioning market, it would take a person to sell almost $4 billion worth of stock. How would a sale that size move the market itself? It occurred to her that it would cost Roger a lot more than $4 billion worth of assets to come up with $4 billion worth of Bitcoin, or whatever crypto the Reckoners were using, on such short notice. Maybe that was why Sir Alexander's and Viv's interest rates had been so high on Roger's loans to them.

At last Vitaly brought Roger back to the ballroom. Roger looked like a man who had just won an award for eating an expired sandwich. He gave his wife the thumbs-up, then beckoned her to come with him. "I'll take them to change into their flight suits," Vitaly announced to Dion.

It was obvious to Kassie that Roger had less interest in being liked than most people she had encountered. Even among the billionaires, she had watched practically all the guests give Roger the side-eye on an almost daily basis during their weeks training together. Jessica, on the other hand, had seemed fun.

Or potentially fun—she and Kassie had been paired together in training a few times, and she had had a talent for throwing herself gamely into whatever ridiculous position the training might call for, like an improv comic or a clumsy cheerleader. There was something about her audacity that had made them both laugh. But the language barrier was a high climb for both of them. Kassie had thought at first that she'd have a chance to finally improve her Spanish, but she had soon realized that it was a long way from *Juan y Marta van a la playa* to talking about anything real.

Roger and Jessica returned a few minutes later, dressed in the garish red of the CisLunar flight suits, carrying helmets under their arms. The suits seemed less flattering now, lumpier around the butt, than they had been on the trip up. Maybe they were wearing astronaut diapers. It dawned on Kassie that the two might be in the capsule for a while.

"Bridge, this is ballroom," Dion said into his transmitter. "Give us a heads-up when the money is in the wallet."

While they waited, Vitaly followed Samir and Nicholas out to begin the liquidation of $3 billion of their wealth. "No dawdling," Dion said in a tone that seemed almost jocular but not really.

Kassie wasn't sure how much time had passed. She wondered if she had drifted off for a minute. But then she was startled by hearing Dion acknowledge some message from the bridge. The man looked down at Roger and Jessica.

"The money has cleared; you're free to go."

The pair got up to leave. Roger offered an awkward wave to the rest of the hostages. "Where is the capsule dropping us?"

"The medevac will orbit the Earth until it can make an insertion for one of its preset landing areas. As long as you don't mess with the presets, you should come down within a hundred miles or so of the Florida coast, the Southern California coast, the Bay of Biscay—there are a dozen pickup points. You'll want to make radio contact with OrbitalVentures on your way down so that they can send a rescue. Remember your training?"

Roger narrowed his eyes as though committing Dion's face to memory. He and Jessica walked out before Nina into the corridor.

Kassie wondered whether she would feel the launch of the medevac capsule from *Imperium*. Would she hear the capsule's rocket boosters? Would she just feel a faint vibration through her body as the force of the launch propagated through the floor?

"Go ahead, bridge." Dion was speaking low into his transmitter. His voice dropped again and he covered his mouth as he conferred with another of the Reckoners.

The other billionaires awaited the launch with what seemed like a resigned irritation. Viv stared out the windows at a star many light-years away.

Kassie had still felt nothing when Nina came back into the ballroom. "They're locked in tight. I have them on channel one."

Dion turned a dial on a device strapped to his chest and spoke into his headset. "Come in, medevac capsule. This is *Imperium*."

He paused for the Van Cleaves' answer, then spoke again: "We will be clearing you for launch momentarily. It appears that someone has changed the preset splashdown coordinates for the medevac capsule. As soon as we retrieve the original coordinate set, you'll be good to go."

It gave Kassie a small, perverse joy to imagine Roger inconvenienced, even briefly. She searched Dion's face as he listened, hoping to see some intimation of how Roger had reacted to this delay.

"The new coordinates are a long way from anywhere if you

are trying to get rescued," Dion eventually responded. "You would splash down in the Pacific near Villings somewhere."

A minute later, after fielding whatever whining or abuse was coming back at him over channel one, Dion answered, "If you don't care, don't let me stop you. But if you want to live, I suggest that you wait for us to recover the original coordinate set for the medevac. Dion out."

"Bridge, this is ballroom," Dion transmitted. "Any word on those presets for the medevac?"

Dion's lips tightened to a thin, tense line as he listened to the response from the bridge. He stood in silence a minute, contemplating. Then he walked over to stand between Nina and Vitaly. The three spoke in low voices. "Leave them on the medevac for now," Kassie heard Dion say. "They're more secure there."

They seemed to confer as though they were planning something; they had grown as somber as they had been at the beginning of the ordeal. Vitaly shook his head as though in debate with them. ". . . doesn't have that much ammunition," Kassie heard him whisper. Nina and Vitaly each turned to regard Dion again and again as they listened—it was as though they could not keep their eyes on the hostages for very long.

At last, Dion took a few steps away from the circle. He turned the dial again on his communicator and began speaking with someone in a voice Kassie could not hear.

The exchange was terse, at least from Dion's end. Even without being able to see his eyes, Kassie could see Dion growing exasperated with whoever he was speaking with. His voice took on a peevish timbre she had not heard from him before: "Do you think I enjoy this? You can come out anytime—this can all be over."

Kassie realized he was speaking again with Chloe. There was another pause as Dion listened; then he shot back, "Really?

Really? Okay, fine. Another one goes out the airlock in twenty minutes. Come out when you're ready for it to end. Dion out." With a cool precision, he pressed a button on his wristwatch, as though he had never lost his temper before in his life.

There was another low breaker of gasps from among the hostages. Kassie felt a rushing in her ears, as though a phantom sea were pouring into *Imperium* in another part of the station.

She wondered whether she had any chance of being a sacrificial victim. More chance than some, she supposed. She speculated for a moment, in her hubbub of racing thoughts, whether there was some clause in the contract that designated that the victims would come from one of the hostages who had failed to pay some minimum. She had listened as carefully as she could when the contract was being read out, but contracts being what they are, she hadn't understood every clause and phrase. A memory intruded on her horrible contemplation: a college friend of hers, after graduating law school last year, had once told her with a tipsy swagger that there was nothing special to becoming a lawyer except learning to read things carefully. Perhaps the billionaires had sold out the rest of them, their secret plan hiding in the plain sight of the text of the contract, and she was only now seeing the plot fulfilled.

This, she realized after a minute, was crazy talk. The billionaires as much as anyone had seemed to regard the contract as concluded business, the beginning of the end of the ordeal. And anyway, the three terrorists—thieves, revolutionaries, whoever they were—had seemed during their conference to be oddly uninterested in the hostages: Dion had been tracing lines on his open palm for Nina and Vitaly like a backyard quarterback while they watched with stern gravity.

At length Nina and Vitaly nodded crisply to Dion and walked out of the Fortuna Ballroom. Kassie wondered at the differences from the last time Dion had threatened to kill one of them, when Erik had been cast out.

Sir Alexander spoke up: "I thought we'd settled this. We're ready to pay."

As though shushing an impertinent student at the final exam, Dion slowly lifted a finger to his lips, his face remote behind his glasses.

Several of the hostages had begun to cry again, low, stifled sobs. But as the minutes dragged on, five, ten, fifteen, an unforeseen sense of detachment began to creep into Kassie's mind. She turned over and over the incongruities of what she had seen. Of course, the people with the guns could kill the hostages however they wanted to—why would they complicate such a straightforward thing as killing them by leaving the ballroom?

A boom like an infernal kettledrum resonated far off. The hostages tensed like startled deer. Dion stood, poised and distant. A flurry of pops, what Kassie knew now to be gunfire, followed. Dion spoke something into the communicator. The only words Kassie could make out were "bridge, support . . ."

Kassie realized then that the threat Dion had made over the communicator fifteen minutes before had been a ruse. Nina and Vitaly had launched some kind of sneak attack on Dr. Chloe. Kassie closed her eyes and waited for the shooting to stop.

The shooting continued.

"You all are settled with us as soon as you've paid," Dion said quietly to the group, as if in answer to Sir Alexander's earlier comment. "We're securing the station, and then we can all go about getting ourselves back to Earth."

It occurred to Kassie that he didn't have to say anything, that this was, she supposed, Dion's attempt at comforting them.

Suddenly an emergency claxon began sounding over the

faint staccato backbeat of the gunfire. Its sound was deeper, less shrill, than the smoke alarm that had gone off earlier, like three repeated notes from a fiendish and discordant trumpet. The computerized voice of *Imperium*'s public-address system began repeating between the blaring of the horn: "Hull breach detected, laboratory wing."

Dion pulled off his aviators. His eyes narrowed as he lifted one hand to his earpiece: "Come again, Vitaly?" The claxon flooded the space with its harsh broadcast. The pops of gunfire continued. "I'm on my way."

Dion shot them all a stern look. "I expect you to be sitting right there when I get back." Then he walked out of the Fortuna Ballroom. With his key fob he closed the sliding glass doors of the ballroom. In the open sonic space between blasts of the claxon, Kassie heard the doors latch.

The hostages looked at one another, some in horror, some in baffled silence. "And now we have a decompression event," Nicholas muttered acidly.

"The warning would be different if it were a decompression event," Tirzah reassured him. "And there's no unusual airflow down here—whatever hull breach is going on must have already been sealed off. All they had to do was close a security hatch."

Kassie felt a surprising nervous energy rising within her, like a long-compressed spring releasing energy into her limbs. She scanned the blank ballroom around her. Could she break down the doors? Where were the HVAC ducts?

She stood up and began scanning the perimeter of the room. "Sit down," Viv said. "What are you doing?"

Indeed, what was she doing? Kassie didn't have an answer ready, not even for herself. Some intuition she couldn't explain told her that the ground underneath their feet had changed. The conditions of the contract, the agreement with Dion and his men, these seemed wholly unsupported by whatever shift in the organizational center of gravity was going on right now; the contract and Dion's assurances seemed as empty and irrelevant as the original itinerary for the guests' second day on *Imperium*.

"I want to get a message to the police," she said, though this was not the thought that was driving her.

"Everybody Earthside already knows we've been taken hostage," Samir said. "We've been raising ransom money, remember? It's not going to speed up a rescue mission for you to get yourself killed."

This eminently reasonable advice remained unsatisfying to her. This firefight that she could still hear far off, the urgency of the warning claxons, had changed her calculus in ways that she could not articulate—it seemed like the most breathtakingly foolish course of action imaginable would be to sit and wait for a group of killers to come back and point guns at them.

From behind the closed glass doors, she peered as far as she could in both directions up the main corridor. The hallway remained cool blue, empty, still. Even the stink of the grease fire was diminished now that the doors were sealed. The doors were not made of ordinary glass, and maybe not glass at all. In any event, she saw no chairs, no fire extinguisher, nothing in the ballroom massive enough to shatter whatever the material was.

She counted four HVAC registers, or maybe intakes, and she pulled on the grille of each while the other hostages squawked at her with increasingly loud, scandalized voices. "You're going to make things worse for all of us," Viv said.

That was when Kassie noticed the housing for one of the holograph projectors in the floor at the base of the sleek black bar. She could feel hinges along one end of the floor panel there. She reached her narrow arm into the hole where the projector lens emerged, found a hidden latch. The entire floor panel, almost a meter square, hinged up to reveal the projector, controller, and a mass of cables snaking back under the floor.

The entire crawl space could not be much more than forty centimeters high, and she couldn't see how far back it went. But when she craned her head as far as she could down the crawl space, she saw—or imagined she saw—a dim gray light somewhere ahead.

Sir Alexander had approached her as she regarded the narrow tunnel in the floor. "Please," he implored her, "you are going to get us all killed."

"They won't kill you," she said. "They want your money, remember?" Without reflecting further on where it led, Kassie slipped on her belly into the crawl space with a resolute amphibian shimmy. "If you close the floor panel behind me, he might not even notice I'm gone."

Kassie heard the floor panel shut and latch behind her when she had gotten a meter or so into the tunnel, dimming the ambient light around her almost to blackness. Yet now there was no doubt, as she crawled her way over cables and splitters and past a black, lightless side tunnel, that the gray glow ahead of her was real. She crept toward it.

She had gone twenty meters or so straight along the tunnel toward that light before she recognized a skein of cables plugging into the back of another hologram projector—a projector that pointed out of an identical aperture in the floor into another dimly lit room. The floor panel was mounted with an identical latch in an identical spot; she pulled it and pushed the panel up on identical hinges. She pulled herself out into another room.

The space was maybe half the size of the Fortuna Ballroom, perhaps could be made to form part of the Fortuna Ballroom if the wall behind her was retractable. Besides a long table, encircled by a swoop of curved chairs on armatures, the place was empty. There was no view of Earth here; the only light flooded in from the main corridor through the glass double doors. The claxons still rang out like the deafening strokes of a mountainous clock. The frequency of the snaps of gunfire had diminished, she thought, but not by much, like popcorn in its final minute in a microwave.

Kassie took barely a second to wonder why the Earth's first orbital hotel, a place with only eight guests and a capacity for no more than thirty, would have so many conference rooms. If she and any of the OrbitalVentures employees survived, she would ask one of them about it. But for now, the sound of the gunfire told her in its wordless way to keep moving.

She tried the doors. If they were locked, they had not been secured the same way that Dion had locked the doors to the Fortuna Ballroom: Kassie was still able to push them open from inside. She poked her head out into the corridor. The presence of security cameras throughout *Imperium*—one of them scarcely fifteen meters up the hallway from her—had not registered in the inarticulate plan that she had formed.

Whatever fire had tripped the alarms before was stinking now in the silky blue hallway. Moving unreflectively, by a kind of intestinal intuition, Kassie padded up the corridor, then ran. The location of the firefight was hard to pinpoint, but if it was occurring on the ring of the main corridor, she didn't believe it was occurring near her.

As she approached the landing of the gamma spoke ladder, she heard another thunderous boom, pinpointing for her that the battle was unfolding somewhere at the other end of the ladder, somewhere on the hub. Yet that was the last noise she heard beyond the wail of the claxons.

She dashed farther up the hall. Just ahead, the doors to the library stood open, just as she had first seen them the day before. Within, an abandoned silence hung over the space, a leather-and-walnut simulacrum of an English gentleman's library, a museum of potted palms and framed iridescent beetles and taxidermized songbirds in cases, all before what seemed like a mullioned bay window looking out toward the hub, rotating against the blackness of space and the inconceivably distant stars. The faint, acrid stench of the grease fire was almost beneath her awareness here.

As she paused here, an unnerving calm descended over the hall: the warning claxon had ceased.

At two of the long reading tables—which, Tirzah had said during the tour, had been purchased from the library of Merton College, Oxford—there was a bank of computers. She had given no thought to what call for help she might post to her Instagram followers. Lack of premeditation had never stopped her before, however: she had made thousands of posts on the fly, walking out of a coffee shop or the gym and saying whatever was on her mind. Some of her most viral posts had begun that way.

She woke up one of the machines and opened the browser. The cute little dinosaur, or whatever creature it was, appeared on the screen to inform her that she was not connected to the internet.

Kassie searched out the available networks. All three of them—*Imperium-Guest, Imperium-Admin, Imperium-Lab*—were password protected. That was new. She remembered how stupid it had seemed to her the day before that the guests' network was *not* password protected, before she had realized sheepishly that there were no other human beings for miles around to poach internet from a space hotel.

Now she contended with a feeling of even greater foolishness: of course Dion would have password protected the internet. What could have possessed her to risk so much just to post a story? Samir had been right—her going to Instagram wasn't going to speed up any rescue operation.

It occurred to her that this was one of the rooms where Vitaly might have been bringing the wealthy hostages. There was no way to tell—the browser history was blank when she checked it—but she realized that one of the rooms with internet access was not the best place for her to hide. She wished she still had her key fob; she wished for a dark corner where she could lie low.

Kassie heard the approach of footsteps out in the corridor.

CHAPTER SEVEN

TWENTY MINUTES EARLIER

Chloe wondered at Dion's voice, what he had said and not said. Before he signed off, his voice had sounded angry in a way she had not heard it before—petulant, like a teenager's sniping hidden in Dion's basso profundo. And now she had twenty minutes to surrender before the second of the hostages was to die.

If Dion had been hoping to guilt her into taking responsibility for the death of the first hostage, whoever that lost soul had been, he had misread her. Whatever emotion Dion had been trying to fish out of her—Compassion? Codependence?—was hard for Chloe to call up even in the best of times, much less now.

She wondered who that first hostage had been. They had killed one of the males—she could tell that much from the man's bellowing in his last seconds—but her view of him as he was flushed out of one of the rim airlocks had been from a hundred meters away. All she could say for sure was that he was a male, that he hadn't suffered in silence, and that he seemed to die quickly.

She had been a fool to have ever mentioned the Starliner to Dion. Probably she'd been a fool to have responded to him at all. But she had been so angry, spiteful, even, that she had just blurted out the trump card she had been holding before it was clear to her how much of a trump card it was. What had her spite cost her? And how had she harmed Dion? If, evolutionarily speaking, her threat had cost her more than it had cost him, was her emotion even spite at all?

She had spent the time between the first hostage's death and the threat of the next by fortifying the lab wing as best she could. She had closed and locked the hatches at either end of the lab access corridor that connected to the Axle. She had used all her masking tape to obscure the lenses of each of the lab security cameras.

She had scoured her lab for anything more she might put to use. Tweezers. A plastic jerrican of deionized water. Latex gloves. A plastic bin of potting soil, a plastic bin of fertilizer. If the fertilizer had been ammonium nitrate, she could have made quite a bomb with it.

Of course, she didn't need quite a bomb—she wasn't trying to kill herself or blow a hole in *Imperium*. But if she could cook up a small explosion, perhaps out of something that had been left behind in the closeouts of lab module four in preparation for the return of the Penn State group, she might concoct a bit of pyrotechnics to confuse an attacker for a critical moment.

So she had returned once more to lab module four. Within the materials lockers was a whole chemistry set of acids and solvents and flammables: nitric acid, acetone, methanol, pentane. She took the flask of pentane, a plastic liter squeeze bottle, the little portable Bunsen burner that looked like a backpacking stove.

And like a ghoul, she rifled once more through the pockets

of Angel's corpse. Now that she understood what she was looking for, she found his key fob sitting right in his hip pocket. If
the woman on the bridge hadn't thought to deactivate it, the
fob might still be coded to all the locked hatches on the station.
Chloe lamented once more the trouble she could have saved
herself if she'd simply snapped up the man's fob the first time.
But a person makes a lot of mistakes in a panic. The woman
on the bridge was making her own mistakes: had she been able
to keep her head, the woman could have closed and locked the
hatches to the lab wing during Chloe's ill-starred adventure on
the rim. Chloe wouldn't have been able to get back in, then.

With Angel's fob on her belt now, she might even be able
to let herself into a secured room before the bridge figured out
what was going on. Maybe she should try to get aboard the Starliner after all. Or if she could get into the hotel administration
office on the rim, she could probably deactivate Dion's fob, or
anybody's. She might even be able to lock the terrorists into one
of the rooms on *Imperium* until rescue arrived.

As she had mused on these options, a realization arrested
her. If the terrorists had given themselves full entry access on
their fobs—and why wouldn't they have?—it did her no good to
have locked the hatches in the access corridor. If anything, closing those hatches put her in greater danger, in that they sealed
her off from the rest of *Imperium*. If they had a mind to, Dion's
team could open the second airlock and decompress the whole
lab wing. She would probably be able to get into her pressure
suit in time, but no guarantees: if the bay doors and inner hatch
of the airlock opened quickly enough, she might very well lose
consciousness before she got the suit on.

That revelation had spurred her to pull the pressure suit out
of her lab closet and to put it on. Practically every room on *Imperium* had a cabinet with a couple of emergency pressure suits

hanging in it. Thick, bulky balloon skins that a person of nearly any size could don. Yet the emergency cabinet in Chloe's own lab contained a suit fitted for her, just like the one hanging in her cabin. One of the perks of having her own lab. She could do yoga in such a suit, if she were the kind of person to practice yoga. But even the fitted suit restricted her field of vision a little, bound up her movements in ways she couldn't always predict. As she donned the suit, she noticed again her ball cap; she must have put it on without thinking when she had awakened in the night. She let it drift out of her hand, and it spun slowly across the lab like a sad Frisbee.

Chloe noticed, too, that the gauntlets of the pressure suit were not designed for shooting—the fingers of the gloves were almost too thick to fit safely through the Glock's trigger guard.

The dearth of pockets on the pressure suit had bothered her almost as much as the gauntlets had. She had spent much of the time between Dion's threats arranging some provision for her motley gear, including the pistol that Angel had inexplicably not carried in a holster. She had gone through every storage cabinet of every lab module. Most of the stuff sacks had been empty, though there was another roll of tape, actual duct tape, left behind in the webbing of lab module two. She fashioned a duct tape sheath for her screwdriver, and she had gathered two of the stuff sacks from her module. One of these she had taped to her hip with a makeshift belt of duct tape; the other she had looped over her shoulder to use as a holster for the fire extinguisher she had taken from the cafeteria.

Then, using the blade of the plastic scraper she had scrounged as an armature, Chloe had wrapped layer after layer of duct tape into a rough envelope that would hold the pistol. An hour would have been enough to make it handsome, but the five minutes she took were enough to create something ugly and functional: the rudiments of a holster that covered the trigger guard. She had strapped the crude arrangement to her thigh, finally, with more duct tape.

She fashioned her bomb, a Rube Goldberg device of a plastic squeeze bottle filled with pentane, duct-taped to the sliding panel of the hatch to the access corridor. She lit the Bunsen burner and taped it down to the doorjamb opposite. When the hatch slid open, if it opened, the bottle would move with the hatch until it was above the burner, which would be squeezed against the jamb, and would hopefully burst adjacent to the burner's flame.

And now she had, according to Dion's pompous whining, twenty minutes. Less than twenty—perhaps only fifteen. She wished it had occurred to her to start a timer when Dion first made his threat.

She wondered whether she might use her lab laptop to crack the new network password and send a distress call to Earth. This line of inquiry, she knew, was just so much spinning of her wheels that she would do well to forget about the prospect: she was no hacker, and whoever was on the bridge wasn't about to fall for a spear-phishing attack.

It was then that Chloe heard a noise nearby. The telltale rushing exhalation of an airlock emptying told her that they must be decompressing the lab wing. She dropped into the script of her training: she reached reflexively, without even waiting for the rush of air that betokened a decompression, to close the visor of her helmet. Still no rush of air. She braced herself.

Her mind raced to understand their tactics. If they were decompressing the lab wing, why had the bridge opened the airlock bay door to the outside but not the inner hatch leading into the wing? If this was a decompression attack, they were going about it the dumbest way possible.

An insight beneath the level of reflection, as thoughtless as a diamondback's warning rattle, signaled that she would need her weapon. She pulled the Glock from its duct tape holster.

She considered for a moment raising the visor of her helmet. No time, she thought. As best she could through her narrowed field of vision, she took in the main hallway of the lab wing from the hatchway of her lab. Three or four meters to her left stood the hatch that led to the access hallway; that way led to the Axle and the rest of *Imperium*. The two halves of her makeshift bomb were duct-taped to the hatch and bulkhead like a pair of barnacles. Directly across from her was the hatchway to lab module four; Angel floated there like the carcass of a becalmed sea creature. To her right, on the same side of the hallway as her lab, stood the hatch that led to lab module two, and beyond it to the airlock where the Starliner was docked.

It was from across the hall and to the right, beyond the hatch to lab module three, the old Kamara-Zhou lab, that Chloe had heard the noise from the airlock beyond.

She had a brief, heartbreaking pang of regret that she had never answered Dion's bid to parley over channel eight: now that they knew she was listening in, her attackers must have begun communicating over another channel. She scanned about her for a position that might take in both directions at once. In the same moment that she arrived at the provisional conclusion that there was no such position, she saw and heard the hatch of lab module three open a hand's breadth, watched a cylinder like a black camping lantern sail into the corridor like a clumsily thrown football.

She knew that object, remembered her father's showing her when she was ten years old what a flash-bang grenade looked like and what it did. With one hand she pulled down the glare visor on her helmet while she pushed off with her legs against the jamb of the hatch to put herself behind the bulkhead of her laboratory.

The boom of the flash bang amazed her. She didn't think she was deafened, though: the grenade must have gone off on the other side of the bulkhead from her. The sound overwhelmed the noise cancellation in her earbuds, but the shock wave didn't buffet her directly and was baffled somewhat by her Snoopy cap and helmet. The flash of light, too, was not as effectual from the other side of the bulkhead, shining into her lab through the half-closed hatch; through her glare visor, she might have been looking at the sunset of a star much dimmer than the sun.

She pulled herself back into a position in the hatchway of her lab when she saw the light change to her left—another hatch opening, probably the hatch leading from the Axle to the lab wing access hallway. Attackers were approaching her from two directions.

She heard Dion's voice come over her earbuds like a tiny, tiny insect chirping in a cloud of cotton wool: "Bridge, support the attack on Dr. Bonilla in the lab wing. She may try to come out into the Axle." She was not deaf after all. And, stranger still, they must still be using channel eight for their communications.

"Copy that," Meredith replied.

Chloe's bomb did nothing. Or at least it was reacting too slowly to achieve her hoped-for effect with it. They would come in firing, she knew.

She had one last moment of heartbreak that her cockamamie pyrotechnics had not gone off. It had been an experiment worth trying. There is no animal quite so willing to experiment as a cornered mammal.

Then her little bomb made a sound more like the whooshing of a gigantic, stately fart than a device designed to intimidate an enemy. Yet she heard the banging of the plastic flask as it clattered and ricocheted around the corridor, heard a yelp of surprise from a man's blunt voice. With her left arm looped through the handhold on her side of the bulkhead, Chloe swung around to fire.

She took in the hallway for a moment. Vitaly was sailing directly across the hall from her, higher and far to the right of where she'd expected he would be, his body rotating slowly; he reached out to grasp one of the handholds next to the hatchway to lab module four, his jumpsuit scorched along his broad back. She swung the Glock up to point at him, but before she could squeeze off a shot, he had pulled himself into lab module four across the hall with a single lithe sweep of his great arm.

She saw no defensible position for herself that didn't involve being cornered in her laboratory. Without further reflection than that, she pushed herself out into the hallway and backed herself up against the doorjamb of her lab as she began firing at the open hatchways of lab modules three and four without seeing her targets, laying down a cover for herself.

She heard and saw nothing from the lab modules—her attackers were either lying low, waiting her out, or moving in stealth toward some vantage she could not imagine. The instability of her position—its metastability, a geologist would call it—troubled her: at her rate of fire, she could hold this position for no more than two or three minutes even if she was able to reload.

Just then, the warning claxons of *Imperium* began to bray all around her: "Hull breach detected, laboratory wing," intoned the solemn, matronly voice of the station's computer.

She pushed herself from her doorjamb toward the scorched hatch to the access hall, firing twice, wildly, to maintain the illusion of cover fire as she spun and caught the handle next to the bulkhead. She looked out into the access hallway beyond.

At the other end of the hallway, an athletic, hard-faced

woman in an OrbitalVentures uniform—Meredith—glided toward the bulkhead like a person diving underwater. She held her pistol in both hands before her like the horn of a narwhal.

Chloe ducked behind the bulkhead as two, three, four bullets slammed against the reinforced steel that separated her from Meredith.

Perhaps she had panicked to see Chloe while floating along the length of the corridor in her unanchored, critically vulnerable state. Whatever Meredith's reason for firing, she had done one of the more foolish things she could have done at that moment. Once she had pulled the trigger, her pistol—and she, connected to it—had to obey Newton's laws of motion just as scrupulously as any other object in the cosmos. The weapon's kickback worked like a retrothruster, slowing down Meredith's approach to her destination to the gentle drift of a duck sitting in the middle of a pond.

Holding the handle of the bulkhead to brace herself, Chloe fired at her. Meredith was five meters away when the bullet struck her in the center of her forehead.

Chloe looked behind herself once more, shot four more times with her back braced against the bulkhead, toward the empty hatchways to lab modules three and four. Then she swung past the hatchway to the access corridor and launched herself down its length.

As she passed, she reached out for the pistol of the dead woman with her left hand. But Chloe had not launched herself on a collision course with Meredith's corpse; rather, she had pushed off as quickly as she could on as clear a flight path as she could, looking behind her; only as an afterthought, as she was passing by, did she grasp at Meredith's weapon, but it was just out of Chloe's reach, and the two women, the quick and the dead, sailed past one another like boats on a swell.

While she floated down the length of the hallway, she pointed her weapon below her, between her feet, and fired three more times toward the bulkhead she had launched from. Her pistol had to obey the same Newtonian laws that had undone Meredith, now in use to boost Chloe's speed a bit down the hallway. She wondered how many bullets had punctured the hull of *Imperium*. Perhaps just one if she was lucky.

She passed out of the access hallway and crashed softly into the curved wall of the Axle. She expected at any moment to look back and see another attacker swing a weapon around the opening to the access hallway that she had just left. She stole a glance ahead of her: The Axle was flocked with ragged scraps of cloud from the fire extinguisher she had used hours ago, now congregating at the air vents like froth around a storm drain. But the place was clear of people as far as the access hallways for the bridge and the Levitas Reception Hall at the other end.

More quickly than she was able to comment on it, Chloe considered the data that was available to her. Based on what she had been able to tell from the chatter on channel eight, there had been only one person on the bridge after she had hidden herself in the cabinet of lab module four: Meredith. The woman with the Midwestern accent, floating in the access corridor with a bullet in her brain.

It was time to take a blind risk of her own. She hauled on the handhold to launch herself up all thirty meters of the Axle. As she trained the pistol between her feet, looking back every other second in expectation that one of the attackers would emerge to begin firing on her, she wondered how many bullets were left in the magazine. Not many, she knew—probably fewer than ten. She shot once at the open doorway behind her, then shot once more, to cover herself.

She didn't like that she could be perforating the hull of

Imperium like a watering can. The claxon blared the same whether she had punctured the hull once or ten times. Her father, a traditionalist on the subject of ballistics, would have told her that even a 9mm weapon like the Glock was too heavy-handed for combat in an environment like *Imperium*, where a stray shot even with a hollow-point bullet might clip through the hull like a hole punch—to say nothing of the difficulty of maintaining a stable position while firing in zero gravity. A smaller caliber weapon, like a .32, would have made a great deal more sense, especially on the hub. Chloe had noted in passing Meredith's corpse that Meredith had carried something that looked like a .32.

Then Chloe remembered her other gear. From her shoulder stuff sack, she drew out the fire extinguisher again. She pointed the nozzle behind her and sprayed.

A great lumpy cone of foam spread out beneath her feet. It did not look so different, she thought as she sped up, from the burgeoning mushroom of exhaust that came out of the tail of a launching rocket. Two seconds later, she glided past the landings of beta and gamma spokes and the door to the alpha spoke elevator; in fact, she was speeding faster than she liked toward the far end of the Axle.

In the final few meters of her flight, she tucked her body and turned to face the wall she approached; she shot the extinguisher ahead of her as a brake. She realized she had misjudged the physics of the approach just as she slammed into the other end of the corridor. She heard a sickening crunch, felt a sharp pain along the crown of her head. Yet she realized almost immediately that she was not dazed; the crushing sound she had heard must have been the headlamp in her helmet impacting against the wall. A constellation of plastic shards formed a nimbus around her head.

Two hallways opened on either side at this end, one to the Levitas Reception Hall, one to the bridge. Chloe looked behind her one last time down the length of the Axle. She saw the moment that Vitaly's head and arm popped out into the Axle to fire on her. She sprayed the extinguisher to her side to launch herself up the access hallway to the bridge; she took a parting shot down the Axle at Vitaly as she disappeared from his view.

She realized as she sailed up the access corridor toward the bridge that Vitaly had missed her. She had almost certainly missed him as well—neither of them had had much of a moment in which to aim. The bridge hatch was closed, and she stopped hard against it.

"Meredith's down," she heard Nina saying over her earbuds. "Chloe's headed for the bridge."

"That's checkmate for her," Dion responded. He sounded neither particularly happy nor triumphant. "She's locked out. Take up positions in the landings for beta and gamma spoke where you have view of the bridge access corridor. I'm coming up alpha—we'll smoke her out."

She looked through the porthole, wondering whether Dion or one of his people could shoot her through the glass. Perhaps, but the glass was very thick: she suspected a hollow point wouldn't penetrate easily—assuming that all the terrorists were shooting dumdums to minimize overpenetration into the hull of *Imperium*. Of course, a hollow point could pierce a great deal of material—if you got lucky, or unlucky, a hollow point could punch through the hull. The emergency claxons still wailed as though to scold Chloe for having fired so many rounds. The bridge looked empty within.

The hatch was locked. As she pulled up Angel's key fob from the string hanging from her impromptu duct tape belt, she hoped that the key was in fact coded for universal access.

The hatch slid open for Angel's fob. She pulled herself in, closed the door behind her, and locked it down manually.

She stared in horror at the banks of controls, the keypads and monitors and displays that she had seen many times before but never personally needed. She could see the security camera views running in six small slideshows over one monitor. Some slides were black when they came up—the cameras she had disabled, she presumed—but after a few seconds, a feed of one of the cameras on the Axle appeared in one quarter of the screen. She tapped the view of that feed, and from the menu that popped up she pinned that view to the screen. She could see Vitaly and Nina pulling themselves along the Axle by hand-holds, floating into the openings to the beta elevator and the gamma ladder like ghosts dropping into two wells. If Vitaly had been harmed by Chloe's little bomb, he didn't look it. Nina was dressed in a pressure suit, the visor of her helmet up. Another stun grenade was clipped with a carabiner to a utility belt she wore outside her suit.

Chloe struggled to collect her thoughts under the blaring importunity of the warning claxon. She tried the keyboard of the main terminal, tried the mouse pad. On the central moni-tor were crowded dozens of menus for displays and command prompts. She hunted through them for some kind of commu-nication channel: radio, an internet browser, Skype. There were station schematics she could pull up, displays for life support, status reports on the airlocks, interfaces on electricity supply and usage, a log of the usage of each key fob and the door access for each user. A red warning banner flashed across the top of each of the monitors on the bridge: *Hull breach: lab wing. Atmospheric pressure dropping at 73.4 kPa/min.*

She found a dedicated radio on the control panel, as well as a browser on the computer. But her attention was arrested when she saw the icon for the key-access program on the menu she was looking at.

She pulled the application open. A seine of submenus presented itself. Out of the net she picked the one marked *Current location*. A two-dimensional map of the hub, shaped like a barbell, appeared on the left side of the screen; the ring of the rim appeared on the right. The two maps were connected by three schematic dotted lines to represent the spokes, marked *Alpha, Beta, Gamma*. Each map was clustered with location pins.

She hovered the mouse pointer over each of the five pins in the map of the hub. The pin labeled *Angel* was on the bridge; the pin marking Meredith still took up the center of the access hallway to the lab wing. The pins for Dion, Nina, and Vitaly congregated at the midpoint of the Axle. Chloe checked the security camera monitor—the doors of the alpha spoke elevator were half-open, Dion's head and shoulders visible above the aperture as though he were looking out from the turret of a tank.

On the map of the rim, Chloe saw a congregation of pins in one of the staterooms, each pin labeled with the name of a guest or an employee. Chloe wondered how so many hostages could be crammed into a single stateroom before it dawned on her that the hostage takers had probably removed everyone's key fobs and stowed them somewhere inaccessible to them. She would have to search for the hostages on the security cameras.

"The game's over, Chloe."

Dion's voice came over channel eight, calm and solemn. Even compassionate, it seemed to her.

She didn't answer. She floated over once more to peek out of the porthole of the bulkhead into the access hallway, as though she had heard him call to her from just outside the door.

"Throw your weapons out into the Axle where we can see them. We won't harm you."

She wondered for a stray moment whether the imitation of compassion was an adaptive evolutionary strategy for certain species. If compassion was adaptive for *Homo sapiens*, might the faking of compassion be adaptive for some humans? She supposed the issue revolved around the question of whether group-level selection operated as a force in evolution or not. She remembered the dictum of the two Wilsons: *Selfishness beats altruism within groups. Altruistic groups beat selfish groups. Everything else is commentary.* She might devote the rest of her life to studying the accuracy or inaccuracy of that proposition. If she survived, of course.

"Chloe, the station is losing oxygen. Neither of us wants these hostages to die. I give you my word that nobody, including you, will be hurt if you come out."

If she had known how to do it, Chloe would have opened the bay of the Levitas Reception Hall airlock in that moment, flushed Dion and Vitaly and Nina out of the Axle into space. She would have tried to, anyway. But she had barely trained on the airlock-control program. She had certainly never used it before: it was one of those applications that had sat on her laptop before the takeover, before Meredith had changed all the access passwords to the network. But even back when she could have opened the program on her laptop, she had entrusted the workings of that program to the folks on the bridge, hoping that she would never find herself having to open and close hatches remotely in an emergency.

"Chloe, our time is shorter than you think," Dion said over the communicators. His voice reminded her of a concerned therapist's. "We need to deal with the hull breach. We'll be forced to disable you if you don't throw down your weapon now."

Like a frantic magician rifling through a deck of cards for the right one, Chloe kept swiping the mouse through the menus

and submenus of the key-access application. The silence that
followed Dion's offer seemed to fray in her imagination.

"This didn't have to end so badly, Chloe," he said after a
silent minute. "I'm sorry we couldn't come to some agreement."

At last she found what she had hoped to find: a submenu
titled *Permissions*.

A list of the twenty-one active key fobs on *Imperium* appeared on the screen. Next to each one was a drop-down menu
with the user's security designation, as well as another drop-
down that, she presumed, identified which rooms the user could
open with their fob. Her eye ran down the list, past her own
name, past names of the dead, to Dion Stubblefield.

His designation was *Crew: All Access*. She opened the drop-
down menu. There were several designations on the list—*Crew,
Researcher, Hospitality Staff, Guest, VIP Guest*. And at the bottom
of the menu, in red, there was a final designation, perhaps intended for belligerent drunks or guests in a mental health crisis,
a designation that caused her to smile for the first time in some
hours: *Security Risk: Access Rescinded*.

Chloe gave Dion Stubblefield's key fob its new designation.

Chloe heard in that moment, even over the droning of the
claxon, a dull, shocking thud outside the bridge bulkhead. A
flash of light poured through the porthole. One of them had
thrown another stun grenade.

On the security monitor of the Axle, she could see Dion
and Nina covering Vitaly as he glided forward with his weapon
drawn.

It took Chloe only seconds to find the access designations
for Vitaly Poliashov and Nina Jones. She changed their designations as well—*Security Risk: Access Rescinded*.

As she turned to face the hatch that separated her from
Vitaly, she caught one more glimpse on the security monitor of

the big man swinging his body around the corner of the Axle on a handhold to point his weapon into the empty access corridor. She positioned herself next to the hatch and a couple of meters away, against the bulkhead and out of view of the porthole; she braced herself. She hoped she had been right about the porthole glass being bulletproof; she hoped she had altered her enemies' key permissions correctly. She hoped they weren't carrying other kinds of grenades besides flash-bangs.

She heard nothing but the wailing of the claxon. From where she hid, Chloe craned her neck around to peek at the security monitor on the console. Dion was approaching the access corridor as well. Vitaly was scanning about him as though expecting Chloe to pop out from some nonexistent hiding place in the access corridor, as though he was unable even to contemplate the most parsimonious explanation: that she had gotten herself onto the bridge with Angel's key fob.

In the pauses between the bleatings of the emergency claxon, she could hear them conferring in low voices on the other side of the hatch. One of the two men uttered a low curse about his now-useless key fob. Chloe crouched with her weapon trained on the door.

Nothing.

At last, Chloe ventured to take her eyes off the porthole long enough to glance back at the security monitor. Dion, Vitaly, and Nina had returned to the Axle; they were moving quickly now. Vitaly was hauling himself down the length of the Axle toward the lab wing. Dion dropped into gamma spoke. Only Nina remained directly beneath the security camera at the end of the Axle, turned toward the access hallway to the bridge, braced to fire on Chloe if she opened the hatch.

She had bought herself a few minutes, Chloe hoped. She returned to the bridge console, began clicking through security

feeds to find the cameras trained on her attackers. She was reminded immediately of having disabled the lab wing cameras,
which brought up in her a weird, grim empathy for Meredith
and how frustrated she must have been not to be able to see
Chloe holed up in the lab wing. The gamma spoke camera
showed Dion descending toward the rim of *Imperium*, floating
like a vampire down from the rafters with a baleful serenity.

Chloe began a furious search through the apps and menus
for the controls to the airlocks and hatches. If she found them
quickly enough, she might be able to flush Vitaly out of the station through the lab module three airlock, seal off the lab wing
to isolate the hull breach. Or she could try to flush Nina out
through the Levitas Reception Hall airlock. Or she might shut
Vitaly in between two locked hatches, now that they had no key
access. If she ejected him, eight months of her research, her in-
trepid little bean sprouts growing in the BRIC-X, would also be
lost in a vacuum. But her research was likely to be lost anyway
if she needed to seal off the lab wing to contain the hull breach.

She clicked on an icon she didn't recognize, one that had
never appeared on her laptop when it was connected to the
network. *Crypsis*, it was called—some kind of messaging or
conferencing app. The call log showed just one call, from only
a few minutes ago, with a single contact: the username *Tsadok*
appeared beneath a thumbnail avatar of what seemed a pale and
impassive clay mask.

Just then, the warning claxon stopped ringing. *Hull breach
isolated*, intoned the computerized voice over the PA, though the
red warning banner continued flashing across one of the monitors. Chloe saw on the security monitor that Vitaly had closed
the hatch to the lab wing access hallway behind him. *Goodbye,
little sprouts*, she thought.

She managed to find the airlock-control program in a forest

of tiles on the screen. When she opened the application, another station schematic came up, a dizzying carnival in miniature: flashing yellow arrows, red exes, sections in green, sections in a kind of undulating orange. Opening an airlock from the bridge was not so simple, she saw immediately, as changing a crew member's key access. She began hunting through the help documentation for a tutorial on opening airlocks remotely.

A vague dread began to gnaw at her as she studied. She took a moment to try to pin down Dion's and Vitaly's locations. The key-access schematic placed Vitaly in the blacked-out lab wing; she found Dion walking at a clip along the main corridor of the rim. At the door of one of the crew cabins (his own, Chloe suspected from her unfamiliar overhead vantage of the security camera), he stopped. Unlike the security hatches—those thick, reinforced sliding doors that could be sealed to contain a hull breach—the cabin and stateroom doors were little more than upholstered privacy screens, programmed to whisk open at the presentation of the user's key fob as though in some kind of Trekkie cosplay. Dion stepped back a pace and, with a distillation of violence tensing through his whole form, kicked at the leftmost edge of the door.

The camera feed showed Dion attempting to pry back the door panel. The door resisted. After several moments of ineffectual tugging, Dion's shoulders slumped with a hangdog resignation that, for the first time in their acquaintance, gave Chloe the impression of a man treated harshly by fortune. But the man stepped back, took a long breath like one in meditation, then aimed and kicked the door twice more.

The third kick seemed to have deformed the door or the frame or both enough that he was able to gain purchase on the door's edge with his fingers. With a fluid, almost balletic motion, he peeled back the door panel as though it were the lid of a man-size sardine can. He climbed into his cabin. A few moments later he pushed a large, heavy duffel through the awkward hole into the corridor, then slipped out again himself.

Watching Dion striding down the corridor again, pistol in one hand and the massive duffel in the other, Chloe understood that whatever he and Vitaly were doing would come back to haunt her. If Dion returned with something other than flashbangs—C-4 explosive, perhaps, or even a rifle of large enough caliber—they would be able to punch through the bridge security hatch.

She had to get a message out. She picked up the radio transmitter, sent out on the emergency channel: "*Imperium* to OrbitalVentures operations center—come in, operations center."

She waited a second, three seconds, five, for a response. She wondered what time it was in California right now.

The gravelly voice of a young man finally came back to her: "This is ops center—*Imperium*, what is your status?"

"This is Chloe Bonilla—I'm part of the research crew. The station has been taken over by Commander Dion Stubblefield. I think most of the guests and employees have been taken hostage. We have fatalities. We need rescue."

"We're aware of the hostage situation, Dr. Bonilla. We're assembling a rescue mission right now. Where on the station are you?"

Chloe wondered how much information the operations center had, wondered how they had come by it. Since Dion had taken hostages, he had probably made some kind of demand. "I'm locked on the bridge. I don't know how long I'll be able to stay holed up in here. What's the ETA on rescue?"

There was a deflating pause. "We're about . . . three hours from launch."

Chloe knew then that a hostage taking was not the kind

of eventuality for which the OrbitalVentures Corporation had planned. Even if the company did have a contingency plan for such a disaster, Dion must have timed the takeover for an hour that was as far from an OrbitalVentures launch window as possible. She wondered how long he and the others had been preparing.

I'm dead anyway, she thought. Three hours until the launch, another God knew how long for a rescue ship to dock with the station—it took hours to line the moving bodies up favorably—she could be dead for a long time, then, by the time a rescue mission boarded, if they even had a protocol for a hostile boarding.

"Dr. Bonilla, are you hidden?"

As the young man asked her this over the radio, Chloe could see Vitaly on the security monitor, floating back out into the Axle.

"Hidden on the bridge? No, I'm not hidden on the bridge. Stand by, ops center—I'll contact you again if I can. Bonilla out."

She switched the radio off.

Vitaly glided up the Axle to Nina's position. They exchanged a few words in low voices; Chloe couldn't hear them through the hatch of the bridge. Then Vitaly turned and pushed off toward gamma spoke, which he entered.

"Chief, this is Vitaly," Chloe heard over channel eight. "I'm coming down to report."

Chloe had to do something, had to get herself off the bridge and into hiding. If Dion returned to the bridge hatch with his mysterious cargo, she would regret having holed up here. Yet Nina's presence on the security monitor, and her unseen presence behind the hatch, pinning Chloe down, stopped with a shudder every idea that shot across Chloe's brain. Chloe imagined opening the hatch a few centimeters, using the narrow opening as a murder hole. But Nina would be a lot harder to kill than Meredith had been: Meredith had been sailing unanchored up the middle of a corridor, while the security monitor showed Nina holding fast to one of the teardrop-shaped handholds on the other side of the access corridor bulkhead. Nina would be able to shield herself behind that bulkhead almost as well as Chloe could hide behind the bridge hatch.

Nearly frantic, Chloe returned to the airlock-control program. If she could find some way in the airlock controls to seal off the hub of *Imperium* from the rim, and if she could get both the exterior hatch and the bay door open in the Levitas Reception Hall—she might be able to blow Nina out into space as well as keep Dion and Vitaly locked out, down on the rim.

Two big *ifs*. Nina was gripping a handhold; she wouldn't just be swept away even if the depressurization surprised her. But Chloe also realized that a depressurization of the hub would force Dion and Vitaly to suit up if they wanted to come after her. Flushing out the air would pose a minor inconvenience for them in the long run, but it might buy her a few more minutes.

And, she also realized, Nina would need a moment to prepare for a depressurization. Nina had succumbed to the same temptation nearly everyone did when confronted with the restricted field of vision presented by the helmets: she had opened her visor once she had reboarded the station. With one hand, she could close the visor again and seal her helmet quickly enough, but Nina would only be able to do that by either holstering her gun or letting go of the handhold. If Chloe paid attention, she would have a critical second to act.

Chloe reviewed the help documentation on the airlock-control program. The command for sealing a hatch was more straightforward—or at least it seemed more straightforward—than she had first thought. The command sequence for opening a hatch was somewhat more elaborate, an incantatory ritual of pop-up warnings and confirmations, but the series of choices was not, she hoped, beyond her. She was hesitant to begin punching buttons in hopes of summoning the exact sequence of hatch closures and openings: if she left open a hatch that had to be closed, she could kill off all the hostages. Yet Chloe knew that if she was the only armed hostage on *Imperium*—and she almost certainly was—there was some risk to be taken if the rest were to come out alive.

She studied the station schematic that showed the bulkheads and sliding hatches of *Imperium*, every segment of the station that might be sealed or unsealed. Her task reminded her of an old sliding-tile puzzle: seal off the hub at the spokes; open the bay doors to the Levitas Reception Hall, then the hall's interior hatch; open the hatch to the bridge; if she was lucky, shoot Nina while she was still trying to seal her helmet. Find the darkest corner of *Imperium* to hide in.

Chloe began her order of operations. She disconnected two of the three keyboard interfaces on the bridge. She slid these into the awkward stuff sack at her hip. She exposed the connector of the last keyboard, the one she was still using, so that she could remove it quickly when she punched in the last command.

There were two sliding hatches at either end of each spoke. Those at the ends of the elevator spokes were closed, but the hatches at the ends of the gamma spoke ladder were open. She took a deep breath and keyed the first command. She wondered whether Nina was able to hear the hatch at the bottom of gamma spoke slide closed.

She keyed the follow-on commands. The bay doors of the Levitas Reception Hall began to open.

When she keyed in the final commands on the hatch-management utility, the warning message about an impending decompression flashed on the screen. Chloe hoped she had managed to override the station's programming regarding the warning claxon. Then, with a final keystroke, she indicated that yes, she did intend to open the interior hatch of the Levitas Reception Hall, just as Nina's voice broke in, tense and urgent, over channel eight. "I think she's decompressing the hub, chief." The old familiar claxon, thankfully, remained silent.

Things moved quickly then. Chloe caught one last glimpse of Nina on the security monitor: whether she had failed to grasp the handhold tightly enough or had taken too long to seal the visor of her helmet, the torrent of air pushing by her had swept Nina toward the Levitas Reception Hall.

Chloe shut down all security camera feeds from the monitoring program; then she yanked the last keyboard away from its connector. She leaped over to the security hatch that separated her from Nina.

Chloe punched the hatch-open button with the end of the keyboard in her left hand, raised her weapon at Nina as the hatch slid open. A burst of wind, less powerful now, pushed Chloe from behind, against the jamb of the bulkhead, as the air cleared out of the bridge toward the Levitas Reception Hall.

But Nina was not where Chloe had expected her to be. The decompression had pushed Nina almost entirely out of her sight: Chloe could see only a single glove gripping at the lip of the hatch that separated the access corridor from the Levitas Reception Hall. Beyond, Chloe could see the bay doors gaping on the great zero of space.

Chloe aimed at the one part of Nina she could see, the glove whose grip on the edge of the hatch prevented her from being blown out into space. But then Chloe's mind swerved. Something about firing on that lone hand, that solitary grip connecting Nina to the world of humans, called up for a single moment a strange and unaccountable compassion in Chloe.

Then, before Chloe could remember herself and shoot, Nina's hand released its grip and disappeared behind the bulkhead. Chloe noticed that the wind of a few seconds before had faded to a thready nothing, the merest suggestion of a breeze. She felt again her exposure, her nearness to death, come flooding back to settle around her.

She had to move. She pushed herself from the open bridge hatch toward the Axle, her gun trained on the open hatchway to the Levitas Reception Hall.

She launched herself up the Axle, looking behind her, weapon trained on where Nina might return. If Chloe was going to hide herself, she'd be better off on the rim, now that she had disabled the security cameras on the bridge. She didn't like the prospect of using any of the spokes, however. Dion and Vitaly had taken the gamma spoke ladder and might try to return that way. Yet she wasn't about to wait around in the Axle for an elevator to arrive.

She dropped into the gamma spoke shaft, closed the hatch behind her manually. There was no chatter from Nina on the communicator as Chloe descended the ladder, hauling on the rungs to speed her almost as quickly as when she had fled down the same spoke hours before. Would Nina have cried out to Dion if she had been ejected from the station?

Chloe slowed herself on the rungs of the ladder until she could climb the last few rungs to the security hatch at the bottom of the spoke. Now that she had weight, leaning over on the ladder to open the hatch was a good deal harder—she had to turn herself almost upside down on the ladder to turn the hand crank. Just as the door spiraled open on its interior springs, and a gust of air buffeted her as the air pressure of the rim rushed to fill the vacuum of the spoke, she heard Nina at last on channel eight: "I've got the hub sealed off, chief. The bridge is open. Chloe's escaped."

There was a long silence, which Chloe abstained from interpreting. "Roger that," Dion finally returned. "Retake the bridge and wait for my orders."

Chloe scrambled down the last few rungs of the ladder, reclosed the security hatch, and dropped to the corridor. She carried so much now—fire extinguisher, pistol, spare magazine, three computer keyboards, screwdriver, permanent marker, all that duct tape, not to mention the pressure suit she wore— that a jolt of pain shot through her ankles and knees when she dropped to the floor of the main rim corridor. She berated herself silently for risking a twisted ankle in the simplest and safest moment of her escape. But her joints did not rebel any further, and she made for her destination.

She lifted her visor again, pulled out her weapon. She could make out a strange tapping close by, like the knocking of old plumbing. Maybe one of the ventilators had been damaged by the pressure changes in all the openings and closings of hatches. The nearest room with a reinforced hatch was the hotel administration office about fifty meters up the corridor. She regretted not having had a little more time with the security monitors on the bridge to suss out where the hostages were being kept. If they were being kept in the Fortuna Ballroom, that was close by— barely out of her way as she headed for the hotel admin office. But there was no time for that now: she wasn't sure which direction Dion would be coming from up the corridor, and she wanted to be well hidden in the admin office if he passed this way.

She heard Dion again over channel eight: "Give us a visual on her location. We don't want her hitting us in the legs before we can even see her."

She could hear that she was passing close by the source of the tapping. It seemed to be coming from the medevac capsule airlock, a tense, almost regular metallic clacking, as though someone were tapping a nickel on her window to draw her attention.

She could still take the medevac. She wasn't under video surveillance now; no one would know until she was gone.

But once again, she decided that she would not take the medevac. She did not in that moment reflect on her decision, the unconscious tallying up of reasons not to flee, that she was one armed person who knew the station, standing between killers and helpless people.

The corridor remained clear as she padded past the airlock, staff cabins, another useless conference room. The security cameras glared blindly at her. "Uh, chief—we've got a situation on the bridge," Nina was saying over the communicators.

As she passed the entryway of the library, Chloe heard a movement that made her turn and ready her weapon. The room was still and empty—from the corridor she could see the lit cases, the gorgeous long study tables, the laptops, and chairs. But she had not imagined the sound.

Her pistol out in front of her, she crouched to look under the study table nearest the entryway. Someone was crouched there, silent as a rabbit or a leopard.

A small voice whispered from beneath the table: "Please don't kill me."

CHAPTER EIGHT

TEN MINUTES EARLIER

Dion was grateful, at least, that Roger Van Cleave had stopped hailing him over the communicators. Roger's pleas for assistance—first affronted, then cajoling, finally pathetic—had distracted Dion during moments when his attention was needed elsewhere. It was a relief at last to hear nothing—no claxons, no whining.

Of all the unproductive emotions, Dion understood despair to be the most troublesome. It was a more tenacious passion even than anger and fear, those two instincts that he had spent a whole life weeding out of his character. Despair, though, was a feeling that committed a man to more stupidities than anger and fear put together. As Augustine had said somewhere, despair was the only unforgivable sin.

When he had found the Reckoners locked out of the bridge, his team's key fobs deactivated, another team member dead, Dion had contended for a few moments with the same kind of despair that a chess player confronts when surprised by the loss of a rook. In silence he had had to remind himself, as he floated outside the bridge hatch with Nina and Vitaly, that many games of chess are won by players who are down a rook, notwithstanding that God generally favors the player with more rooks.

Most frustrating of all was that this endless wrangling with Chloe had been so unnecessary to begin with. He had not lied to her, at least not about what he would do if she surrendered: he had had no intention of killing her if she had laid down her weapons. Even now, he wouldn't harm a hair on her head if she would simply let the Reckoners finish their business.

But there was no sense, he knew, in wishing for what might have been. Time to pick himself up and regroup. He had been so concerned about the Starliner before, when Chloe was holed up in the lab wing and could get to the shuttle more easily than they could. Intentionally or not, she had drawn the Reckoners out into a more vulnerable position with her antics. And now Chloe could get into a lot more mischief on the bridge than she could have done before, even in the lab wing. Even if Nina kept her pinned down there, she could—

Could what? Dion wondered. Would the launch window for a rescue come any more quickly with Chloe on the bridge? Was she likely to decompress the whole station when there were hostages aboard? Did it matter that she had revoked their key access? Most doors on the rim could be forced open with a pry bar, and they had more than enough explosives to break open the security hatches separating the Reckoners from the Starliner. Their goals would be more difficult to accomplish after the loss of Meredith and the bridge, but hardly impossible.

He supposed that if she wanted to, Chloe could shut down the internet router to the rim from where she was. That would stop the transfer of wealth, alas. But Dion did his best to take the perspective of his opponent, to imagine her fears and desires: given the bind she was in, the danger she perceived, fairly or not, was it likely to occur to her how much the Reckoners needed the internet right now? At any rate, supposing for the sake of argument that she did have such an insight, how would her shutting down the router affect their operation now? They had already collected nearly half of the ransom, a reasonable success for the Reckoners' first mission.

Dion slowed down his pace a moment as he strode down the central corridor of the rim with his duffel. They had committed a few unforced errors, having to react to Chloe's mischief. He could spare a minute now to weigh their options. For one, they could go forward with a frontal assault on the bridge. They had brought the C-4 charges aboard for that very purpose, in the event that things did not go according to plan: the breaking open of a reinforced hatch. Much could go wrong with C-4 up here, though. An explosion of that magnitude would certainly risk another hull breach, perhaps one far worse than a stray pistol round punching through the walls of the station. Then there was possible damage to the bridge's command and data-handling system, which could tip over into any number of other system failures on *Imperium*. And not least, Chloe had proved herself an uncommonly persistent fighter—best to assume now that she would not go down right away. Any or all of the Reckoners might be shot in a firefight, even if they managed to take her out.

Alternatively, they could ignore her. While he and Vitaly kept moving the hostages through their fire sale of stocks to raise their ransoms, he could leave Nina posted where she was, babysitting the bridge hatch, keeping Chloe in time-out. Chloe might, if it occurred to her, try to flush out the hub through the Levitas bay door and expel Nina, but Nina was suited up and knew what to do in a decompression event.

Dion had pulled the duffel from his cabin in anticipation

of the frontal assault. He had been angry, he realized now: he felt a boyish chagrin for having torn the door of his cabin off its track like a drunken lout.

But now, as he weighed the Reckoners' options, as he walked along the endless wheel of the rim, the attractions of the alternative strategy became more and more apparent. Their goals, after all, were not to neutralize Chloe. Ignoring Chloe kept the Reckoners' focus where it belonged, kept their eyes on the prize.

Vitaly dropped out of the gamma spoke ladder a little way ahead of him in the corridor. "What's the status on the hull breach?" Dion asked.

Vitaly made the OK sign. At least, that was what it seemed to Dion at first, until he realized that Vitaly was estimating for him the size of the hole in the hull, a breach about the size of a dime. "A lot of trouble over that little hole," he said. "If we had any duct tape, we could tape a patch over it. For now, I've just sealed the hatch to the lab wing."

Then, as if as an afterthought: "Angel and Meredith don't look so good in there."

"Dead?"

"Very dead."

"I think we should reassess our next step," Dion began. The duffel seemed suddenly heavy to him now, his bag of tricks stuffed with C-4 charges, cables, and detonators; the charger for the active denial device; the .50-caliber rifle and ammunition, if things really spun out of control and they had to repel the approach of a rescue craft; more flash-bangs; screwdrivers, hex keys, and a pry bar for closeouts and cabinets; a medical kit; and yes, duct tape. He would suggest the duct tape in a minute.

Vitaly set his jaw in that way he did when he disliked an idea.

In that moment, they heard the emergency hatch of gamma

spoke slam shut just above their heads. The two men looked quizzically at one another for a moment.

"Is she initiating a decompression?"

"Maybe," Dion answered. He pulled up the mic of his headset to give the warning just as Nina broke radio silence on channel eight: "I think she's decompressing the hub, chief."

"Is your suit sealed?"

No answer came back. Dion and Vitaly stared at one another in growing alarm: the operation was challenging, but possible, with a team of three, so long as they could keep Chloe pinned down. But if they lost Nina, and if Chloe somehow survived, the job would be nigh impossible with a team of two. "We may need to make for the Starliner," Dion muttered.

He began to consider the emergency pressure suits hanging in the rooms around them. Given their bulk and awkwardness, it was almost certainly worth the delay to head back up the corridor to the crew cabins for their fitted suits.

"Let's get suited up," he told Vitaly.

Vitaly raised an eyebrow. "That's it? We're heading for the Starliner? What about Nina?" Dion didn't like Vitaly's tone. Still, his remark was not openly disdainful, not enough to merit a response at this moment.

"There are a lot of reasons we may need to make for the hub on short notice. And if Chloe opened one of the bay doors, the station will take hours to repressurize after we get it closed again. Nina can rendezvous with us at the Starliner." He did not add what Vitaly surely knew already: Nina could rendezvous with them if she managed not to get sucked out of the station. Vitaly also knew, surely, that of all the things that had gone wrong so far, much more *could* go wrong. Wearing but not needing the pressure suits would be infinitely better than needing but not wearing them.

"We're going to frighten the hostages if they see us," Vitaly said as they made for the crew cabins.

"They're sufficiently frightened already. I doubt the suits will add or detract much."

As they turned back toward the staff cabin section, Dion became aware of a faint sound up the corridor, almost at the edge of his hearing, a strange, irregular tapping that he realized must have been going on for some time. Its tone of insistence needled him.

The sound was like the clicking of a poorly mounted ventilation fan, except that the rhythm of its distant clacking was not so predictable, like someone using a tiny door knocker on a stout, eternally locked door.

It took him a minute to understand what he was hearing: the clacking was exactly what it would sound like if someone was banging an object—a safety belt buckle, for example—against the hatch of the medevac capsule, to be propagated through the walls of the airlock to diffuse into the corridor as a weak, far-off tapping.

Vitaly was giving him a quizzical look in the hallway. "It's the Van Cleaves on the medevac capsule," Dion said.

Vitaly let off a snort. "I suppose they are getting tired of waiting. Should we pull them off?"

Unfortunately for the Van Cleaves, Dion knew that the correct answer was no. Cooling their heels aboard the medevac, even while they were still docked to the station, Roger and Jessica were safer than anyone else on *Imperium*. And anyway, how was anyone going to recover the original splashdown presets for the medevac right now? If Roger and Jessica were foolish enough to launch themselves before the medevac navigation computer was restored to its original presets, they had an excellent chance of drowning somewhere off Villings when the capsule eventually, inevitably sank. The OrbitalVentures retrieval teams wouldn't even know the capsule had launched. The Van Cleaves were better off waiting where they were.

Their tapping haunted him, though, like the beating of the hideous heart under Poe's floorboards. Dion felt a furious undercurrent urge to hit the emergency launch button himself from the infirmary airlock, to send away that shameful, clacking reminder of how the Reckoners' plans were coming apart at the seams.

Shame, though, was another unproductive emotion—there was no more foolish reason on Earth to kill someone. Hadn't he already decided he wouldn't be killing anybody else just to make a point, or to avoid backing down on a threat? He intended to keep his word if he could to the Van Cleaves: they had paid up and would go home first.

And if he couldn't keep his word? He would have to contend with that dishonor himself.

"Negative," Dion replied. "They are safer where they are. Let's suit up."

The two double-timed up the hallway to the door of Vitaly's cabin. Vitaly let out another faint, ironic snort at the sight of the next cabin up the hall from his, the door of which had *Dr. Chloe Bonilla Prieto* on the nameplate.

"It's a pity," Vitaly muttered, nodding at Chloe's door. "She shouldn't line up to fight for those billionaires, just because of her boyfriend."

For a moment Dion envied Vitaly's ability to divide the world into revolutionaries and counterrevolutionaries, Reckoners and propertarians. It had never before occurred to Dion to speculate about what Chloe's politics were.

Dion handed the pry bar to Vitaly, who wrenched open his door panel with a quick, broad-shouldered ferocity. Dion prepared to wriggle through the gash in the doorway of his own cabin three doors down, adjacent to the cabin of Konrad Whittaker, his dead colleague. Dion was not in a position to waste precious attention on the reappearance of Konrad's name in his field of vision now. Someday he would reflect on that name again, he hoped—the Reckoners' work was a tangled knot of means and ends that he would one day, if he was lucky, have the leisure to untie.

As he stooped to pass through into his cabin, Dion felt a fastidious awareness of the main-corridor security camera that looked down on their cabin doors. Perhaps Chloe was watching him even now from the bridge. He thought for a moment about shooting out the camera the way Chloe had done with one of the other cameras in the corridor. But he could not see how the benefits justified the risks: the possibility of another hull breach, the noise and the dead camera feed giving away their position just as surely as if the camera were watching them. Perhaps Chloe had panicked when she shot out the camera near the cafeteria.

Back in his cabin, Dion took his pressure suit from the closet and began to shimmy into the thick, fitted fabric. Just then, Nina's voice broke in again over the communicators: "I've got the hub sealed off, chief. The bridge is open. Chloe's escaped."

Dion's relief at not having lost Nina balanced in a kind of cosmic symmetry with his frustration that Chloe was lost to him again. For all he knew, she could be coming his way just now, when he was halfway into his suit, caught almost literally with his pants down. "Roger that," he answered Nina. "Retake the bridge and wait for my orders."

He realized, as he regarded the hole in his cabin door, that the presence of the duffel had suddenly become a nontrivial problem to him. It would only slow them down in a firefight if he or Vitaly had to lug it around. But he couldn't just leave the thing in his cabin if Chloe was on the loose—the duffel held enough C-4 charges to blast a medevac-size hole in the hull.

"Can you give us a visual on Chloe's location?" he called out to Nina. He hated having Chloe listening in. He wished it had occurred to one of them to change to a different radio channel when the three of them were in the Axle together. But there had been too much to think about, not enough time to think.

"Uh, chief—we've got a situation on the bridge," Nina replied. "Chloe shut down the security monitors and pulled all the keyboards out of the terminals. I can't pull up any apps. I've got no visual."

Dion inhaled, then exhaled, a single passionate breath. Why had he ever taken up the study of Stoicism, that philosophy of shipwrecked men and slaves, if not to bear up under such reversals? Would his Stoicism fail him now? Would he fail his Stoicism? There was, he knew, no extirpating passion, root and branch, from the human heart. *The only thing that we did right was the day we started to fight.*

"Copy that. Stand by."

He needed a moment to think. He stood with his suit half-on, taking in the acrid stink of Chloe's carpet fire, the smoke of which had circulated throughout the rim.

If they could get one of the laptops linked up again to *Imperium*'s command and data-handling network, Nina could access the bridge's systems that way. He wasn't about to announce that over channel eight right now, though. He and Vitaly needed to get suited up, get the duffel secured if they could.

He disliked thinking about all the corners of *Imperium* where Chloe could be now. With the bridge interfaces disabled, it would make sense for her to head for the hotel administration office: there she would have key access and the Reckoners would not. From inside hotel administration, she would be able to pull up the security monitors, would be able to follow the movements of the Reckoners' key fobs, would be able to stay in communication with Earth.

She could be anywhere, though. She could just as easily be sneaking up the main rim corridor from either direction in this moment. Perhaps she was somewhere else entirely, somewhere that he did not expect at all: for all he knew, she might be back hiding in lab module one again. He secured the seal between his helmet and his suit, leaned out of the hole in his cabin door-way, and looked up and down the corridor as the Van Cleaves' airlock tapping ticked like a ruined stopwatch timing his and Vitaly's donning of their suits.

A couple of nerve-jangling minutes had passed before he and Vitaly rendezvoused out in the corridor again, their holsters belted around the outsides of their suits. The duffel weighed down his arm like a sandbag. Vitaly looked shaken, on the verge of tears. Perhaps his relief that Nina had not been lost had over-come his own reserve.

"From here, what do we do?" Vitaly asked.

"From here we go back to collecting the ransoms."

"But what do we do about Chloe?"

It would be wise, Dion knew, to report to Tsadok if he could—his team had abandoned plan A hours ago and had had to improvise plans B and C already. But they did not have world enough and time to consult with Tsadok on an entire alphabet of plans. Dion's idea would at least get the Reckoners reckoning again, taking from the rich to give to the poor. At the end of it all, Tsadok would be grateful for Dion's initiative.

"Unless she tries to interfere, we leave her alone. She's taken up too much of our time already." He looked down at the duffel and knew that without key access, there would be no place to hide the bag where Chloe couldn't find it. And if she was watching them over the security monitors from the hotel administration office, she might even see exactly where they hid it.

"We need to get one of the laptops with access to the bridge computer up to Nina," he continued.

"There are none. We locked the laptops out of the bridge network, remember?"

"I'm saying we need to find a laptop that we can unlock. We can get Nina back onto the bridge computer that way."

Vitaly stared at the ceiling behind Dion, perhaps into the dead eye of the security camera above them. "The library computers are closest, but they never had bridge permissions. I suppose we could get the infirmary laptop."

"That will work. Can you unlock it?"

"Maybe not, chief. I don't know what Meredith did to lock it. Maybe Nina will know how to get into it."

The image of Nina floating on the bridge in her pressure suit, tapping out a password on the laptop key by key with a single fat finger of her glove, seemed to Dion an apt symbol for their condition. Yet the mission would be more secure by far if Nina could get into *Imperium*'s network and observe from the bridge.

Dion and Vitaly made their suited, unwieldy way to the gleaming infirmary. With the pry bar Vitaly wrenched open one of the locked cabinets. Within, they found one of the laptop interfaces for the station's command and data-handling system. Dion noted that Roger's or Jessica's tapping—whoever of the two was doing it—seemed no louder in this room, even though the medevac capsule they were trapped in was docked to an airlock just adjacent to the infirmary. The sound seemed sometimes to come from everywhere and nowhere, like a ghostly presence.

Dion and Vitaly headed back up the corridor, summoned the beta spoke elevator, and tapped through the warning that flashed on the touch screen: in the event of a decompression on the hub or the rim, the elevators had been designed to operate like airlocks. "Come in, Nina," Dion said.

"Nina here—go ahead, chief."

"We're sending up a laptop on the beta elevator—see if you can get it unlocked and reconnected to the bridge network."

"I'll try. It will be slow work in the suit, though."

Dion laid the laptop in the elevator car, pushed the button marked *Hub*, and stepped out into the main corridor before the elevator could close. The team was stretched too thin, he thought as he watched the elevator set off for the Axle.

They returned to the locked glass doors of the Fortuna Ballroom. Vitaly levered open the latch with the pry bar, and one of the doors responded to the insult by shattering into a thousand polygonal sequins of safety glass. Within the dim chamber, one of the hostages yipped an almost strangled shriek, as though she had swallowed a tiny toy trumpet. Dion wasn't sure whether her panicked outburst was in response to the shattering of the door, or to seeing him and Vitaly in pressure suits, or to seeing him and Vitaly at all.

Vitaly took up his position at the entryway. Dion strode in, regarding the positions of the hostages on the floor. He disliked that his pressure suit had no pocket for the active denial device: if he needed to draw his pistol, he would need to hold the active denial piece in his other hand. The active denial, at least, had a large enough button and no trigger guard—easy enough to work even in his gloves.

He suspected that their stiff, almost waddling entry in the suits had had a more bizarre than intimidating effect on their charges. They looked at him and Vitaly with the same looks of seasick dread that they had worn in the first hour of the hostage taking. They looked as though the billionaires had never come to any agreement hours before, as though they had forgotten or disbelieved every assurance Dion had made them.

"People," he declaimed through his open visor, feeling like a medieval king in a suit of armor, "it's time for you to fulfill the terms you all agreed to. As soon as the signatories have moved the funds they committed to our act of reckoning, Vitaly and I will be on our way. We'll leave you to wait for your rescue in peace." He looked over his silent audience.

They appeared stunned. "The revolution isn't going to wait for you," Vitaly added. His voice sounded a bit too menacing, in Dion's opinion.

Samir finally spoke up. "Is *Imperium* losing air? Is that why you're wearing pressure suits?"

"There was a brief decompression event on the hub of the station," Dion explained, "but the breach has been contained. The rim of *Imperium* is totally sealed off. Vitaly and I are suited up because we're ready to head home—as soon as you've made your contributions to social equity." If the hostages found this explanation unsatisfying—they certainly seemed skeptical enough—Dion was pleased to have hit on an economically worded approximation of what was going on.

But something else was different about their mood, he knew. Most of them looked stricken, as though they expected him at any minute to begin searing them with the active denial device. They seemed paralyzed by his presence. He passed his eyes slowly over the miserable collection like a person assembling a jigsaw puzzle, knowing that the piece he needed was somewhere in front of him, waiting to be seen in a new way.

He realized then that one of the pieces was missing. "Where's Ms. Ng?" he asked in a voice as quiet, as serene, as that of a monk discoursing on the nature of the divine.

The undercurrent of terror among the prisoners seemed

almost to take on a physical existence of its own now, flapping around the Fortuna Ballroom like a confused bat. "We tried to stop her," Sir Alexander Dunne blurted.

But Tirzah Fowler had interrupted him before he had even finished his five words. "She couldn't have gone far," Tirzah nearly shouted. "*Imperium* is not that big."

Meanwhile Viv Volterra pointed wordlessly at a spot on the floor. Dion regarded the tiny trapdoor by which one could access the hologram projector. He had wondered about that space before, during the planning. He had concluded then after careful inspection that even someone as small as Kassie Ng would find the space too tight to move in—certainly none of the Reckoners had been small enough to fit. That seemed an interesting part of the plan to have been wrong about.

Samir gave Volterra a look that Dion imagined must contain all the opprobrium and shame of an Old Testament curse.

Yet Dion found the hostages' panic and recrimination unexpectedly amusing. Not because he enjoyed their discomfort especially, but because Kassie Ng was utterly unnecessary for the Reckoners' mission now. The hostages would come up a million dollars short without her. What was a million dollars among billions? For all Dion cared, Kassie could go back to her cabin and live stream makeup tutorials until rescue came.

Was this joy rising within him? Had the Reckoners managed, in spite of their losses and confusion, in spite of this farce of grease fires and sabotaged key fobs, to put the mission to rights? He did not wish to divulge this happiness to the hostages in front of him—not because he enjoyed frightening them but because they were likelier to move quickly, to raise ransom urgently, if they were frightened of him. Yet part of him wanted to shake each of their hands, to hug them and whirl them around the room for joy.

"Messrs. Winters-Qureshi, please go with Vitaly to arrange your ransom." Dion's voice betrayed neither anger nor contentment but (he hoped) conveyed hidden depths that his hostages might take for controlled rage. Both Samir and Nicholas regarded him warily as they stood.

"Nina, what's your status on the bridge?" he said into the communicator as the unkempt venture capitalists stepped into the main corridor in front of Vitaly, who lugged the great duffel with one hand and trained his pistol on Samir and Nicholas with the other.

"I think I've figured out what Meredith did to lock these laptops out," Nina replied. "I'm trying to reestablish the handshake with *Imperium*'s CDH."

"Give me a report when you get things connected."

Dion surveyed his charges as they sat before the wide windows of the ballroom. The station moved over the nightside of the Earth, but in this moment the windows showed that the ballroom was also facing away from Earth, looking out on a black field of stars that Dion had always found tantalizing and inaccessible. One day, he knew, humanity would be a just and wise species. One day, no one would own wealth ten orders of magnitude greater than the rest. Gone would be the color line, gone all such illusory division, gone all stratification, all oppression. And humanity would, in that day, live among the stars. They would think on their ancestors with a bemused pity, reflecting on the groping of Dion's generation through a miserable, benighted age that celebrated every variety of exploitation and parasitism. Humanity in that day would be prone to other follies, certainly, other injustices, but the injustices that so pressed on Dion and animated his actions, the injustices that had given rise to the Reckoners, would be resolved like an untangled knot, like the solution to a child's riddle. The room was so silent that he could even hear the breathing of some of the hostages. The phantom tapping, real or imagined, of the Van Cleaves trapped in the medevac had gone silent.

"Commander Stubblefield," a man addressed him in a soft voice. Dion looked down to see Zhiming Li staring at him with an unsettling focus.

"Commander Stubblefield," Li continued. "I must respectfully insist that you bring Kassie Ng back to the group. We had an agreement: each of the guests would pay some part of the ransom. We have done everything you have asked, and many of us find it unacceptable that Kassie will possibly return without having paid anything. I, for one, refuse to pay her part of the ransom."

Dion stared back at Li, feeling at a loss for how to respond to the man's insistence. What was he to make of Li's unaccountably dignified bearing? He supposed that people like Li did not become billionaires by forgiving anyone a million dollars' debt. But Dion found it irritating, almost shocking, that even as a hostage Li would feel entitled to insist on his wishes being carried out.

Still, Dion had to acknowledge that Li had a point. Kassie's escape represented a literal breach of contract. If Vitaly could bring her back without a lot of fuss, if the contract could be honored—

Just then Nina's voice came over channel eight. "We're back in, chief. We have access to all command and data-handling functions."

"Excellent. Override key-access functions for the hotel administration office." If Chloe was there now, or even if she wasn't, the Reckoners should have shut down computer access for the hotel admin office from the beginning.

"Roger that. Key-access function overridden."

"Now, restrict all key access for all key fobs on *Imperium*, with the exception of yours, mine, and Vitaly's."

There was a pause of a few seconds while Nina transferred the balance of power on the station back to the Reckoners.

"Key access restricted for all but we three."

Dion silently corrected the grammar error for his own benefit: *All but us three.* "Very good. If you can, get a visual on Chloe Bonilla. Kassie Ng too, if you can find her."

"Commander?" Li repeated.

Did Dion dare imagine that he might recapture Kassie, that he might even be able to spare Nina for a few minutes, have her recover the medevac's original splashdown coordinates so that Dion could keep his word to the Van Cleaves?

"No camera feeds from some areas," Nina responded. "No visual on—stand by. I've got visual on Kassie Ng. She's on the main rim corridor, in the vicinity of airlock two, moving toward beta spoke."

At that moment, the station alarm claxon gave three short, piercing blasts.

CHAPTER NINE

"If they discover either of us, I'll give you three short blasts on the station's claxon," Chloe said.

She disliked that Kassie had no communicator, disliked that the general-issue emergency pressure suits in the hotel admin office were several sizes too big for Kassie—who, to be fair, was several sizes smaller than anyone else on *Imperium*. She didn't want Kassie sneaking off to her stateroom just to retrieve the pressure suit that fit her—the whole trip seemed an intolerable risk. Still, it was easy for Chloe to say that the risk was intolerable: Chloe was already wearing her own pressure suit.

"If you hear three short blasts," Chloe continued, repeating herself as though Kassie were one of her college-freshman biology-101 students, "find somewhere dark or with no cameras and take cover. The restrooms, a storage closet, a stateroom, one of the conference rooms, even. Just get yourself out of sight. I'll be watching you on the monitors, and I'll come to you if I can. As soon as you get the suit on, hail me on channel five. Remember that they might be listening in. Say as little as you can."

Kassie nodded with a head-snapping conclusiveness. She put the lanyard, with the new administrative key fob that Chloe had just assigned to her from the hotel administration computer, around her neck. Chloe had given the fob no name, just an asterisk as a label, as though that would fool anyone checking the station schematic on the key-access application on the bridge. She had replaced Angel's name with a single parenthesis on her own fob, too.

Kassie gave Chloe a squeeze on the forearm as if to reassure her, or perhaps herself. Chloe scanned the security monitors once more and gave her the all-clear—Vitaly and Dion were still coming up on the Fortuna Ballroom cameras, and Nina was still on the bridge, tapping away at a laptop. Kassie opened the hatch to the main corridor and dashed out.

This is a horrible idea, Chloe repeated to herself once she was alone. She had tried to impress on Kassie the idea that all living requires the balancing of relative risks. Yes, the people Kassie called the Reckoners might find the two of them holed up in the hotel admin office. And yes, the Reckoners might have explosives. And yes, if they used explosives to blow open the office hatch, they might cause a hull breach. Yes, dying in a vacuum was a risk when you went into space.

But, Chloe had tried to explain, if Dion blew open the office hatch, a hull breach would be the least of Kassie's problems. There were many risks a pressure suit wouldn't protect against, many other risks that Kassie was courting by venturing out for her suit. Chloe would rather by far that they just stayed out of Dion's way.

Kassie had argued that if she could just get to her stateroom and get her pressure suit on, they could find an unused radio channel and communicate through the Snoopy caps of their respective fitted suits if they were separated. Chloe answered that any radio channel on the Snoopy caps could be eavesdropped on by the Reckoners; more importantly, if she wanted to keep from being separated, she shouldn't try to sneak into her stateroom.

But it was clear that Kassie was going to do what she wanted—Chloe wasn't about to pull a gun on her and force her to stay. Chloe wished, not for the first time, that she had managed to scoop up Meredith's weapon when she had sped past Meredith's corpse up on the hub. But Chloe could not have spared a moment then. Now she had the time to spare, but Meredith's pistol might as well be on Earth. Anyway, Kassie had never held a firearm in her life; perhaps it didn't matter that there was no spare weapon to give her. But Chloe hated the idea of Kassie's sneaking around *Imperium* without even the pretense of being armed.

Alone again, sitting amid the clutter she had unloaded from her stuff sacks—the keyboards, the nearly cashed-out fire extinguisher—Chloe wondered over the identity of the person that Meredith had communicated with just before she died. Had Meredith been in too much of a hurry to delete the record of the call before she was called out to get herself shot? Chloe tried to ascribe some meaning to the strange avatar of Tsadok's profile picture, the pale, half-lidded ceramic mask with the imperturbable face of some judgmental idol.

While she watched through the security monitors as the slight, elfin woman—she seemed more girl than woman, really—padded up the corridor, Chloe pondered the information Kassie had shown her. Kassie was cleverer than Chloe had given her credit for, using Chloe's admin permissions to sift through the internet-use logs for the station's computers. The program Meredith had used, Crypsis, seemed also to have accessed *Imperium*'s server several times through someone's— Dion's?—phone. Three calls in the last forty-eight hours, one of them between the hours of the opening gala and the hostage taking. Had these been conferences with Tsadok too?

In their first minutes after finding one another, after holing up in the hotel admin office, Chloe and Kassie had Skyped Hellmund. Even though it had been four in the morning in California, Hellmund had picked right up. He was dressed already, looking rattled—someone from OrbitalVentures had awakened him earlier, as soon as they were aware of Dion's takeover on the ground.

"What the hell is going on up there, Chlo?" Hellmund had asked when he picked up.

Chloe had felt tears rising up in her as soon as she saw his piercing, stricken eyes, the anxiety pulling at the corners of his mouth. She had wished she could reach through the screen to wrap herself around him, hold on, and just cry.

However, Chloe Bonilla had been an expert, from the time she was eight years old, in suppressing the urge to cry. "Dion and a team of employees have taken over the station," she had said, her voice as flat as if she had been reciting data points of radicle lengths for a graduate assistant to write down. "Konrad is dead. Six people are dead, by my count."

He looked utterly at sea for a moment, let out a long, freighted sigh. "Do you know anything about what the hijackers want?" he said at last.

At this, Kassie had broken in: "Dion says they'll leave *Imperium* if we pay eight billion dollars in cryptocurrency. They call themselves the Reckoners."

"The Reckoners," Hellmund had repeated in a tone that Chloe took for disdain, as though to mock the high-handedness of the name. "If what they want is money, then why the hell are they killing people?"

"Two of them, I killed," Chloe had said. "Two Reckoners.

Angel and Meredith." She had felt in that moment another strange welling-up behind her words, a desire to recount all, to explain, to lay out in every detail her claim of self-defense as though she were acting as her own legal counsel before a judge. But at that moment she had also felt intuitively that, however much there was to say about it, there was just as much to say about any killing, about every killing for as long as humans had had language to make sense of the world. Even those murders that one read about in the news, the ones that seemed so senseless and irrational, were final strands in a great web of causes and effects, stretching back across the killer's life, the lives of ancestors, the lives of a great host of strangers and loved ones and enemies who had helped or hindered, or failed to help or to hinder. There was everything to say about every killing, which meant paradoxically that there was nothing to say in this moment about the two killings she had committed.

"When can you send a rescue mission?" Kassie had interjected. Chloe had already explained to her the temporal demands of launch windows, the rare slivers on the clock when it was feasible for a rocket to leave the Earth and rendezvous with a perpetually hurtling orbital station: it was easier by far for a quarterback to land a football directly in the hands of a wide receiver running a fly route fifty yards away. She couldn't blame Kassie, though, for wanting a second opinion.

"We have a rocket on the pad right now, ready to go. We're sending up twenty security personnel. But you can't just launch a rocket whenever you want and link up with your destination. Our launch window won't hit for about two and a half hours."

A leaden, discouraged silence had descended over Kassie then, which Hellmund broke. "Are you two safe right now? Out of sight?"

"We're good," Chloe had said. "But listen: I need you to

do some research for me. The Reckoners have been in touch with someone on the ground with the username Tsadok. Can you find out anything about them? These guys have a lot of equipment up here, and they've been planning this a long time— someone on the ground has to be helping them out."

Hellmund had repeated the name, begun spelling it out. "*Z-A-D-O-K?*"

Chloe had spelled out the name for him.

"I'll do what I can," he had said, staring down at his pad of paper as though to find some hidden meaning in the letters he had spelled. "But you have to do this for me, Chlo: stay out of their way. No gunplay, no stupid heroics. If what these Reckoners want is money, just let them take it and get out of your hair. I'll die if you get yourself killed over some bullshit mugging."

"I'll call you again when I can," Chloe had said. "Just find out what you can about this Tsadok."

Her last glimpse of him when they had signed off was of a man older than he was: owl-eyed, shaky, her boyfriend had seemed on the verge of crying himself. He worried over her, she knew. And, she supposed, he was watching the value of the company he had built melt away to nothing. There was no way that *Imperium* would survive as a luxury hotel after a hostage taking on the inaugural night.

Now, sheltered alone in the hotel admin office, as she watched Kassie running up the rim corridor toward her stateroom, Chloe thought of the glimpse she had had of Hellmund and was filled with an aching sadness. She felt lonely in a way that she had not felt in all the weeks she had worked by herself on *Imperium*, in all the months of solitary fieldwork for her doctoral research in the Dark Divide. It dawned on her with a sudden, stealthy force that her solitude, which she had always felt as a kind of obstinate, prideful hermeticism, was not part of her native personality. Her independence, her ability to be away from Hellmund, from everyone, had been learned. Solitude had emerged in her as an adaptive response to the great loneliness that had been with her since childhood, perhaps since birth. It felt to her as though her mother's constant distance, her volatility, her death, which had dried into Chloe's childhood under the cold sun of her father's silence and emotional color blindness, had drawn her personality into a taut, immobile sinew that wrapped her mind always around the work at hand. Why the sinew had slipped now, why she felt this aching loneliness, when the work at hand was so heavy, was a mystery to her. She looked up at the security camera of the hotel admin office itself, the lens of which she had covered with duct tape in an abundance of caution. As though she were some form of exotic particle, her presence might be inferred—but she would not be seen.

Chloe watched Kassie let herself into her stateroom. A moment later, on another of the monitors, Samir and Nicholas Winters-Qureshi stepped out of the Fortuna Ballroom into the spray of safety glass spangling the corridor where Vitaly had broken open the glass doors with a pry bar a few minutes before. Vitaly walked out after them, his steps fluid and poised in spite of his great bulk and the bulk of the bag he carried, like the pacing of a tiger. Samir and Nicholas chatted together with tense, tight mouths as they walked before Vitaly's drawn weapon, as though they had already grown accustomed to being threatened every minute of their lives.

Chloe watched the three walk the corridor in the same direction that Kassie had gone. Though Kassie's stateroom was at the antipode of Vitaly's current position on the rim, the emergence of one of the Reckoners in the corridor was exactly the situation Chloe had dreaded.

Dion was conferring with Nina over channel eight as they tried to regain access to the bridge computers. The possibility distressed her: from the bridge, Chloe's computer terminal could be overridden; her key fob permissions could be revoked; Dion's permissions could be restored.

If Vitaly was walking them to the library, as Kassie had told her the Reckoners were doing with the hostages, they would be out of the corridor within the next minute or so. Chloe watched on the monitor as the three passed right in front of the hatch to the hotel administration office. They passed so closely that she heard for a moment the low murmur of Samir and Nicholas's chatting.

They were, for a moment, no more than three or four meters away from her. An instinct climbed up her spine, a wordless, unreflective sense that a window of opportunity had opened in front of her. She could, if she acted now, right now, crack open the hatch, if she was lucky, take aim at the center of Vitaly's broad back. Fluidly as a stalking cat, she drew her pistol from its duct tape holster and crept to the hatch.

Then she paused. The chance passed as silently as it had arrived.

What stayed her hand? It was nothing that she had reasoned, though she did have good reasons to pause: she wasn't thinking in that moment about the dangers of overpenetration, even using hollow-point rounds, or that she might have killed Nicholas or Samir as well as Vitaly—or even instead of Vitaly. She wasn't thinking about Dion, also near, also armed—she wasn't thinking about what he might do if she advertised her location like that. She wasn't thinking about Hellmund's advice to steer clear of heroics, or what heroics meant in such a moment, miles from any human community that had ever existed.

What stayed her hand was just as instinctive, as preverbal,

as the urge that had put the weapon in her hand the moment before. As she told herself later, she was not a killer. *That's not me*, she said, many moments after she had let the chance pass, as she tried in retrospect to attribute meanings to her actions and lack of actions. She was not a killer, she told herself, even though she'd shot a woman in the head not an hour before, even though she'd driven a screwdriver into a man's brain earlier that day. But in that moment, wordless, she turned away from the closed hatch, and on the security monitor she found Vitaly and Samir and Nicholas as they walked into the library.

Once Kassie got into her suit, Chloe knew that she could get a warning to her over the communicators, keep her from passing by the library until Vitaly had returned to the ballroom, if he ever did.

She'll get back safe, Chloe told herself. She rehearsed in her memory the time required to don one of the fitted pressure suits. Two minutes to do it right. Chloe switched between channel eight, where Dion and Nina still conferred over the handshake between laptop and server, and channel five. "Come in, Kassie," she whispered.

Nothing.

Chloe listened to the dead air of channel five as long as she dared. Had they agreed to use channel five? She wasn't misremembering? She scanned the security monitors for any sign of Kassie, as though she would find a new, undiscovered camera feed spying on Kassie's stateroom.

When she could no longer bear the wait, Chloe switched back to channel eight.

". . . restricted for all but we three," Nina was saying.

"Very good," responded Dion. "If you can, get a visual on Chloe Bonilla. Kassie Ng too, if you can find her."

Chloe did not know what Nina had just said, besides the

fact that Dion had found the news very good. She felt again the nightmarish rush of adrenaline, that transcendent, animal clarity that breaks in upon pursued prey. She darted one more glance at the security camera lens in the office, mummified in duct tape.

"No camera feeds from some areas," Nina began, her voice tentative and thoughtful. "No visual on—stand by—" and in the same moment that Nina announced Kassie's appearance to Dion and Vitaly, she showed up on Chloe's monitor, running along the corridor from her stateroom door toward the hotel admin office. She didn't have her suit on.

Chloe gave three short, piercing blasts on the station alarm claxon.

Chloe had a talent for moving beyond regret more easily than most human beings. Yet even she felt buffeted by regret that Kassie had ever stepped out of the hotel admin office. If the Reckoners were smart, they had surely revoked her key fob access by now, as well as Kassie's; she knew, too, that the hotel administration office computer could be overridden by the bridge in an emergency. There was only one place on the rim that controlled the emergency claxons—they knew now where she was. No matter.

"Kassie's running now," Nina announced over the communicators. "She's carrying something under her arm. Looks like a pressure suit."

"Any weapons that you can see?" Dion responded.

"Negative on weapons."

It was impossible for Chloe to know where Kassie was running—every location on the rim faced that eternally visible ring of the corridor. She ran the way she had come, as though she was returning to the hotel admin office by the same long route, in a way that would pass the library and avoid the Fortuna Ballroom. Chloe wondered if Kassie was panicking and had forgotten to hide. Anyway, what good would hiding do her now that she had been spotted?

Chloe watched Kassie try her key fob on the door of the solarium. She seemed to accept her revoked access—or was Chloe merely imagining Kassie's equanimity? Had she expected Kassie to react with a petulant foot stomp or with anime-eyed, tearful mugging for the security camera? How she might have chronicled such a setback in one of her Instagram videos was totally unlike the intense, chill hurry with which she swiped the fob, swiped again, looked up the corridor in both directions, scanned the options available to her. She regarded the open entryway to the fitness center on one side of the hall, spun around, assessed the three private locker room doors across from it, and dashed through the middle door.

"She's gone into the middle changing room," Nina announced with the tone of a woman playing three-card monte at Fisherman's Wharf.

"Do you have a visual on the hotel admin office?" Dion asked.

"Negative—that feed is dark, chief."

"Roger that, bridge," Dion replied. "Cut computer access to hotel admin."

Chloe watched as the windows of the security monitor, the key-access program, and all the utilities folded up. They left behind the blank blue wallpaper of the OrbitalVentures IT system. The color reminded Chloe of the blue screen of death that afflicted old Windows machines when they crashed. Of course they knew where she was, whether they could see her on the security cameras or not. She and Kassie might have been wise to have simply locked themselves in one of the changing rooms from the beginning. They might have stayed hidden a while longer that way, maybe until rescue.

In the silence of the hotel admin office, Chloe could hear once again the faint tapping, like the distant, plaintive knocking of a slow-moving woodpecker, that she had heard in the corridor before. If it was the clacking of a malfunctioning fan, it might knock until the end of the world before anyone got to it. *She* wouldn't be the one repairing it, whether she lived or died, whether *Imperium* one day became a storied old hotel for dowagers, like some kind of orbital Grand Plaza, or turned into the most expensive piece of space junk in the history of the world.

"Keep an eye on the hotel admin hatches," Dion ordered. "And keep us apprised of Kassie's movements."

"Roger that."

Minutes passed in silence. At first, Chloe felt relieved to hear nothing, no coordination between Nina and Vitaly and Dion like some sinister three-body problem. The silence began to trouble her soon enough, though. The last attack had come in silence. Perhaps Vitaly and Dion had begun using a different channel.

She clicked through the other channels, heard nothing. She sat on the floor by the bulkhead and pressed her ear against the hatch to the corridor. Besides the far-off clacking, sometimes louder, sometimes so soft that it barely grazed her hearing, there was no other sound in the corridor.

She wondered what the hell they were doing in the rest of the station. If they had resolved to ignore her, or if they had in secret planned another fake-out by which they would blow the hatches of the hotel admin office and take her out, she would be hearing the same silence right now.

In that moment she heard, when she pressed her ear against the hatch, footsteps out in the corridor, the clicking of a knee or ankle as somebody walked. Was it one person or more than one? Were they stopping at her door or passing by?

Chloe wished, incongruously, that she could use the blank computer on the desk to call Hellmund again, to see his face for one more minute. She wouldn't be calling anyone on that computer, though. She might as well be trying to call her dead father.

Chloe wrestled for a few minutes with the desire to remain behind reinforced hatches while the Reckoners did whatever they had come to *Imperium* to do. Would she be safer here? What story would she tell herself in a year, in thirty years, if Kassie was recaptured? If they punished her? If they flushed her out one of the airlocks?

At the same time, what could she do to help Kassie? Would Chloe give up one defensible position to join Kassie in a less defensible one? Chloe thought about Hellmund's advice, how little his words seemed to fit the circumstances of her existence. Like so many communications with Earth over her months on *Imperium*, Hellmund's words had been just more opinions from ground-control folks about a situation they didn't seem to understand.

Chloe found herself contemplating the same old bargain: all life required the balancing of relative risks. The fitness center was across the hall from the locker rooms: if she and Kassie could take up positions behind the weight stacks and keep the wall-to-wall picture windows looking out on space behind them, the Reckoners wouldn't fire into the gym, toward all that glass. They wouldn't get much of a ransom from anybody if they caused a decompression event on the rim. Maybe Chloe and Kassie could hole up there for a few hours. Chloe wasn't sure she'd be any less safe than she was now. Kassie would almost certainly be safer.

Once Chloe decided, she saw no point in delay. She dropped Angel's old key fob on the bar of the reception desk. Why carry something that wouldn't open any doors anymore but would advertise her location to anyone on the bridge?

"She's running," Nina shouted into channel eight as Chloe burst out of the hatch into the main corridor, running full bore for the locker rooms. She could not attend to Dion's answer, however: she looked to her right as she sprinted, training her pistol on the doorway to the library. In the fragment of a glimpse that she had, she could not tell whether anyone was there. She kept running.

She benefited from the rise of the ring corridor before and behind her. She guessed as she ran that a pursuer would have to be following within fifty meters on this hamster wheel to have a shot at her from an upright position; for anyone farther away, whether before or behind her, the sloping curve of the ceiling concealed her.

Nina called out her progress: "She's passed gamma spoke, heading toward beta."

"Roger that," Dion responded. "Vitaly, heads up."

Chloe spared a single glance behind her as she ran. The corridor was empty, shining in baleful blue light. As she passed the cafeteria, her footfalls squelched through the soaked, charred carpet of the grease fire she had set hours before. In that moment, she had a strange sense that she was traveling along the curve of a terrible karmic wheel, forced into an eternal circular path like an ironic punishment the ancient Greeks might fabulate for the afterlife of an evil king.

She was approaching the changing rooms. She would bang on the door and call out to Kassie; if she came out quickly, perhaps they could make it across the corridor into the fitness center without being fired on. Chloe passed gamma spoke, her stride bounding in the .85 g as though she were a college athlete on the runway for the long jump.

But Chloe knew something was up as soon as the locker room entrances came into view. The door of the middle locker

room stood open, its sliding panel deformed into a gentle si-
nusoidal curl. As Chloe slowed down to consider what she had
not expected, Vitaly stepped out of the locker room into the
corridor.

In the moment Chloe took aim, she saw that he had Kassie
Ng headlocked in his burly arm. Chloe hesitated a half second,
watched Vitaly begin to raise the pistol in his other hand.

Chloe turned to drop back. As she turned, she caught a
glimpse of Kassie twisting herself in Vitaly's clumsy headlock.
Chloe scrambled back the way she had come, watched as a gash
in the carpet appeared a couple of feet in front of her, and then
another, as Vitaly fired on her. She took off running, expecting
at any moment the shot that would take her down from behind,
as she cast her mind about like a trapped rat for where she might,
without a key, hide in a dark, defensible space.

"She's turned back toward beta, chief," Nina said over the
communicators.

She heard another shot two seconds later. Yet she felt herself sprinting unimpeded, unshot, toward the pillar of the beta
spoke elevator.

Dion's low voice came over channel eight. "Vitaly, hold your
position. I'm heading her off."

Chloe did not wonder in that moment who was watching the hostages if Dion was running toward her. She thought
of nothing: didn't wonder why Vitaly's last shot had not hit
her, didn't regret having left the hotel administration office.
One door, the only door nearby that she knew she could open,
was within her reach: the door to the beta spoke elevator. She
punched the button to call the elevator car.

"She's going into the beta spoke elevator," Nina called out.

"Kassie Ng is down," Vitaly reported in a voice curiously
smoothed of emotional contours.

"Come again, Vitaly?" Chloe could hear Dion's heavy breathing over the communicators as he ran toward her.

Chloe tried to force what Vitaly had said from her mind, even as he repeated himself. She had a few seconds—maybe five, maybe twenty—before Dion would come upon her here. The touch screen above the elevator call button warned her about the lack of atmosphere on the hub. Her finger jabbed through the message-acknowledgment screen. The doors opened for her.

As she boarded and the doors slid closed behind her, Chloe pulled the rip cord at her waist that began the emergency pressurization of her suit.

"She's boarded the beta spoke elevator," Nina announced.

Her suit stiffened, filled with a personal atmosphere. She heard Dion over channel eight. For a man who had just been running, who had just learned that one of his underlings had shot one of the hostages, his voice seemed a placid skin, a skiff of ice over a lake filled with many-toothed fish in the bottom mud: "Vitaly, I need you here. Nina, secure the bridge. Take up a position in the elevator landing for beta spoke on the Axle. Neutralize Chloe."

CHAPTER
TEN

FIVE MINUTES EARLIER

Vitaly was ready to go home. He had liked the idea of space once, sure. When he was a kid, maybe. This mission had cured him of that feeling, though.

Samir and Nicholas had moved the money fast. From what Vitaly could tell, the couple's asset manager had set everything up before their second call. Samir put up their collateral, and they secured the loan. The collateral properties were all in places Vitaly had never been and wasn't able to visualize. He wasn't even sure where some of the places were.

If the rest of the hostages could get their ransoms so quickly, the team would be done, Vitaly and Nina could go home, and the first phase of the revolution would be underway.

Now he had brought Samir and Nicholas back to the For-tuna Ballroom. Dion motioned Vitaly over, pulled the pry bar from that tedious duffel, and dropped the tool into Vitaly's hand.

"Head over to the middle dressing room and bring back Kassie," Dion said. "Keep your eyes open for Chloe."

Dion hadn't needed to say that last part. Over the last twelve hours, Chloe had transformed in Vitaly's imagination from a factor almost beneath his notice, to a serious inconvenience, to the bitch who had almost killed Nina.

He moved up the corridor. The only thing he would miss about space was how effortlessly he could run in the .85 g; he jogged along the track of the big hamster wheel, feeling quick as a much smaller man, the way Messi used to dash up the right touchline on a counterattack for FC Barcelona.

He checked each way up the corridor when he arrived at the dressing rooms, holstered his weapon, rammed the pry bar into the seam between door panel and doorjamb. He wrenched at the door panel. The latch sheared off with a metallic whine. He pulled his gun out again, using the crook of the pry bar to peel open the panel, which slid halfway on its track before it jammed.

Vitaly ducked and stepped sideways into the opening. Kassie sat wide-eyed on the bench at the back of the dressing room, her knees drawn up to her chin. Vitaly made a wry smile at her; he shook his head like she was a kid out after curfew that he had caught.

That was when Vitaly heard Nina call over channel eight: "She's running." Once again, Chloe had made something simple a lot more complicated for Vitaly. He stood over Kassie, considering his options now that that woman was loose again.

Vitaly had once imagined, when he imagined anything, that once the revolution began he would be fighting official thugs. Police, security guards, eventually even regular troops—people in uniforms that the propertarians had hired or fooled into serving them. Vitaly didn't like having to fight a regular crew member wearing the same jumpsuit he wore, someone without a badge or any reason to help out a billionaire. Still, he knew enough not to underestimate her now, and if she wanted to stand in the way of the revolution, what business was that of his?

Nina's voice came over the radio again: "She's passed gamma spoke, heading toward beta."

"Roger that," Dion responded. "Vitaly, heads up."

Vitaly gave the question no more thought. He slipped the crook of the pry bar into his belt, reached out, pulled Kassie to her feet with his free hand. He appreciated that she moved quickly, without crying or whimpering.

Vitaly drew the tiny woman into a headlock. "Don't do anything stupid, and I won't hurt you."

She was so small that he could feel her feet flailing, lifting off the floor while he returned with her to the ruined door. His first impression was that she was lighter and easier to maneuver than that damn duffel had been.

He ducked out into the hall, careful not to crush Kassie Ng in the crook of his arm, when he saw Chloe up the corridor from him, braking with a stutter of her feet as he appeared. Chloe looked them over with a distant, clinical eye as she raised her pistol, then seemed to decide all at once to juke and scramble back the way she had come.

Vitaly raised his pistol, took aim. He could feel Kassie Ng writhing in the crook of his other arm, lively as a fish. She kicked at the side of his knee ineffectually; still, she was troubling his concentration. He overshot Chloe, missed her by a meter or more.

Vitaly had never wanted children. But Kassie wriggling in his headlock felt like what he imagined it would be like to deal with an unruly son or daughter. A son of his would be Kassie's size by the time he was eight years old. He aimed again, felt the jabbing of her heel against the outside of his thigh, felt a strange building sharpness at the base of his biceps.

Just as he was squeezing off his second shot, he could tell that Kassie was biting his arm. Even through the thickness of his pressure suit, she had latched on, clamped herself to his arm with a force that impressed and infuriated him. The second shot went wide.

His first impulse was to bear down on the headlock, to break the teeth out of her mouth with the force of his arm, perhaps snap her neck. But the pain in his arm was intensifying, and she dropped out of his headlock as soon as he tried to adjust her position.

An old rage flooded through Vitaly's limbs then. Chloe still ran from him; Kassie scrambled across the floor in the opposite direction down the corridor. But Vitaly's mind had contracted to an ancient, limbic fury. The nest of words constructed around him from birth, from before birth, around his whole life, fell away, insubstantial: a Babel of gossip, advertising, gauzy pop lyrics; maxims of the Bible-sotted parents who seemed from the beginning not to know what to make of him; teachers' subtle remonstrances that he knew inarticulately to be a kind of ridicule; thousands of night hours in a kind of autodidactic creation of himself at the computer, reading and disputing with the finest minds he was capable of understanding and many he couldn't, people the world couldn't be bothered to publish or even to recognize; slogans about pain on the posters in dojos and on the T-shirts of other meatheads in weight rooms; the chorus of all the human beings he had met, who, save one, had never bothered trying to understand him—none of this slow formation and deformation of Vitaly's soul had any word to say now. All the necessary words and silences had come and gone long ago.

Vitaly turned and raised the pistol without reflection just as Kassie Ng was rising from a crouch into a full-bore run. A quick, thoughtless shot crumpled her as he turned to train his weapon once more on Chloe.

He heard Dion's voice over the communicator. The words,

almost nonsense to him, nonetheless called him out of his storm of adrenaline and back into a human world of language and plans. "Vitaly, hold your position. I'm heading her off."

In that moment, Chloe passed far enough up the wheel of the corridor that she slipped from his sight. Dion's order snapped taut like a cord between Vitaly and the rest of humanity. Vitaly could consider at last what he had just done; the act settled upon him like a bitter gray haze. He turned to regard his handiwork, looked down at Kassie as the blood began to soak the white of her jumpsuit. Her breath was panicked; she still writhed.

It had not been a very good shot, Vitaly remarked to himself. An impulse rose in him, which he neither understood nor knew the origin of, to shoot her again, and again, to put as many bullets in her as necessary to make her stop writhing like a stricken snake.

Nina said something over the communicator as he pointed the gun. Had she been speaking to him? Nina's voice, whatever it had said, seemed to call him to account, to lay bare his mistake.

"Kassie Ng is down," he said into the communicator.

"Come again, Vitaly?" It was Dion asking now.

"I said Kassie Ng is down. She tried to escape, and I shot her." He raised the pistol once more, took aim.

In that moment, he heard Nina again. He could hear a hint of panic in her voice. Perhaps another would not have recognized it, but the sound anguished him. "She's boarded the beta spoke elevator."

"Vitaly, I need you here," Dion ordered.

Vitaly listened to the tone of Dion's voice as he continued giving orders to Nina. It was this quiet, cool timbre, more than anything that Dion had actually ordered, that persuaded Vitaly to raise his weapon, to turn, to run up the corridor toward the beta spoke elevator.

CHAPTER ELEVEN

The faint popping of gunshots sounded from up the corridor somewhere. As he listened, Sir Alexander Dunne surveyed his domain. The parts he could see of his domain, anyway: at the moment, what he could see were the bare walls of one of *Imperium*'s many conference rooms. The Fortuna Ballroom, at least, had $300,000 worth of graceful, curvilinear design touches; the Fortuna Ballroom also had views of Earth every couple of minutes. Now, though, Dion had hustled them up the corridor at gunpoint, lugging that corpse-size duffel; he had locked them all in a far drearier chamber, one with a solid sliding hatch that locked, a room so windowless and spartan that Sir Alexander was sure the hotel staff had never intended that the guests would spend any time there. What kind of space hotel needed four conference rooms? No, one day this blank box of a space would have been the spot for an arcade, a whiskey lounge, a film studio, a bondage club—for something, that is, that OrbitalVentures had been hoping to put in once the hotel started making money. Sir Alexander consoled himself that at least there were chairs in this room.

Sir Alexander had been in worse scrapes than this. Not as a

hostage—he had never had that particular honor before, true. But financially, he had once found himself staring back at this much financial ruin and worse, back in his wild days. To be sure, a hostage taking in the first twenty-four hours of operation of the world's first orbital hotel would, he surmised, exert some downward pressure on the stock price of the hotel's parent company. But how much downward pressure? Would the price bounce around for a few months before the company righted itself? Or was the stock a meteor that he was riding down to a deafening impact with Earth?

OrbitalVentures could right itself, he thought. If he could get them back to leasing the station to the university labs, or if they could secure some incubation money for zero-g manufacturers, the hotel could wait until it was ready. *Imperium* hadn't been close to ready as a hotel. If it had been ready, there wouldn't have been an overloaded electrical circuit during the group space walk; if it had been ready, he wouldn't be sitting around a conference table right now with a crowd of other hostages in party dresses and pajamas, listening to gunfire out in the hallway.

Like a man who can't stop picking at a scab, Sir Alexander cataloged how he would have OrbitalVentures handle things differently when they tried the hotel again. The orbital market was not the Wild West, not some race between tribes of Viking raiders. What had it benefited the company to open *Imperium* before Hesperus or Axiom or Orion Span could get to market? He wanted no more *move fast and break things* cheerleading at OrbitalVentures; he would allow no more corner cutting. For a start, he wanted much more robust background checks— seriously, what did it say about the company that both the commanding officer and security chief of *Imperium*, as well as both of the medical staffers, turned out to be hijackers and thieves?

Something within him—doggedness, his biographer might call it, or perhaps delusion—would not allow Sir Alexander to imagine any other outcome than the reopening of the hotel. It was that doggedness or delusion that had kept him afloat through his bankruptcy the last time, during the dot-com bubble. He was much older now, of course, less inclined to work into the small hours, more thoughtful, he hoped, about taking risks on the fly. But what he might have lost in speed he had gained in wisdom: he was a wily old fox now, one who had learned the scent of every trap he had encountered.

He had to admit that he was caught in a new sort of trap. But he would learn the scent of this one, too. He would not be caught again this way.

He had counted only three shots in the corridor, then silence. Three shots, compared to the dozens that had been fired during the hull breach two hours ago, constituted an improvement in his opinion. He felt a peculiar distance from himself, from the plain conference room around him, as though he were observing his ordeal happening to another person. He had been weighing out a number of likely outcomes for this person he observed, this aging libertine in a vomitous wizard's robe. In one outcome, the man would sit tight, trust to the word of Dion and his henchmen, lackeys—whoever they were. Pirates, maybe. Dion and his pirates would squeeze the shitcoin out of them all, then fly off in the Starliner. All Sir Alexander would need to do was await rescue.

But Sir Alexander didn't, in fact, trust Dion. Gunfire is not a sound that one associates with a well-run hostage taking. Who were they shooting now? He expected that at any moment Dion or Vitaly would burst in, covered in blood perhaps, to tell them once again that everything was running smoothly.

Sir Alexander was disinclined to wait around for another

flaccid reassurance like that. But what were the alternatives available to him? Could he shinny out of some as-yet-undiscovered crawl space in this room the way Kassie had slipped out of the ballroom? That, too, struck him as a foolish course of action: he wondered what the chances were that one of those three gunshots he had just heard had killed Kassie. He felt a pang of grief for the imagined death of this beautiful girl that he had only known a few weeks but who, in another world, might one day have been charmed into seeing something in him. Dion seemed unlikely to kill one of the billionaires if what he really wanted was ransom, but Kassie's portion of the ransom was so paltry as to be inconsequential. Killing her might even motivate some of the wealthier hostages: if Dion walked in here and threw Kassie's corpse on the table, Li would unload his stock for crypto in a hurry.

In this new room, Sir Alexander had taken a seat in the far corner, set away from most of the others. Across from him, staring at the table in front of her like an unpopular girl in the lunchroom, sat Viv Volterra. Sir Alexander looked at her with new eyes, as though she were some kind of flower that had been planted in his garden for twenty years that he had noticed for the first time just now because it happened to be in bloom when he passed by (this, too, had happened to him, as he often went many months without setting foot in his garden). She was no beauty of Kassie Ng's caliber. However, the same could be said of most human beings on the planet. And now that he was regarding Viv in the absence of the dearly imagined recent gunshot victim, Sir Alexander remarked to himself that Ms. Volterra had a kind of poise that could, on many occasions, substitute admirably for beauty.

At that moment, as though she were aware of Sir Alexander's musings, Viv raised her eyes to meet his. She arched her brow as though she were issuing a challenge, or perhaps posing a question. One corner of her pert, lopsided mouth lifted in the hint of a smile.

"Are you ready to pay?" Sir Alexander asked her.

"I doubt that Dion Stubblefield is all that concerned about my contribution," she said in her quiet, mordant contralto. "But yes, I was ready hours ago." She swept a stray strand of hair behind her ear. "And you? Are you ready?"

"I suppose I am, if there's nothing else for it." This was, he supposed, essentially true. However, it was only on answering the question posed so directly that Sir Alexander realized that he was still on the hunt for an alternative, for some opportunity worth snatching.

"Part of me . . ." he continued, "part of me feels like just making a run for the Starliner."

Viv's mouth curled into a wry but unmistakable smile now. "You're going to escape through a decompressed part of the station in your wizard robe?"

"If the chance came, I might take it. Every room has an emergency pressure suit."

He couldn't tell whether she was humoring him or pitying him. She might even have been a little charmed. "What was your personal best for getting into the emergency suits back in training?" she asked.

"One minute, forty-one seconds."

"That's a very long time to be allowed out without a chaperone."

He shrugged. "Our chaperones have been gone for at least a couple of minutes now."

She glanced around the room with a wide-eyed theatricality, like Clara Bow playing a dominatrix. "You're ready to get into the pressure suit, then?"

Sir Alexander noticed for the first time that this conference room did not have the heretofore-ubiquitous closet containing the emergency pressure suit. No fire extinguisher, either. He was right, then: no one had expected this room to be used for some imagined orbital conference. Why, then, were there chairs and a conference table? And why were there no chairs in the ballroom? Had Dion kept them there just to make them sit on the floor?

"Would you come with me if we got the chance?" he asked.

He found the smile she gave him both inscrutable and intoxicating. He saw at once how easily she could have hoodwinked her investors for so long. "You'd have to find a suit for me as well," she said. "And I'm not a fan of the emergency suits—they make me look like the Michelin Man."

The bulk of the suits did present a nontrivial problem for his escape fantasy. Not the look of them, of course—Sir Alexander Dunne had never spent a minute worrying about what he looked like—but the suits' clumsiness, like those novelty sumo-wrestler outfits that people wear at American funfairs, made them extremely difficult to maneuver in. He would present a fat target to anyone within a hundred meters. It occurred to him that he still had no idea how many pirates there were. Dion, Vitaly, Nina, likely at least one other, maybe a whole phalanx of them that he didn't know about. How many would get a shot at him bouncing along in the plump beach ball of an emergency suit?

"So let's say we find a way to get into our fitted suits. Come with me then?"

"This really *is* an elaborate fantasy," she shot back. "I don't remember reading that you've ever flown a Starliner."

"It's true—I haven't. But flying a Starliner is not so different from flying the *Morgenstern*," he offered.

"I suppose I'll have to take your word for it as a pilot. The two seem quite different to me."

She was, in fact, correct. The Starliner was as different from the space plane he had once flown on as it was from a weather balloon. And anyway, to be scrupulously accurate, Sir Alexander had never actually flown the *Morgenstern*. Contrary to all the press releases from Hesperus Aerospace, Sir Alexander had been copilot in name only. His great accomplishment in the *Morgenstern*'s first publicized orbital flight was that he had survived it. That, and more human beings had watched him puke than anyone else in history. "You'll really just have to trust a pilot with these things, you know."

Li scowled from across the table. "A lot of us trusted you, Sir Alexander."

"That's not fair," Tirzah Fowler broke in. "Sir Alexander wasn't even associated with OrbitalVentures when you signed up for this trip."

"Will all of you, please, just shut up?" Nicholas said with what seemed an infinite weariness. "If you haven't paid your ransom, please just shut up and pay it when they come back."

This did in fact shut everybody up. Viv concluded her conversation with Sir Alexander with an eye roll worthy of a saucy teenager. He winked back as though something momentous had been agreed to between them.

Sir Alexander also found himself feeling an unanticipated access of tenderness for Tirzah Fowler, talking back to one of the guests on his behalf. He supposed that she was technically standing up for her boss—or at least for the majority shareholder in her company—which could of course have complicated her motives. But her defense had been an unsought kindness.

The door slid open at that moment. All the dolorous company of conference room C looked up to see Dion come in. "I will not accept another delay," he announced, his voice both quiet and bristling with a frightening subterranean energy. It seemed to Sir Alexander that something had happened to the man, or to his plans, in those minutes out in the corridor. He stood arms akimbo as the door slid shut behind him; the strange apparatus that he had used to cause Roger Van Cleave such agony was in his hand; the great duffel was apparently elsewhere. And with no further preface, he pointed the slender object at Li and pressed the switch.

"Mr. Li, you will come with me, and you will hurry," he said with a livid tension in his voice as Li writhed in his seat like a netted eel. Whatever currency the strange device minted, Dion paid it out for three seconds, four seconds, more, until Li fell to the floor with the yelp of an injured dog. Only then did Dion lower the odd wand and draw his pistol. The others at the table had the good sense not even to gasp.

From his fetal position on the floor, Li kept his eyes averted, though he raised his hands in supplication, as though his instincts had informed him that Dion had a pistol aimed at his head. "Get up," Dion said with a malignant calm.

As Li scrambled to his feet, Dion took in the rest of the hostages at the table. "I will brook no more stalling," he said. "Our time is short, and I will shoot any of you that tries to escape. Is that clear?"

Sir Alexander nodded vigorously before he realized that Dion's question had been rhetorical. He had shepherded Li out of the room and locked the door behind them.

Left to themselves once more, the hostages stared at one another in a silence that they all seemed frightened to break. In the stillness, Sir Alexander could hear the tiny, ghostly tapping that propagated through the walls of the station from somewhere nearby. The sound reminded him of the knocking of distant plumbing, the background noise of an old down-at-heel hotel rather than whatever OrbitalVentures was pretending at with *Imperium*. The rhythm would persist for thirty seconds, a minute, enough to set his nerves on edge. Then the sound would stop for a few seconds, a minute.

Perhaps half an hour passed. In that long silence, Sir Alexander returned to contemplating his alternatives. His share of the ransom was the next largest after Li, since practically all of Viv Volterra's ransom had been financed by the Van Cleaves; Sir Alexander expected, then, that if these brigands kept to their pattern, they would lead him away next. He wondered whether he had cut a favorable bargain with Roger Van Cleave, agreeing to borrow so much of his share of the ransom to be repaid at twenty-five percent interest. The wisdom or folly of what Sir Alexander had bargained depended more than anything on what was going to happen to the stock prices of OrbitalVentures and Hesperus. And he could no more predict the future value of his companies than he could predict the weather a year hence.

Whether the bargain had been shrewd or not, Sir Alexander found himself accepting the reality of payment, both what he would pay to Dion and company and what he would owe Roger Van Cleave later, without a moment's grief. The money was just so much paper—less than paper, nothing more than a promise of future value that he was pissing away to others in exchange for his life. He regarded his own ability to make money, even in the autumn of his life, as an essentially limitless resource. He was troubled more, or far more immediately, by the thought of physical torment coming out of the tip of whatever disruptor Dion was carrying.

And yet, and yet. Was his fear of Dion and his weapons and his henchmen based on anything more real than the money he had promised away? Dion had killed people, true. But had he killed any of the people who had a ransom to pay? Perhaps Kassie Ng. But Sir Alexander had no evidence that she was dead, and even if Dion *had* killed her, Kassie had committed only a million dollars. Would Dion actually kill him when he was committed to pay almost 250 times as much?

He could see plainly enough that Dion's enterprise was not going to plan: during the first hours of the ordeal, the hostages had huddled on the floor under the gaze of three captors; now Dion locked them in a windowless room without supervision for an hour at a time. And something had obviously upset Dion's applecart—he was a man in a hurry, prone to making mistakes, maybe. During one of their unsupervised lock-ins, Samir and Nicholas had whispered of the conversations they had had with their financial advisers: OrbitalVentures had known of the hostage taking for hours now. Surely some kind of rescue would come as soon as a launch window opened. If the weather cooperated on Earth, the launch window could open anytime.

Though he had been cooped up under guard, locked in one room or another, for hours now, Sir Alexander felt a teasing, aching awareness of possibility, of opportunity, rising up from the pit of his stomach. He had felt much the same ripple within himself when it had first occurred to him to make a tender offer for OrbitalVentures.

He asked himself, silently, the question that had been sneaking around behind the arras in his mind: *Will I try to escape?* But before he could answer himself, or resolve any of the other mysteries about where he might hide and whether Kassie had been killed, the door opened once again. Li stumbled in with his head down and dropped into a chair with a tired and graceless thump. The evidence of his ordeal with Dion's device appeared in garish strokes across his face like invisible ink that had revealed itself. Dion himself stood in the doorway. "Alexander Dunne," he said with that familiar cool tranquility. Yet given the device in Dion's hand, his voice frightened Sir Alexander more than if his captor had been screaming at him. Sir Alexander sprang to his feet and scampered toward the door with his hands raised before his face. He winced to imagine what was to come at any moment from this man who seemed to have been made capricious by whatever had transpired over the last few hours.

But for now Dion did not point the peculiar miniature coffin at him. "To the library," was all Dion said.

Sir Alexander walked before him at a brisk clip, as though he were a child trying to walk ahead of a parent. The fear of the man with the gun, which he had regarded with a kind of academic distance when he was locked in the conference room, now threatened to give him a panic attack: he wondered whether there was enough oxygen left in this section of the station as he gulped at the air. He imagined Dion's pistol trained on him as they walked.

They entered the library. Dion shut the hatch behind them and directed him to a chair in front of one of the open laptops on the grand study table. "We'll try this the easy way," Dion said. "You will begin contacting your primary financial adviser; she should be expecting your call. You will begin liquidating assets as quickly as you can. Don't worry about the price you are getting when you sell; sell at whatever price will help you survive. If your advisers are wise, they've already begun making inquiries about buyers for real estate you own. You should be able to move things along quickly."

Dion walked around the table so that he faced Sir Alexander, looming over him from behind the laptop. "If I begin to suspect that you are slowing down the process," he said, "we'll proceed the hard way." If Dion pulled out one of his weapons for theatrical effect or made some threatening grimace, Sir Alexander saw nothing but the walnut of the tabletop where he fixed his gaze.

But Sir Alexander did manage to exert enough self-control

to nod. He stared at the blank screen of the laptop in horror. Was he supposed to Skype Ursula, his principal asset manager? FaceTime with her? Set up a Zoom meeting? WhatsApp? Google Messages? Was he supposed to Google Ursula's name and find her phone number, which, like every other phone number he'd called in the last thirty years, he had not memorized? He was afraid to look up at Dion, who was beginning to move around to stand behind him. Sir Alexander opened his mouth to ask what he was to do, but only a squeak like a rusty hinge emerged from his constricted throat.

"Whoops," Dion said affably. "I've left you in the dark." He stood beside Sir Alexander and motioned with his disruptor at the bottom of the screen: "Move the mouse down there, and your menu should come up." Closer up, the device seemed less to Sir Alexander like a little coffin and more like a brushed-steel ray gun in an art deco, Flash Gordon aesthetic, with a narrow, fluted trumpet bell of a muzzle, like a penstemon blossom made of gunmetal.

Sir Alexander looked over the task bar that appeared. Among the icons was a folder with his name on it. He opened the folder; within was only a single document titled *Contacts* and a Skype shortcut. The document listed the Skype username, phone number, and email of Ursula Butler, as well as usernames and numbers for three of Ursula Butler's assistants and several names he did not immediately recognize but that he realized a minute later must belong to some of his property managers.

How the Reckoners had come by all this information was a mystery to him. Sir Alexander felt the return of a dread that had plagued him all day, dread that people who wished him harm had been studying him for some time, perhaps for weeks, perhaps from the moment he'd applied to become one of the first guests of *Imperium*.

He clicked the Skype shortcut. The somewhat frazzled-looking, matronly visage of his financial adviser came up almost immediately on the screen. "Hello, Sir Alexander," she said in a tone that struck him as both sympathetic to his plight and incongruously casual. "I was told that you'd be calling."

"I need to come up with two hundred and forty-nine million dollars as quickly as possible," he blurted.

If Ursula was taken aback, she didn't let on. "As you know, that's a difficult figure to move quickly. It will involve discounting a significant fraction of your assets. However, I have secured preliminary approval of a loan from Barclays; I will inform them of the amount you will be borrowing, to be paid, pending your authorization, by a transfer of stock in the following index funds . . ."

As Ursula Butler recited the names of his money market accounts that would be sucked dry to pay the loan of his ransom money, Sir Alexander considered how the great wheels of the transaction, like massive interlocking gears, seemed to have been in motion a long time without his approval or even knowledge. It was a feeling he had encountered before in reverse, the sense of his net worth multiplying well beyond the inputs of time and energy he had devoted to growing his fortune. In a sense, he had become a kind of approval machine whose only function in the ecosystem of his empire was to authorize or decline to authorize activities that various underlings brought to him.

"You have my authorization," he found himself croaking.

"Very well, sir," Ursula replied. "You may tell your captors that within the next hour they will see two hundred and forty-nine million dollars' worth of Algolcoin in the wallet I was provided."

Sir Alexander wondered what had taken Roger Van Cleave and the Winters-Qureshis and Li so long when they had been brought into the library. Of course, they had a great deal more money to move. Sir Alexander thanked his asset manager and managed to work up a wan approximation of a smile. He stared awkwardly at the woman on the screen: In the fifteen years they had worked together, since she had taken over his accounts after the retirement of his last asset manager, he had never invited Ursula Butler to dinner. In fact, he had never bought her so much as a coffee that he could remember. He had, of course, paid her very well for her services—better, he was sure, than the salaries of ninety-nine percent of the asset managers in the world—but after fifteen years she meant no more to him than a familiar postal clerk or a regular waiter at a favorite restaurant might. Yet he looked at her now, thousands of miles away, with all the tenderness he might have felt for a spouse or sister or daughter, if he had ever had such a person in his life. Ursula Butler seemed to him a solitary connection to the world of gravity and open air, of skies full of rain, of an old assumption that he would not be shot at when he stepped out of his door. He wished for the call never to end; he wished to weep and blubber to Ursula Butler about how much he had always loved her and had only now realized it.

But Dion was standing again before him at the other side of the table, lifting up his Buck Rogers ray gun as though he were pausing in the moment before pointing it at Sir Alexander. Dion drew a finger across his throat in silence.

Sir Alexander ended the call without a profession of love. Though Dion had not pointed the device at him, Sir Alexander brought his hands once more in front of his face, grimacing already against whatever agony was coming for him. It was in that moment that an insight rose up out of his predicament, a sudden knowledge of his own bravery and cowardice. He had been able to descend to the abyssal zone of the Pacific in his own research submarine; he had circumnavigated Great Britain alone in a sea kayak; he had flown into orbit in an experimental space plane. In all those moments of heroism or folly, he had forged ahead without a doubt because it had never occurred to him viscerally that he would be hurt. Far from being enemies, the oceans and atmospheres he had traversed were, to him, no more than neutral media that held his charmed life as a bird's nest shelters an egg. Now, though, facing the armed man before him, he could barely maintain the presence of mind to keep from cowering under the table. Dion was a creature with the grace and threat of God's avenging angel; Sir Alexander quailed in his presence.

But when Sir Alexander stole a glance through the unruly mess of his hair, he saw that Dion had turned away from him. Sir Alexander looked up then to see Vitaly in the doorway: the big man had the look of an ancient butcher or field surgeon, his pressure suit smeared and spattered with blood, his gloves soaked dark.

"She's gone," Vitaly said.

Sir Alexander couldn't see Dion's face, or indeed anything about his reaction; he heard nothing except for a frightening silence that had settled about the man. At length Sir Alexander heard a slow, deep exhalation, like the breathing of a whale.

Vitaly stood at attention with the massive duffel bag in one hand and his pistol in the other. A pry bar was stashed in his belt, by his holster.

"I'm calling an end to the operation," Dion said at last. Sir Alexander heard in his voice the same placid veneer, the same undercurrent of deep malice, speaking to Vitaly as Dion used with the hostages. "I'm going to prepare the Starliner for launch. You lock the hostages in, retrieve the body, and rendezvous at lab module two at fourteen twenty hours. Do you think you can do that without shooting anybody else?"

"Yes, sir."

Dion turned to look down at Sir Alexander. "I think we're done here, comrade." He offered an incongruous little nod, as though in approval of Sir Alexander's behavior, or by way of goodbye. He strode past Vitaly without a word; Vitaly stepped aside for him to pass.

Vitaly motioned for Sir Alexander to rise; he passed through the entryway into the main corridor and walked a few steps ahead of the bloodstained gunman toward their holding pen in the conference room.

Vitaly unlocked the door for him. Sir Alexander noticed as he passed through into the room a stale funk of body odor that he had been only dimly aware of in the hours he had sat among the hostages. Someone gasped.

Vitaly addressed them from the open door. "We thank you for your cooperation, people. A rescue mission is on its way from OrbitalVentures. The launch window should arrive within the next hour or so. It will take them a few hours to dock; that's normal. If you need to visit the restroom in the next few hours, now is the time."

To Sir Alexander's surprise, no one spoke up. Perhaps there were some who would rather pee their pants than walk alone with someone who looked as Vitaly did now. Then, just as Vitaly opened his mouth to speak, Viv Volterra spoke.

"I suppose if we're going to be waiting that long, I should go."

"I should as well," Samir said.

"Me too," said Nicholas.

Vitaly pursed his lips as though he was contemplating a trial of great unpleasantness. "All right, then," he said. "You first, Volterra." She went out before him, and a moment later the door slid closed behind them.

CHAPTER TWELVE

FORTY-EIGHT MINUTES EARLIER

The elevator car pulled Chloe along the cylinder of beta spoke as she listened to Dion's pronouncement of her death sentence over channel eight. "Neutralize Chloe," he said, deploying that odd bureaucratic euphemism for what was to be done to her, as though Chloe were some acidic solution being titrated with a buffer. The image was apt in one way, at least: Chloe's talent, more than any other, was her knack for suspending, briefly, the stories that the mind will spin, those confections of anxiety and doubt and guilt and resentment that punctuate the actions of all human beings to one degree or another and that paralyze many. She was in that moment as thoughtless as an acidic solution stirred in an Erlenmeyer flask, as automatic in her works as a hydrogen ion cleaving through its universe of water.

She assumed that Vitaly and Dion were standing in the rim corridor just outside the entrance to the elevator. They wouldn't be able to open that door, at least not without a great deal of force: *Imperium* treated each of the exterior elevator doors as airlock hatches. Above her, at the other end of the spoke, another fortified hatch separated beta spoke from the Axle. That hatch, being the destination of the elevator, could be opened.

Chloe was suspicious of that hatch at the other end, the hub end. Nina might have enough time to leave the bridge and make her way in near vacuum toward that hatch, where she could use it as a murder hole in much the same way that Chloe had killed Meredith.

Chloe assessed the second door of the elevator car, the one above her head that would dock with the hatch at the hub. In that moment, the elevator stopped. The display screen read *51% of Earth's Gravity—Prepare to Grasp a Handhold*—the car had gone only about a third of the way up the spoke. Nina was the only one in a position to have stopped the car, assuming she had not yet left the bridge. In a few moments, though, she would float off the bridge into the Axle, open the landing doors to the elevator, and begin perforating the car with gunfire like a stage magician piercing a box with a dozen swords. Alternatively, Vitaly and Dion could blast through the elevator doors below her, assuming they had something in that bag of tricks to punch through the steel of the doors, and they could do the same from below.

She didn't have time to deal with the elevator car's security camera. She hoped only that Nina had turned from the bridge and was not watching her as she moved. She hooked a foot into one of the handholds of the elevator as though she were stepping into a stirrup. Then she vaulted toward the ceiling, grasped the manual-access knob to the upper hatch. She popped the hatch open like a trapdoor.

She pulled herself out of the elevator car into the pitch black of the shaft. In the dim light that emerged from the car through the hatch opening, she took her bearings. Then she shut the hatch behind her and slid her way in darkness behind the cab, between the rails of the emergency ladder and the guide rails of the car.

She waited. In the threadbare atmosphere of the spoke, she could hear nothing. When the firing started, all Chloe felt was the rocking of the elevator car on its guide rails, the plinking of bullets almost beyond her hearing, like the dropping of far-away coins. She didn't know whether the gunfire was coming from Nina at the hub end of the shaft or Vitaly or Dion at the rim end; she didn't know whether the walls of the car presented enough of a barrier to prevent overpenetration of the bullets. She suspected that they didn't.

And yet, whoever was firing seemed to be peppering either the roof or the floor of the elevator from a perpendicular angle or nearly so, rather than firing obliquely at the walls of the shaft. Chloe realized, when she opened her eyes, that there was a dim gray oscillating glow above her as the car shook. She had a fleeting sense of waiting for a train to pass over her; the wall of the elevator car rocked in the near darkness only a few centimeters in front of her face.

How many shots had there been? A dozen? Twenty? She could not hear them. But Chloe was aware of a pause in the shuddering of the elevator car.

She took her chance. In the close space she drew her weapon, moved quickly up the three rungs of the ladder to climb past the elevator car. The landing door of the elevator was cracked open above her, flooding the end of the shaft in dim light.

She saw no one in the opening.

She noticed, too, that no light came from the perforated ceiling of the elevator car—it was too dark, in fact, to see the bullet holes themselves. Nina must have shot out the lights in the car during the barrage.

There was no chatter over channel eight. Chloe leaned against the top of the car, resting her elbows and taking aim.

There was a stillness of a few seconds, barely long enough for Chloe to wonder whether her hunch was correct.

Then a shadow appeared again in the handbreadth's opening of the hatch at the elevator landing, and Chloe knew that she had guessed correctly: Nina had been reloading. Chloe fired, and as she saw the shadow jerk in reaction, Chloe felt the fleeting satisfaction of being able to see someone who could not see her. She watched Nina's form back away from the opening.

Chloe hesitated only a moment, backed down behind the ruined elevator car like a hiding crab. She heard Nina's voice, hyperventilating, come over channel eight. "I've been hit—trying to seal off my suit."

Chloe moved quickly. She dashed up the ladder, pumping herself up each rung with her legs as she guided her ascent with her left hand. She had not climbed thirty rungs before the pull of that false gravity had diminished sufficiently for her to scramble over rungs, skipping rungs, nearly leaping upward, until with a final push of her right leg and a heave of her left arm, she was launched, rising like a shark out of the darkness.

Vitaly's voice came more frantic than Chloe had ever heard it before over the communicators: "Where in the Axle, baby?"

"I'm—*fuck*. Won't stop."

Chloe slowed herself with the rungs of the ladder just below the open landing of the elevator. She hesitated. In the aperture of the landing, Chloe could see from her angle a sparkling cloud of Nina's spent cartridges, floating like a tiny asteroid field.

She heard nothing more from Nina over the communicators. "Sit tight," Dion said. "Vitaly is on his way."

Chloe ran through her options. She could try to descend the shaft again, climb past the elevator car to the rim end, hide out there. Or she could attempt to secure the Axle, maybe catch Vitaly unawares.

Neither option appealed to her. If she climbed back down the shaft, she had no idea who might be on the other side of the elevator doors at the rim end. For all she knew, Dion had set himself up in the corridor, ready to blow open the doors with explosives or a high-powered rifle. And if he wasn't there, would she be able to get out that way if she had to? If there was some way to cajole the doors open from her end, she didn't know it.

But she disliked just as much the idea of escaping out the hub end of the spoke into the Axle: Nina was still grunting up there. Lots of people get shot and still feel like fighting. And even if Nina had become incapacitated by now from panic or blood loss or depressurization of her suit, Vitaly would be arriving any minute.

She did not pause for long before she decided to push herself down the spoke the way she had come. She grasped the rungs of the ladder again when she had floated halfway down the shaft, then climbed gingerly back to her redoubt behind the elevator cab. In the dim twilight of the shaft, bits of detritus— shards of the punctured elevator hatch, scraps of upholstery from the car—floated about in the wispy air and low gravity like marine snow.

Below her, on the other side of the hatch, she knew, parts of *Imperium* were still beautiful, still unburned, still a glowing nimbus of svelte curves and arctic-blue light. Here in the shaft, though, in this place that a guest would never have been invited to enter, the spoke was abyssally dark.

"Chief, this is Vitaly," she heard over channel eight. "Nina has a chest wound. I want to get her down to infirmary—could you meet us with the gurney at the bottom of alpha spoke?"

"Copy that, Vitaly. Bringing the gurney."

Chloe thought once more about whether to move or stay put. If Dion was meeting Vitaly and Nina at the alpha spoke elevator, she would be free to return to the rim through the doors of the beta elevator—if she could figure out a way to get them open from this side. It was worth inspecting the doors, at least—was there some manual override that she hadn't remembered? She climbed a few more rungs down the ladder, into the pitch black of the lower shaft. She questioned whether she was safe to light her headlamp, whether Vitaly and Nina had boarded the elevator yet. Her time was short. Chloe steeled her nerves—what is life but a series of calculated risks?—and reached up to light her lamp. Then she felt the jagged edge on the crest of her helmet, remembered her collision hours before with the wall up on the Axle, the crunching sound, the spray of plastic shards. The darkness around her wouldn't be answered; for all the human ingenuity available to Chloe, the darkness might have stretched out forever, over the distance between the galaxies.

It didn't take her long to realize that she shouldn't stay where she was. This elevator shaft was her last known location to them. It would be a tough spot to escape if one Reckoner was posted at each end of the spoke, which might happen again soon enough.

Once Vitaly and Nina descended, she would have the hub to herself. She imagined how much time it would take Vitaly to call the alpha spoke elevator, guessing at how much time had passed since his last communication. She took the risk again, climbed again, pulling herself until she floated to the top of the elevator shaft.

She looked out with her gun drawn. The Axle was bright, gleaming, empty. If she could get down the alpha spoke elevator while the Reckoners were on their way to the infirmary, she might slip out, could find herself another place to hide.

The alpha spoke elevator was at the rim. She called it, drawing her gun on the doors as they opened for her. But the car was empty, pristine except for a single smear of blood on one azure satin wall.

The elevator descended quickly. The doors opened on the empty corridor of the rim. The silence of channel eight gave her some satisfaction: it meant, she hoped, that there was no one left on the bridge to communicate with. She had little time to waste on hoping for things, but she moved up the corridor beneath the security cameras in the hope that she was unobserved.

She moved counterclockwise around the rim, in the opposite direction that Dion and Vitaly would have taken to get Nina to the infirmary. Chloe passed toward the locker rooms, the gym, toward that spot where she had watched Kassie squirming in Vitaly's headlock. The corridor was empty now. But then, as she approached the broken-open sliding door of the middle dressing room, she saw a dark thread trailing along the carpet. The trail drew a thin, broken line toward the fitness center.

Chloe looked through the open entryway of the gym. The place seemed empty. She saw, though, the thread of blood leading deeper into the room; she opened the visor of her helmet, scanned around. When she stopped her own breath, she could hear the small, ragged breathing of another.

Chloe came around one of the treadmills and found Kassie there, lying on her side with the fitness center's first aid kit pulled down from the wall, its contents strewn about her. A great peony blossom of blood had spread across the white outer thigh of her jumpsuit, close by her hip. She did not look up when Chloe came into view but rather seemed to be trying to hold a gym towel over the wound.

Chloe knelt beside her. "It's okay, Kassie—I've got you," she said, though she did not feel that either of those assertions was true. She leaned over Kassie's thigh, using one hand to press the blood-soaked towel against the wound at the back of her leg. She saw immediately that there were two wounds: the bullet had passed out of the front of her thigh about fifteen centimeters away. Kassie had been trying to cover both wounds with one towel.

Chloe grabbed another towel, began pressing against the wound at the back of Kassie's thigh with her knee while she mashed the other towel against the wound at the front with her hand. With her foot, Chloe dragged over the tumbled first aid kit. She took the surgical dressing scissors still lying in the case and began cutting open the leg of Kassie's jumpsuit. The work felt awkward in the gloves of her pressure suit, with only one hand free, as though she were a little girl using scissors for the first time.

Kassie made a low, keening cry, as if she was suddenly distraught over the loss of the jumpsuit, or as though she was only now aware of Chloe's presence. "Shhh—I've got you," Chloe said. Kassie continued moaning.

Chloe peeled back the incised fabric of the jumpsuit and began to pack each wound with gauze. Kassie screamed in agony, or perhaps in horror, as Chloe found herself thinking back, incongruously, to the silent cadavers of the Santa Rosa Junior College anatomy and physiology lab: gaunt cancer victims, octogenarians felled by heart disease or stroke, each body embalmed as meticulously as a pharaoh's. Whatever was different now—the warmth, the air about Kassie free of aldehydes and methanol, the elasticity of her tissues—added up to something, Chloe knew. She would not call it the soul, which she didn't believe in, nor any other mysticism like *the vital spark* or *animal magnetism*. But some mystery was there, some emergent property that kept Kassie writhing even now and that kept Chloe probing her fingers into the mouth of each wound like some doubting Thomas.

As she worked, she worried about the noise Kassie was making—if Dion or Vitaly heard her, would they be more likely to come help her or to come harm her? "I'm going to get you home," Chloe said. This assurance was not, she thought, strictly impossible. If the bullet had hit her femoral artery, Kassie would have bled out already. Here on the outside of her thigh, though, the gauze Chloe was sliding into the wound with her finger was beginning to stanch the flow of blood. To judge by the imagined line that connected the wounds through the leg, Chloe supposed that the bullet might have shattered the femur, or at least ricocheted off the bone.

"I need you to stay quiet," Chloe said. Kassie nodded; she had at least stopped screaming now that the wound was packed, had dropped her breath to a whimper. Still too loud, Chloe thought, but at least she couldn't be heard throughout the whole rim of the station.

Chloe rolled a towel under Kassie's head for a pillow and started rummaging around the welter of spilled first aid supplies for some kind of painkiller. It occurred to her as she hunted that Kamara, long gone home from lab module three, was a medical doctor. Not a trauma surgeon, perhaps, but certainly better equipped to manage a gunshot wound than she was. It seemed strange to her that a company charging visitors $82 million a head would have kept only two EMTs on staff. It was then that she realized the two were Angel and Nina.

Chloe tried to draw Kassie's attention away for a moment. "Why the hell didn't you put your pressure suit on? I was trying to contact you on channel five."

"I couldn't get the suit on," she panted. "Those suits are hard to get on."

This was not Chloe's experience with the fitted pressure suits. It wasn't as though Kassie had tried to strap herself into a PMU. Then a pill bottle that had rolled under the treadmill captured Chloe's attention.

Acetaminophen tablets, two hundred milligrams. Chloe

disliked the idea of giving Kassie Tylenol for a gunshot wound. However, she disliked even more the idea of sneaking to the infirmary in search of morphine.

The rescue mission might take another hour to hit its launch window, by her estimate. Perhaps ninety minutes. Who knew how long it would take a rescue detail to dock, to board, to secure the station? Her intuition told her that Kassie would survive that long—she had a decent chance, Chloe thought, of not bleeding out. Assuming, of course, that nobody found her and shot her again.

But if Chloe could get Kassie in the medevac—and herself, for that matter—they could be Earthside in an hour. A helicopter could have Kassie at LA General an hour after that, maybe less. The medevac was docked close by the infirmary—Chloe didn't like its proximity to Vitaly and Dion. But could she sneak Kassie out behind their backs? Were the Reckoners likely to use the medevac for themselves?

"I need you to hang tight," she whispered to Kassie. "I'm going to see if we have a clear path to the medevac."

Kassie shook her head with what seemed like dread. "No," she exhaled. "No, that won't work."

Chloe shushed her. "I'll be right back—stay as quiet as you can."

"No—Roger and Jessica were on the medevac. I'm sure they've launched it by now."

Kassie spoke with such conviction that it wasn't clear whether she was speaking lucidly. "I will check on that," Chloe said, humoring her. "For now, let me see if the medevac is still there and if we have a clear path to it."

"Fine, go ahead," Kassie sighed in a tone that said she knew Chloe was wasting her time. "Just hurry."

Chloe looked up and down the main corridor of the rim. Her

communicator had been silent since she had last heard Vitaly's exchange with Dion. Did that mean Vitaly and Dion and Nina were in the same room together? Or had they finally changed the channel they were using? She listened in for a few moments on each of the other channels, hearing nothing. Maybe they were observing radio silence, or maybe she just wasn't lucky enough to catch them talking.

The medevac airlock was at the antipode of the fitness center, just down the corridor from the library. Reckoners territory. She knew, though, that there was nowhere on a circular track that one could hide for very long from any of them. Chloe found herself again disliking the choices that were before her.

She drew her weapon and began to slink down the corridor, eyeing each hatch and doorway as she approached.

Then she saw something that chilled her. As she passed the pillar of the beta spoke elevator, she noticed that along the seam of the doors, a white putty had been affixed like a crude spackling job. Dion and Vitaly had been carrying around C-4 in that duffel bag. If she had remained in the elevator shaft, if she hadn't gotten a lucky shot at Nina, they would have blown open the elevator doors below her.

Once more Chloe banished the sense of her looming mortality, returned to the path before her. She began to move quickly now—there was no good reason for one of the Reckoners to be hiding in the cafeteria, a storage closet, one of the surplus conference rooms, on the off chance that she would pass this way.

When she had gotten close enough to see the hatch of the medevac airlock, the bottoms of the entryways to the infirmary and the library were visible up the curve of the corridor. She stopped, crouched, watched, hearing nothing. A minute she waited, steeling her courage. Then, as she was about to slip down the last meters toward the airlock, she saw someone emerge from the infirmary.

From the looks of the feet and the legs, the great duffel bag—the only parts she could see from her vantage—the man was Vitaly. His legs crossed the corridor to the library and passed in.

Chloe decided in that moment that she would return to the fitness center. She would give Kassie a large dose of acetaminophen from the first aid kit and hope for the best; they would wait for the Reckoners to leave, if they did leave; they would wait for the rescue mission, whenever that was coming. She and Kassie might yet survive. Perhaps the others would, too, those that had managed to live this long.

Then, just as she began to turn back the way she had come, she saw a different pair of feet emerge from the library, stepping crisply away from her down the corridor. She watched them recede from view until they disappeared.

A few moments later, she watched a third pair of feet—Sir Alexander's, she was sure, nearly hidden behind the hem of his wizard's robe—walk out of the library and up the corridor, followed by the legs of Vitaly and his swinging duffel.

A brave impulse, really nothing more than the perception of an opportunity worth grasping, flashed for a moment in Chloe. There were opiates in the infirmary, a gurney. Nina, if she still lived, must have slowed down a good deal by now.

Chloe took one last look up and down the corridor and slipped into the infirmary.

She saw Nina at once, a bloody mess on the gurney. Her pressure suit and jumpsuit had been cut open; blood-soaked gauze pads still rested on a spot above her right breast. She would have bled very quickly in the near vacuum of the hub, Chloe knew. Or perhaps she had died first from decompression, the bullet having perforated the pressure suit before it entered her body. Her face, that gate through which all humanity had evolved to communicate its joys and sorrows, its fears and serenities, expressed nothing now.

The room was a confusion of opened wrappers and discarded implements. The three cabinets against the wall all stood open—their doors pried open, it looked like—and had been rifled through. Chloe scanned quickly over the medication packs, disremembering which colored box corresponded to medications for which ailment. It was in the red pack that she found the painkillers: lidocaine, benzocaine, more acetaminophen, hydrocodone.

She dropped the bottle of hydrocodone into the makeshift pocket at her duct tape belt. She was relieved to see that despite *Imperium's* carnival of bloodshed, the infirmary's second gurney was empty. She released the brakes and began wheeling it out. She spared one last look at the ruin of Nina. Nina's key fob remained on the belt of her pressure suit. And beneath the sliced-open flaps of the suit, in the breast pocket of the jumpsuit, Chloe spied the beveled edge of a cell phone.

She had another intimation that she had found something that might come in handy: even without the access code, she would have been grateful for a cell phone flashlight when she was stuck in the elevator shaft. Chloe slipped the phone into the pocket with the painkillers and Nina's fob.

She wheeled the gurney to the doorway, once more scanned the corridor, then pushed the gurney out into the hall and ran it back toward the fitness center.

She found Kassie groaning where she had left her. Kassie grimaced with what seemed like pitying disdain for Chloe on seeing the gurney: "I told you—the medevac is gone."

Chloe realized only then that she had been so engrossed with the opportunity of finding the infirmary empty that she had not followed her own plan. "You told me," Chloe repeated in the tone of a parent comforting a sick child. Chloe looked around for something she could use as a cup for the water fountain. The canister of methyl salicylate spray among the first aid supplies had a plastic lid that might hold half an ounce of water. She filled the cup and knelt over Kassie to give her two ten-milligram tablets.

"I didn't know you had a cell phone with you," Kassie said. Chloe's pouch had dangled near Kassie's head as she took the hydrocodone. "You should try to call Hellmund again—see when the launch is happening."

"It's not my phone. I found it on Nina's body. I took it in case we need a flashlight."

Kassie stared at the phone as though she were regarding an omen that had appeared to her. "I think that's Erik's phone," she finally said. "The PIN is *007007*."

Chloe concluded that Kassie was probably in shock. "I'll try that, okay? But right now, I want to get you onto this gurney and into the medevac capsule."

"You're not listening to me," Kassie groaned, punctuating each word as though she were speaking to a drunk or a child. "The medevac is gone. Everyone made a bid for it, and the Van Cleaves won—I'm sure they launched it hours ago."

Chloe remembered the ghostly tapping she had heard in the corridor. She began to wonder whether there was more to the medevac than she knew.

"Really, try *007007* to unlock that phone—I'm fucking serious."

"All right, fine—I'm trying it." Chloe punched in the numbers, and the phone opened up like a dream. Apparently Erik *had* chosen one of humanity's dumbest possible PINs. "How did you know that?" she asked Kassie.

"I saw Nina using it after they killed Erik." She took a deep breath and closed her eyes, surfing some wave of pain that had passed over her. "Can you Skype Hellmund with it?"

Chloe gave it a try. Most likely, Hellmund wasn't expecting a call from Erik's phone. Then again, he was probably glued to his Skype right now.

Hellmund picked right up. He was scowling when he first appeared on the screen, sitting in his study, his disordered, over-populated bookshelves stretching off behind him as far as the hallway, which was mounted with totems and masks he had collected from throughout the Americas. Hellmund had the frown of someone who had received a lot of bad news lately. But his face softened to a bemused, stricken look when he recognized Chloe.

"Chlo—how did you get Erik Rasmussen's phone?"

"It's a long story," Chloe said. "Listen—things are bad up here. What's the status on that rescue launch?"

"T-minus . . . fifty-four minutes. Can't you just stay out of their way for that long?"

"I'm trying to do that," Chloe answered, offering a fleeting censorious glare at Kassie. "But we've got a situation here. Kassie's been shot, and we need to get her Earthside. I was hoping to get her aboard the medevac, but she tells me it's been launched already."

"I can check on that for you, but I'm pretty sure the medevac hasn't launched," he said. "Ground control would have received an alert on that."

Chloe shot another glance down at Kassie, who was shaking her head with a twisted expression that might convey disapproval or denial or misery. "I'll look into the medevac," Chloe said. "You might let ground control know that we'll be trying to launch as soon as we can."

"What did you find out about Tsadok?" Kassie called out from the floor.

Hellmund seemed as surprised to hear Kassie's question as Chloe was. "I really haven't had much time to dig into that. Once everyone is safe at home, we can get to the bottom of all those leads."

"Ron, I'm going to try to get us on the medevac. I think we're better off getting Kassie Earthside as soon as we can."

Hellmund looked faded and defeated beneath his wall of books. "If you can do it without crossing the hostage takers, go ahead. But you're better off hunkering down where you are." Then, as if realizing only in that moment that he could neither forbid nor permit anything Chloe might want to do, he said, "Please, Chlo, just keep yourself safe. I would never forgive myself if something happened to you."

For a moment after he signed off, the grainy still image of Hellmund in his study, the hallway in the background with the masks and totems staring out at her, remained on the screen of the dead man's cell phone. Chloe regarded it as she might a curious snapshot.

"I swear to you," Kassie said, "Dion auctioned off the seats on the medevac. Roger and Jessica won them."

"I believe you. But Ron would have known by now if the medevac had launched. If Roger and Jessica are still aboard *Imperium*, I want to get them off the medevac and see if I can get you home on it."

Kassie looked past Chloe, up at the ceiling, with a miserable resignation. For her part, Chloe wasn't sure that her plan was such a good one either. They were likely much safer where they were, out of Dion's way and hopefully—if the bridge remained empty—out of sight. Could they wait for rescue here? Then again, Chloe had no idea how OrbitalVentures' rescue mission was going to work: Would Dion and Vitaly have escaped the station by then? Would there be another shootout? What was to keep Dion from killing everyone aboard if he wanted to? What would keep him from blowing up *Imperium*? Meanwhile, Kassie had bled a great deal: it wasn't clear to Chloe that she would live another hour, much less another eighteen, or however long it would take OrbitalVentures to secure the station and ferry them back to Earth.

Chloe passed sips of water to Kassie, half ounce by half ounce in the cap of the analgesic spray can. Kassie took each tiny gulp greedily. Chloe wished that it had occurred to her to take a water bottle from the infirmary, the latest incarnation of a regret that kept manifesting in one form or another today. Yet she knew that no one could anticipate all things. She took consolation in the knowledge that there was much that Dion and his people had failed to anticipate, too.

Moving Kassie to the gurney would have been a challenge for a pair of EMTs. Even in the opiate haze that was descending on her, she was in agony being moved by a single person, one half of her body at a time. At one point she cried out with such guttural force that Chloe wondered whether she had made a mistake to try and move her.

Kassie looked at her with an exhausted, pleading stare. "Please just let me rest a minute. Please. Please just see if the medevac is there. If it's there, you can put me on it. Just give me a minute."

Chloe had assumed, when she tempted fate the first time, that she would make one trip to the infirmary for the gurney, another with Kassie on the gurney to the medevac, not that she would be shuttling back and forth, back and forth, as Vitaly and Dion prowled about. Yet the mystery of the medevac capsule—whether it was there or not—troubled her as well. She weighed whether she wanted to wheel Kassie into Reckoners territory on a hunch.

"I'll be back as soon as I can," Chloe said. She reached out to brush the hair from Kassie's forehead with what she hoped, or imagined, conveyed affection to the girl. Chloe felt in that moment like some fantastically complex machine that had been invented to imitate mammalian impulses and behaviors. Someday, if she lived that long, she would contend with her grief and would, perhaps, feel like a mammal for real.

As she drew her pistol again and began the long walk along the wheel to the medevac airlock, Chloe had a sudden, unexpected urge to reach out to Dion on channel eight, as though she were some State Department official negotiating with a hostile regime over the fate of a prisoner. Perhaps they could talk like adults about the medevac capsule, come to some agreement about getting Kassie to a hospital—how would that possibly interfere with Dion's goals?

"Come in, Dion," she hailed him over the communicator.

She continued creeping up the corridor, attending to the silence over channel eight.

"Dion here," she heard at last. "Go ahead, Chloe."

"I don't want trouble. I just want to get Kassie Ng onto the medevac capsule. Can we negotiate safe passage for her?"

There was another long pause. "That's not going to work."

"What the hell do you want, Dion?"

"There's nothing I want from you or Kassie," he replied. "The medevac is currently occupied."

"Come on, man. Kassie's been shot."

"That was a regrettable consequence of her attempt to escape."

"Screw you, Dion. Just take your money—or Tsadok's money—and leave us the hell alone. We're not trying to stand in the way of your fucking revolution."

"You don't know me," he said at length, "and you don't know the revolution. If you did, you would let us go about our business. We're fighting for people like you."

"You could have fooled me."

"I'm serious: Did your father deserve to die protecting a wealthy man's property? What was his reward for a career keeping the underclass out of the malls and gated subdivisions? Did any of that property he was protecting come to you? You still owe fifty thousand dollars in student loans, if I'm not mistaken."

In fact, it had occurred to her more than once, as she nursed a nameless sadness late at night, or as she sat raw nerved in freeway traffic, that her father's job had essentially been to protect the wealthy from the poor. Some in her position, perhaps most, harden their commitment over time to those rules, to that law and order—how else would she make sense of her father's life and death? And yet, some lonely clarity in her character had always refused to make sense of something senseless. The system that had killed her father was in fact broken.

But Chloe soon came back to herself. "Look, I didn't call to discuss politics with you. I just want to put Kassie on the medevac."

Dion's voice had a resignation that disarmed her. "Take my advice: if you want her to live, don't put Kassie on the medevac. Somebody sabotaged the splashdown presets: Kassie will just end up in the middle of the Pacific somewhere if you send her down that way.

"But I won't stop you," he added at last. "Dion out."

The medevac airlock had two secure hatches: one that opened onto the main corridor and a bay door that docked with the medevac capsule itself, attached to the rim of *Imperium* like a remora to a gigantic, heedless shark. Chloe made a quick inspection up and down the corridor, checking again the doorways to the library and infirmary, then turned her attention to the medevac airlock hatch. The reading on the hatch display reported that the airlock was pressurized; through the porthole she could see that the bay door was also closed. She waved Nina's key fob over the latch and let herself in.

The tapping was louder within. The airlock was empty, a utilitarian metal vestibule at odds with the design of much of the rim. She walked across the chamber to the exterior hatch; through its porthole, she could see the hatch of the medevac capsule, still docked to *Imperium*. The insistent tapping vibrated through her fingers when she touched the handle.

Chloe opened the hatch and rapped on the closed hatch of the capsule.

The capsule opened. Within was a cramped, low-ceilinged space, like the bed of a camper van. Roger and Jessica Van Cleave looked out like two bleary-eyed owls.

"Where the fuck is Dion?" Roger asked. "We've been crammed in here for—" Then his voice trailed off. Chloe appreciated suddenly the sight she presented with the gun in her hand, the bloodstains soaked into her suit; the feeling was like the sight of a fun-house hall of mirrors that, in the midst of many distorted reflections, presents a single image of shocking accuracy.

It occurred to Chloe as Roger and Jessica began clambering out of the capsule into the airlock that there was no safe place on *Imperium* to put the two. Perhaps she could use Nina's key fob to hide them in an out-of-the-way space. "Listen," she said, "let's get you locked up into one of—"

"No way," Roger interrupted as he pulled Jessica from the capsule. "We want to talk to Dion."

"Please listen—it's not safe out here," Chloe protested, but the two had moved past her, sliding the visors of their helmets open with an exasperated flourish.

"You tell Dion that we want to talk to him," Roger snapped as they strode into the hallway.

Chloe realized only now, as she followed the two out, that they believed her to be one of the Reckoners.

When the interior hatch of the airlock snapped shut behind her and she stepped into the rim corridor again, she saw Vitaly. He was walking in her direction, lugging the old fateful duffel. He stood perhaps ten meters away, just on the other side of the library and the infirmary from her.

It registered on her quickly that Vitaly seemed at least as surprised as she was. As he raised his weapon, Chloe fired at him and dove for the only cover anywhere nearby: toward him, into the open doorway of the infirmary a couple of meters up the hallway. Jessica Van Cleave let out a scream behind her; the duffel hit the floor with a thud. Whether her bullet struck him or went wide, Chloe didn't stay to find out.

Chloe landed on the floor inside the infirmary. The gurney where Nina's corpse lay in repose loomed in front of her. She scrambled to turn over and aim her weapon just as Vitaly's form appeared in the doorway. She had, she thought, hit him with her shot in the corridor: his right hand hung empty at an odd angle. Yet he moved with a kind of painless, predatory grace. In his left hand was the pry bar she had seen him and Dion use when she had watched them through the security monitors in those moments, hours ago, in which she'd felt herself to be in danger but which had been, she knew now, moments of relative safety.

She fired again as he pounced upon her. She knew that this shot had hit him—a gut shot, she believed. And yet, before she could fire again, she felt the nerves of her weapon hand explode in a flash of pain as the pry bar swung into it like a baseball bat. She heard her pistol clatter against the far wall of the infirmary; she regarded the sound with a kind of resigned melancholy, as though she were listening to a solitary rock bouncing down a talus cliff of a distant, lonely mountain.

She attempted to squirm out from under Vitaly, who had dropped to a knee on top of her. He knelt on her thigh and swung the pry bar again. She lifted her left arm to parry; the blow glanced off her arm with another jolt of fantastic pain, then bounced into the side of her helmet. Even under her helmet, the glancing blow sent a flurry of sparks across her vision.

She flipped herself over as he leaned back to swing at her once more. She scrambled out from under him before he could bring the pry bar down upon her again. She pushed herself to her feet with her aching forearms—she noticed with a kind of clinical detachment that she could not bear weight with her right hand—and dashed out into the corridor. Even dazed as she was, she could tell that Vitaly had been slowed down. And yet, she could hear him grunting like an enraged boar somewhere behind the labored breathing she heard in her own helmet.

She ran as quickly as she was able, her head pounding, her right hand numb. Ahead she saw Jessica and Roger running away from the gunfire, moving beyond her field of vision in the corridor. She shot a glance back toward the infirmary; she could see Vitaly, blood soaking the front of his pressure suit, staggering into the corridor toward the duffel he had dropped. She heard the pry bar clatter to the floor.

Chloe, too, staggered. She felt blinded by the pain above her ear. She knew, or some observing part of her mind knew, that she must attend to the present moment, had to think, that her life and the lives of others depended on it.

Where was she going? She couldn't lead Vitaly back to the fitness center—why, then, was she running that way? And there were so few decent hiding places between here and there. As though in a dream, she knew that she had had this realization more than once already.

He was behind her. She doubted that he could run very fast, given his blood loss—but there were at least two pistols he could have picked up. He could almost certainly live long enough to shoot her.

She looked to the staff cabins as she passed by them. The hatches to Dion's and Vitaly's cabins had been torn away—could she hide in one of those? Whether by dull instinct or the evil associations her buffeted brain drew with the names on the broken doors, Chloe passed those by, kept staggering up the hallway.

Thirty meters farther on, she saw the scorched, noisome cafeteria where she had hidden from Nina a few hours before. Or had she hidden there days before? Up through the fog of her confusion, she remembered the cafeteria as a horrible place to hide.

Yet that was the dark, quiet space she made for. Hopefully she had outrun Vitaly enough that he wouldn't see her duck in. Yet when she hazarded one more glance up the corridor, she saw him: he was not thirty meters behind her. He had lowered the visor of the helmet on his pressure suit; a pistol was holstered at his hip. In his good hand was a small squarish device—a walkie-talkie? An old handheld radio? Chloe felt as though the object's function was nearly accessible to her mind, another dream memory that she had begun to forget upon waking.

She ran as best she could. Some deep insight, perhaps no more conscious than the firing of motor neurons, led her to lower the visor on her banged-up helmet.

In that moment, a great shudder rolled beneath her feet. A flash of light glared like the sun far ahead along the corridor, followed a moment later by a concussive roll of thunder that drowned out everything. She found herself thrown to the floor.

That was it, she told herself, as though she were only now beginning to understand a joke that had been told at her expense: the object in Vitaly's hand was a wireless detonator. In a visionary encirclement tactic, or perhaps in some access of suicidal spite, he had detonated the C-4 around the elevator doors at the beta spoke pillar. Chloe felt the urgent need to turn herself over, to get to her feet, to move. The lights had failed in the section of corridor where she lay; even in her suit she could feel a breeze passing over her, as though *Imperium* itself had suffered a sucking chest wound. The claxons began to wail again, distantly: the closest loudspeaker must have shorted out, and she was hearing the alarm from farther up or down the corridor. "Decompression event, beta spoke," the computer voice was saying. "Ammonia leak detected in ring corridor."

She pushed herself to her side. She saw that in the direction she had come from, one of the corridor's emergency hatches was closing like a massive garage door: the station was trying to seal off the hull breach that the explosion had caused. On the same side of the corridor, soon to be locked in with her, was Vitaly. He was attempting to roll to his knees by pushing with one elbow against the floor, one of his hands dangling like a rag doll, the other clasped over his abdomen. She saw both of his gloves steeped in blood.

She rolled to her arms and knees, scrambled crawling toward the cafeteria. She heard a shot, but nothing hit her as she dashed behind the wall of the entryway.

The cafeteria was deep in darkness now that so many of the nearby lights in the corridor had gone out. She pulled herself to standing with the help of a chair, then wobbled and felt her way toward the swinging door to the kitchen, which puffed open as the air within the room was slowly sucked toward the station's newest hull breach.

She passed through into the pitch black of the kitchen. She hoped that the lights were shorted out here, too. She felt along as she groped toward a hiding place. With her good hand, she reached gingerly to the magnetized rack that her sense memory of the kitchen had placed above her head. Her glove passed over the slim blade of a boning knife. She took it up and lurched the last few steps to the edge of the stove. She crouched in the space between the stove and the butcher block, the knife out before her in the blackness.

The noise of the far-off claxons had diminished almost to nothing, a sign that much of the atmosphere in this section of the rim had already bled out into space. She did not hear the swinging door of the kitchen as it opened again—rather, she registered Vitaly's entry only as a faint infiltration of a distant gray glow from outside the kitchen.

Then the darkness prevailed again. If Vitaly had tried the switch, the lights must have shorted out in here as well. She wished that she had taken a position from which she could fight: crouched on the floor where she was, the best she could do would be to punch out with the knife while Vitaly stood above her, putting a bullet in her head. Through the haze of concussion, through the shadows of blood and violence that clouded her memory, she accepted the likelihood of her death with a sleepy indifference, with no more terror or sadness than if she had awoken in the middle of the night to find that one of her experimental beans had failed to germinate.

She heard—or, more accurately, felt through the floor—Vitaly's slow, stumbling steps into the kitchen, like the staggering of a drunkard. She prepared herself for one last moment; in her imagination, he stood perhaps two meters away.

She did not hear him take another step. With a kind of mindless desperation, Chloe punched out in front of her with the knife. But there was nothing to strike, nothing to sense—no sounds, no vibrations. She stabbed again, thrusting the knife upward in front of her. She felt nothing, not even a whisper of air.

A minute passed. Then five minutes. In the silence and waiting, Chloe became aware of the numbness in her right hand giving way to an increasingly insistent pain. She worried for a moment about the ring of her father's lapel badge cutting off the circulation in her swelling finger; then she remembered that she had moved that ring to her left hand. She pressed her thumb against her ring finger, felt the band pressing back against her under the thick skin of the glove.

She didn't know how long she waited before she felt curious enough to set the knife down next to her and fish Erik Rasmussen's cell phone from her pouch. She lit up the flashlight and leaned forward to shine it around.

Vitaly was sitting next to her, no more than a meter away, in much the same position that she had been: crouching, his back propped against the door of the stove, his head tilted back as though in exhaustion. Vitaly's arms were crossed over his belly as though he were nursing a stomachache. In profile she could see his still face, looking out into the darkness as though regarding a far-off mountain.

His pistol lay next to him. It was another Glock 18, she noted. Or perhaps it was the same gun she had been using before Vitaly had broken her hand. She could have reached out and picked up the weapon from where she sat.

The claxons had gone silent now—Chloe was in a vacuum, or near vacuum. She couldn't remember where the rim corridor's emergency hatch was positioned on the other side of beta spoke. If the fitness center was on the other side of that emergency hatch, she told herself, Kassie might live. If the gym was on this side of that hatch, she would certainly be dead by now.

That coolant leak was new, too—there was no telling how dangerous that was. If the leak had sprung where the hull breach had occurred, the ammonia might simply bleed off into space. Without the heat-exchanging function of the ammonia, the station would get very hot, or very cold, or both hot and cold in sequence as *Imperium* rotated, but everyone aboard might be able to live through the temperature extremes for a couple of hours until rescue arrived. But if the leak had cropped up elsewhere as a result of the shaking of the station, the gas leak could kill anyone who couldn't get into a pressure suit. If, again, they weren't dead already.

Chloe's hand was throbbing now, immovable in its glove. She wished she had a couple more of the hydrocodone tablets she had given to Kassie a few minutes ago. The side of her head, too, gave off a distant, otherworldly throbbing. She felt an unexpected yearning to lie down, to rest, as though a broken hand and a knock on the head with a crowbar were nothing more than fleeting setbacks that would resolve themselves with a good night's sleep.

But several aspects of her reality refused to let her sleep in peace. Kassie, for example, was one of those who couldn't get into a pressure suit. Nobody—none of the hostages, none of the putative rescuers, not Hellmund, maybe not even Dion— knew where Chloe was right now. And she had no more than twenty minutes' worth of oxygen in this suit without her having to plug into an umbilical.

She reached across her body with her good hand, took the pistol that lay between her and Vitaly, holstered it at her thigh. She picked up her phone-flashlight again, and with a sickening pain she lifted herself to her feet with her quadriceps by sliding her back up the wall behind her. As she picked her steps over Vitaly's corpse, she noted that her movements were no surer than his had been in his final moments: she tottered her way toward the door, holding her broken hand against her sternum as if in an imaginary sling.

She emerged into the new darkness and vacuum of the corridor she had once run. She made her way toward beta spoke. When she saw it, she knew that she would not have survived if Vitaly had timed his blast better: the hatch to beta spoke was blown into a pandemonium of shards that had gouged out great rents of scorched upholstery, exposed dangling wires, torn light fixtures from their sockets. There were two odd debris piles that she registered after a moment as bodies. She realized as she approached that she would not need to check for a pulse on either of them: Jessica's corpse lay splayed in an unnatural, blood-soaked backbend. Roger lay a few meters beyond, nearly sheared in two at the waist. His face, profoundly ugly, grimaced at the dark ceiling.

Chloe peered with the light of Erik's cell phone up into the beta spoke elevator shaft through the ruined doors. She could see that the spoke itself had been subjected to intense spallation: the lowest three rungs of the emergency-access ladder were bent out of shape, and she could see in the wall of the spoke a hole the size of a human heart gaping out into space.

Chloe passed on up the corridor, beyond the second rim airlock, where Erik had been cast out, toward the fitness center. That was when she saw a stroke of good luck: the emergency hatch had closed off the corridor just beyond the conservatory, separating the blasted section she was in from the rest of the rim. The fitness center lay on the other side of that hatch. Kassie might still be alive.

At least, she reminded herself, Kassie might still be alive if there was no ammonia leak on that side of the rim. Chloe did her best to remember the layout of radiators and ammonia lines around *Imperium*. She knew the main pump for the rim was mounted on the exterior of the station, just between the two rim airlocks. Wherever the leak was, she could stop it by venting the ammonia from that pump.

If she could get herself plugged into an umbilical in the second rim airlock, from there she could space walk to the pump. She wondered whether she understood all the ramifications of what she was doing; she accepted that she might have been dulled by her injuries. But dulled or not, the engine of reason was the only engine she had. She knew she had no other options than to space walk toward the ammonia pump.

CHAPTER THIRTEEN

ELEVEN MINUTES EARLIER

Dion sat in the captain's chair of the Starliner, patching the capsule's computer system into *Imperium*'s command and data handling. Once he finally accessed the bridge computer system again, he would be able to redirect the hub's overworked oxygen generators to pressurize the capsule while he assessed the status of the station's systems.

Dion reached out over the communicators: "Vitaly, what's the status on the hostages? Do you have an ETA?"

No answer. He disliked having called the operation before its completion. Not that the remaining ransom was worth worrying over—how much additional risk did they want to subject themselves to for Viv Volterra's 120 million, much less Kassie, if she was even still alive, and her single million? What bothered him, rather, was the collapse of the agreement: As much as he despised Roger, Dion had had every intention of honoring their bargain and sending the Van Cleaves home first. Instead, Roger had paid the lion's share for an empty promise. Dion had signed nothing, of course. But how would the Reckoners be regarded in the future, once Roger started spouting off about how he had been cheated?

Dion resolved again to devote less attention to what a reprehensible young billionaire might say about him to the news media. "Come in, Vitaly," he repeated.

The voice that responded was Vitaly's, but husky and distant in a way that made him sound like a different person. "Chloe . . . wounded . . . pursuit . . . toward beta."

"Come again, Vitaly." Dion began keying in the override commands for using *Imperium*'s oxygen generators to pressurize the Starliner.

In that moment, the Starliner shuddered. A sickening tremor shook Dion in the restraints of his safety harness. A shock wave had mushroomed through the hull of *Imperium* and across the capsule.

Dion knew immediately what had happened. It troubled him that someone had seen fit to detonate those charges. And if it was Vitaly—all the irritation Dion had felt with Vitaly for having shot Kassie Ng flooded through him again, an emotional shock wave that mirrored the physical one. The status display of the station began to proclaim the existence of a new hull breach on the rim, as *Imperium*'s computer began closing the emergency hatches in the main rim corridor to seal off the section of the ring near beta spoke.

"Vitaly, report!"

Vitaly made no response, but Dion was confronted by a squad of other warnings broadcast by *Imperium*'s computer: rapid decompression, ammonia leak, orbital perturbation. Dion took a long, hesitant moment to assess how dire *Imperium*'s circumstances had become. He called out to Vitaly once more. Dion wished that he could get at the station's surveillance camera feeds from this terminal and see for himself what was happening down on the rim. If Vitaly had gotten himself blown up by his own overenthusiastic demolition work, there was a kind of Dantean poetic justice in the man's fate. Live by the C-4, die by the C-4.

But Dion knew that he had gotten ahead of himself. There were any number of reasons that Vitaly might not be responding—and he couldn't very well leave the man behind if he was alive. He checked the key-access program through *Imperium*'s computer. Vitaly's fob—and Nina's—came up in the staff kitchen, of all places. At least Vitaly had recovered Nina's body.

He moved quickly. There was so little atmosphere in the hub that he was able to get past the elevator door hatch at the head of beta spoke without even a puff of air. He lit up his headlamp and surveyed the long, dark shaft. He moved down the beta spoke emergency ladder toward the rim. In the dim light flooding down from the hub, he could see the shot-up elevator car that he needed to move past.

Squeezing past the car on the ladder was a tight fit for him. The bottom of the spoke was badly damaged, a mess of twisted metal and scorch marks. The hull breach was close by where he climbed, a jagged rent in the steel of the spoke. He had suspected when he first saw the charges set that Vitaly was being overenthusiastic with the C-4. If he hadn't cared about causing a decompression event, Dion could simply have broken open the elevator doors with the .50-caliber rifle. It would have made less of a mess than he was seeing right now.

Cautiously he picked his way down to the warped end of the ladder, dropped himself past the last few damaged rungs to the blackened deck of the rim. The station looked abandoned here, a ruined, derelict craft from another world that he had boarded. In the charred chaos of the hallway lay one human lump, then another. He recognized the raw-meat coloration of the CisLunar pressure suits. The corpses of the Van Cleaves seemed no more than an oddity now, a curious feature of this unfolding disaster, long past any power now to stir up feelings of honor or shame in him. He drew his weapon in the lonely hallway and made his way toward the kitchen.

Dion's headlamp picked up a smear of blood on the swinging door to the kitchen. He pushed open the door and scanned the room, let his eyes pass over Vitaly's bloody form, suppressing an immediate emotional reaction, clearing each spot in the darkened space where a bad guy—where Chloe—might have hidden herself.

The kitchen was clear. He knelt over Vitaly, took in the profusion of blood that soaked his pressure suit, looked into his visor. His once-handsome, chiseled face had taken on a doughy, bruised cast, as though he had just emerged from a boxing match with an invincible opponent. A track of blood snaked from his nose; another trailed from the corner of each eye, like two dark tears.

Dion allowed himself a single moment of contemplation. He was now what he had always known himself to be: fundamentally, unalterably alone. Vitaly, Nina—where was Nina's body? He checked Vitaly's body for Nina's fob for a few moments before an alternative explanation for the fob's whereabouts occurred to him.

He went back the way he had come, climbing out of the blast zone of beta spoke by the shaky ladder. He returned to the Starliner. As he strapped himself in, he felt neither the grief of his loss nor the triumph of having secured the ransom. There would be a day to feel all things; now, like a well-programmed machine, he began the launch routine again.

He looked once more at *Imperium*'s status readouts. The computer had detected the ammonia leak, not at the site of the explosion itself, where Dion had originally expected it would be, but farther out on the rim. The ammonia lines apparently did not pass that closely to the juncture of beta spoke and the rim: from the computer's schematic, it looked like the feeds passed exclusively around the rim's outside edge. But the shock wave of the explosion had apparently knocked something loose in the system: there was a small leak on the ring nearly midway between alpha and beta spokes. A small leak, but sooner or later all ammonia leaks are deadly: the launch window for the rescue mission was still forty-five minutes away—perhaps three hours would pass, perhaps far more than three, before the rescue mission would be able to dock with *Imperium*. That was more than enough time for an ammonia leak to poison everyone aboard.

The station's cooling system, like its oxygen generators, could not simply be shut down in toto from the computer. Some engineering team at OrbitalVentures had had the insight that there were almost no benign reasons, but a great many malign ones, for a user to order such a shutdown. Dion attempted to shut down only the ammonia pump serving the rim. He found the malfunctioning ammonia circuit on the schematic and began tentatively clicking commands from the drop-down menus. Yet a few moments of investigation failed to turn up any simple command named *Shut down*. He felt a wistfulness come upon him—not regret, precisely, but something like an awareness of irony—that Konrad Whittaker was dead: Konrad had known far better than he how the control application for the cooling system worked.

Dion considered the possibility of leaving the hostages to their own devices. The hostages might be able to get suited up before they were overtaken by ammonia fumes. Or maybe the hostages would die—their deaths did not of necessity imply that he had not kept up his half of the bargain. After all, it was

Vitaly who had caused the explosion, not him. And anyway, he had already broken his word to the Van Cleaves; what did it matter if he failed to keep this other assurance?

Dion knew that these were rationalizations. He stared at the display for a long minute, resisting the conclusion that he already knew he would have to arrive at: he needed to deal with the leak before he left.

If he couldn't figure out how to shut it down from the computer, he would have to manually disconnect the ammonia pump that fed the leaking circuit. From there he would be able to vent the entire reservoir of that circuit into space. He didn't relish the thought of another space walk. But he didn't dread the prospect, either. He felt a stillness that he had not anticipated, as though all the violence and folly of the last hours, for good or for evil, had balanced to a perfect composure in his heart. Whatever he had done, he had done in service of some larger, more cosmic justice. The reckoning had been made; it fell to him now not to let the hostages die.

Dion took up the capsule's emergency tool kit from its locker. He disembarked the Starliner capsule once more, moved to the airlock off lab module two next door. The same PMU he had used the day before hung in its webbing. He strapped himself in, connected the PMU's oxygen pack to the intake in his pressure suit, and opened the bay door of the airlock.

As he maneuvered his way clear of the hub, Dion was struck by the gleaming beauty of *Imperium* viewed from outside. The station was orbiting the dayside of Earth; the sun glinted on the white sheath of the hull as though over a sheet of pure ice. No visitor looking on the station from this vantage would guess how much destruction and chaos had fermented within.

Dion sailed his PMU out from the slow rotation of the hub toward the more quickly spinning wheel of the rim. He had dropped about ten meters beneath the station—or above it, depending on one's point of view—and he took a moment to ascertain which of the ammonia pumps was the main. He manipulated the PMU's thrusters and retrothrusters to watch the edge of the rim rolling above him. He saw the long, brightly lit windows of the fitness center and the darkened, shimmering windows of the observatory approaching his position. Then, a little farther on, the second rim airlock passed by, and thirty meters or so beyond that, the squarish locker of the ammonia pump moved along its arc of rotation toward him.

Just as he began to fire his thrusters to turn, to intercept the movement of the pump the same way a train jumper runs alongside the tracks as the cars pass, Dion saw something he did not expect. A figure was already there, without a personal maneuvering unit, awkwardly poised at the ammonia pump. The figure looked as though they were belayed to some protrusion or spar on the hull of the station; they appeared already to be working on the pump's access panel with what looked for a moment like a pistol but, Dion realized, must be an automatic socket wrench. Whether because of unfamiliarity with the tool or because of the difficulty of their position attached to the wheeling rim of the station by both a belay and a pressure suit umbilical, or for some other reason, the figure had clumsy, misbegotten movements, the awkwardness of a strange child.

Dion hesitated. There was only one person alive on *Imperium* that could have taken it upon themselves to space walk without guidance or supervision. As the figure passed beneath him, he drew his weapon, unsure of his next step in a way he had not yet experienced during his mission on *Imperium*. The figure—Dr. Chloe Bonilla—passed by, rotating with the stricken station, clutching her right arm to her chest like a withered limb.

A brazen, visceral malice rose in him for this frail-looking figure who he might have considered a friend in a different world, to the extent that Dion had friends at all—this woman who had killed Angel, Meredith, Nina. Even that fool Vitaly had not shot *himself* in the stomach. The Reckoners' victory had cost them a great deal, thanks to her: How many cells of Reckoners were out there in the network with as much talent and training as the team that Chloe had broken up?

And yet, what would he accomplish by shooting at her? The Reckoners had come to start a revolution. Their task had been to strike a blow against an inequality of wealth that shocked the conscience. They had come to make an end run, through an act of public theater, around that connivance of banking, finance, and speculative interests that had erected around itself a legal system whose sole purpose was the preservation of those unconscionable inequities. Dion and his Reckoners had redressed that sucker's game of a system, at least as regarded a handful of billionaires foolish enough to spend $82 million to float around orbiting the Earth for two weeks. No one would be spending a dime on something so idiotic as an orbital vacation for a long time to come. And the money they had siphoned off these leeches would recruit and equip a hundred thousand more Reckoners.

How these new recruits would appear, where they would train and emplace themselves—Dion was curious about those questions, but they were hardly his concern. Tsadok was the most senior Reckoner he had spoken with, and even Tsadok was someone about whom he didn't know that much. The man was no more than a shadowy figure in a parking garage that he had spoken with a few times, a disembodied voice on a Crypsis call. The Reckoners' leadership structure was, of necessity, distributed—how else could any change be accomplished in the regime of surveillance capitalism that bore down on most of humanity? The Reckoners had set themselves up in such a way that if any one of them had been captured, or if any of them had defected, nobody would have anything of real value to divulge to the principalities and powers arrayed against them.

Dion had no need to preoccupy himself right now with that larger struggle, the feints and counterpunches in motion around the planet as the Reckoners battled the forces of exploitation that most of humanity simply called *the world as we know it*. Dion had done what he'd come to do; that was enough. He hadn't come to *Imperium* to kill without reason.

As though she had been listening in on his line of thinking, Chloe suddenly swung around on her belay to position the box of the ammonia pump between herself and Dion's PMU. Dion knew that she had seen him: she had let go of the wrench, which floated free now on its tether, while she reached across her body with a graceless jerk toward her weapon. He hit his thrusters to position himself on the other side of the rim from her. As she passed out of his sight, he understood the ungainliness he had noticed in her actions: she couldn't use her right hand. Why else would her holster sit on the hip opposite from the hand that drew the weapon?

He should have shot at her, he realized. In the silence of a vacuum, in a battlespace as broad as the orbit of the Earth, she would never have known that anyone was firing on her. But he was not like Vitaly, one who could kill without reflection. Perhaps, Dion thought, he would have saved himself a lot of trouble if he had been such a person.

Dion maneuvered to the inner side of the rim, just below the path of the revolving spokes of the station, beyond the field of view of Chloe's position. He wished he could simply fly the PMU back to the hub and board the Starliner. Chloe had been handling the leak, however inexpertly. Whatever crisis Vitaly's demolitions had brought on, Dion didn't have to answer for it or make it right.

The ammonia pump had passed beyond him now, maybe a hundred meters away on its rotation, like a model train on a track. He could no longer see Chloe, either, whatever she was doing there, or whether she was moving elsewhere along the rim. He concluded with a deepening dismay that she would have a clean shot at him if he took the PMU from the rim to the hub the same way he had come out. It would be safer for him to travel with one of the spokes between his route and Chloe's position. OrbitalVentures had spent a lot of time training the crew not to move PMUs between the rim and the hub in the same plane as the spokes—collisions were far too easy in that plane, as each spoke swung around like the boom of a sailboat. But with a bit of careful maneuvering to stay on one side of the spoke as it rotated, he could keep himself out of sight. Alpha spoke, which would pass his way again soon enough, could give him cover as he moved. But no matter how he returned to the hub, Chloe could still get a good shot at him when he got to the hub and had to reenter the lab module two airlock.

He also knew that he couldn't stay where he was right now: Chloe could look over either edge of the rim and get a shot at him where he was. He placed himself in the same plane as her, just to the outside of the rim, watching the blank dark windows of the staterooms reflect him as they passed, as Chloe's revolution around the hub took her past the antipode of his position. The thought occurred to him—though he had no time to entertain it—that he was engaged in a pathetic dance with her, a pas de deux that would end in the absurdity of him killing her or her killing him. And it was an absurdity: he had no reason to kill her beyond his own anger, anger being the worst reason to kill anyone; for her part, she would waste precious moments trying to kill a man who would be happy to leave her alone, all while the people aboard *Imperium* asphyxiated in a cloud of ammonia gas that she could have diverted.

There was nothing to be gained by silence now, Dion realized. He reached out to her on channel eight. "Chloe, stand down. I only came out to bleed off the leaking ammonia. If you're doing that already, I won't trouble you."

There was a long pause. Dion prepared himself to face the spot where he had last seen her. Then her voice came back over channel eight: "Fuck you, Dion."

Profanity had always irritated him, ever since he was a boy wading through a sea of it among classmates, neighborhood thugs, adults flapping their jaws carelessly. Cursing was a symptom of a breakdown in communication, a cloaking of one's rational position—or the lack of a rational position—with silly verbal posturing or juvenile theatrics. He was in no position, of course, to lecture Chloe on the subject the way he had Roger Van Cleave. Then again, he had had a point to make to Roger, as well as to the other hostages, that had nothing to do with cursing.

He knew she was no thug. "Chloe, please be reasonable," he called out. "You're only endangering the others by wasting time shooting at me."

"Who am I endangering?" she retorted. "The Van Cleaves? Erik Rasmussen? Why don't you let *me* worry about the people you haven't killed?"

Dion regarded her words, which would have called up such shame or anger in him an hour ago, with a detachment he had not expected. "You're making a mistake," was all he answered.

No matter—he had to prepare for the ammonia pump to appear in his line of sight again and roll beneath him on its arc. He held his weapon in front of his sternum, as near to his center of mass as he could, his arms held closer in than the posture he would assume if he were shooting in gravity. When he fired, he would be propelled backward, but hopefully not into a spin—the great danger in zero-gravity shooting.

The ammonia pump rolled into view again. Chloe was nowhere to be seen. Dion scanned the rim as it rotated a few meters beneath him; as it passed, he saw Chloe's umbilical stretched over the edge of the rim. Like him, she was trying to put the structure of the station between them.

He had to use one hand to turn the PMU to face her position as the rim rotated by. In the final moment, just before that section of the rim rotated out of his view, he saw Chloe's helmet and arm pop up behind the box of the ammonia pump. He heard no sound but his own breathing in his helmet. He felt no shot, but he knew that she had shot at him—there was no other reason to expose herself like that. He returned fire, his pistol off center now in relation to his mass. He listed from the recoil of the shot. As he worked to compensate with the PMU thrusters, he glimpsed the ammonia pump rotating out of sight with a geyser of white flakes erupting from its side. His shot must have punched through one of the ammonia lines in the pump. As he stabilized himself again out of sight of Chloe's position, Dion wondered whether his shot would bleed off the ammonia from the leaking coolant loop in an appreciable way.

The quiet of the predicament they were in was eerie to him. The two of them could fire on one another until doomsday without either of them ever hearing a sound beyond their own breathing. The knowledge of that silence saddened him.

He called out again: "Chloe, I repeat—stand down. Stand down and I will do the same. I don't want to fight you. The Reckoners are leaving *Imperium* immediately."

"Do you have any idea what a patsy you are, *Reckoner*?" Chloe responded.

Dion had spent many hours steeling himself against the ridicule of the Reckoners that he knew he would face, against the ignorant mischaracterization of his mission, against the derision that was at its root a terror of the revolution to come. Yet despite his hours of meditation, the tone of Chloe's question stung him. He would be lying to himself if he denied ever having had the anxiety that he was still, somehow, a sucker. For him, the Reckoners were both an all-consuming philosophy and an obscure secret society. The organization's physical manifestations, however, were little more than a fevered manifesto that had been compiled by fellow travelers; coded, late-night conversations in fringe discussion forums of the web; a couple of shadowy dead drops with Tsadok, leaving Dion satchels of cash for suppliers that would not take crypto; and his companions of this mission, now lying in their own blood within the corridors of *Imperium*. Who were the Reckoners, really? Had he at any point allowed his imagination to run away with him? Was he, in fact, a patsy?

"I never took you for a propertarian," he countered. "But the enemies of the revolution are not always the obvious ones."

"I could say the same about the Reckoners," she said, breathing hard.

"Chloe, will you please stand down? Let's just back away from each other, and we can both get home alive." Yet as soon as he said it, Dion knew that she was going to keep shooting at him. There was no sense in begging.

And whatever she had meant just now, Dion wasn't such a sucker that he was going to wait around getting shot at. He would get himself back to the Starliner if he could, keeping one of the spokes between himself and her as he maneuvered back to the hub, then keeping the shaft of the hub between him and her as best he could. That meant turning, and moving himself, as the station rotated, matching his rotation exactly to that of the station. The lab module airlocks, though, were on the same side of the station as Chloe's position. In the last moments, she would get another shot if she saw him.

He couldn't see the ammonia pump now—it was at the other side of the rim from his position—but he could see the plume of frozen ammonia bellying out from the pump's location like the exhaust of an old steam train. However, he wasn't about to wait until Chloe came into view and passed out of sight again—he would take his chances now. He dropped below the plane of the revolving spokes and fired the thrusters toward the long pillar of the hub.

As he moved, he kept his eye on the plume of ammonia, scanning for any sign of Chloe emerging to fire on him. He kept his pistol trained on the plume as it traveled before him. If he had to fire on her, he would have to compensate quickly with the thrusters to put himself back on course.

He saw, or thought he saw, a dark shape moving behind the plume of ammonia. Dion fired at the shadow he saw. As he felt himself turning in response to the gun's kickback, he knew, quickly and wordlessly, that if he had seen her, she had seen him; that if she had made herself visible, it was to fire on him; that if he had not hit her—and perhaps even if he had—she had the same chance that he had just taken.

Dion was ready to compensate with the PMU thrusters for the kickback of his shot. But he never got the chance: he felt a shocking, conclusive thud slam into the side of the PMU. Then a great, hot force pushed him from behind, and he felt a searing pain. He spiraled away from his destination, free and clear of *Imperium*, like a bottle rocket corkscrewing into the night.

Dion did not lose consciousness immediately. He had enough presence of mind to know that his PMU had been hit, that Chloe's bullet had likely punctured one of the tanks or valves or feed lines—propellant maybe, or maybe oxygen. He tried to reach up to disconnect himself from the backpack now blowing its contents into space. Yet his arm wouldn't obey his command.

Then Dion felt an equanimity settling upon him, greater than any he had ever felt in all the hours of his striving and meditation. He wondered at the last whether he would be captured by Earth's gravity well and end his existence as a shooting star over someone's night sky, or whether he would spin off into the depths of space, an eternal remnant of ice.

CHAPTER
FOURTEEN

The ammonia pump was easy to shut down. At least, the shutdown was easy once Chloe was alone and could focus her attention on something other than being shot at. She unscrewed the box that served as the cowl of the pump, letting the bolts float away into space, then turned the pump off and disconnected the primary ammonia line. Once free of the pump, a lazy snowdrift of ammonia gushed out of the line for a minute. Chloe wondered whether she had even needed to shut down the pump in the end: Dion's shot had gone clean through the hose, and the holes the bullet had created were bleeding off the ammonia admirably.

All her wellsprings of pain—in her head, her hand, her arm—gushed up in her almost as soon as the ammonia line fell away from the pump. Chloe felt drowned by her pain, scarcely able to reel herself in on the suit's umbilical and return to the rim airlock. She let the umbilical pull her in, slid down to a sitting position against the bulkhead of the airlock as the bay doors closed behind her. Dying there would be a blessed release, she felt.

Death didn't come for her, however. The umbilical kept pumping pressurized air into her suit, powered by the same independent generator that moved the bay doors—they had been designed to work even in the event of a general loss of electricity. She wondered, then, why the umbilicals and bay doors had failed in the second lab module airlock during the guests' space walk—when? A year ago? Had that space walk occurred just yesterday? Perhaps the crowd of them, all plugged in, had simply overloaded the circuit.

She closed her eyes and gave herself over to the synchronized pulsing in her hand and the side of her head.

She heard a voice she didn't know. "Dr. Chloe Bonilla, come in." It was a young man's voice, with the tone of a bored telemarketer calling her on a Sunday afternoon. A few minutes had passed, or a few hours, or several days, since she'd closed her eyes and let her suffering wash over her.

It took her several moments to understand that she was being hailed over channel eight. "This is Chloe Bonilla Prieto," she said. Her voice was husky and clouded, as though she had not spoken for a very long time. "I'm in rim airlock number two, in a depressurized section of the station."

"Copy that, Dr. Bonilla," said the voice. "This is security officer Kenneth Grady of the OrbitalVentures ship *Sphinx*. I can see you through the airlock hatch porthole."

Only then did Chloe open her eyes to see a blue Orbital-Ventures helmet in the little glass window of the hatch.

Chloe had only hazy memories of the next few hours: her extraction on a gurney, rolling through the main corridor to the alpha spoke elevator in what seemed like a totally decompressed station; one of the rescue team explaining to her that the explosion on *Imperium* had critically destabilized the station's orbit, that there had been no one on the bridge to fire thrusters to compensate for the orbital perturbation, that *Imperium* would need to be imploded in order to break it into pieces small enough to burn up in the atmosphere when it fell to Earth; her weeping, inexplicably, for the first time since she was a child when she realized that she would lose the seedlings she had been researching.

She remembered that she was strapped into the gurney on the *Sphinx*. She was the last person to be pulled from the station. A man had been asking her questions, stupid questions: *What are your dreams for the coming year? Are your parents alive? What were their names?* Much later, she understood that he had been assessing her for a concussion; at the time, though, she found the questions both annoying and impossible to bat away.

Someone medicated her. She remembered seeing Kassie Ng, somehow, impossibly, suited up, strapped into a gurney next to her. She remembered hearing the voice of a man somewhere behind her head, muttering something about how they had been cheated. She realized the voice was Nicholas Winters-Qureshi's.

She didn't remember much after that. The destruction of *Imperium* registered in her memory as nothing more than a bright light witnessed from a porthole of the *Sphinx* from kilometers away. The reentry to Earth's atmosphere, which she had sometimes dreaded during moments of exhaustion or boredom over the last months, barely registered on her consciousness: she remembered it later like a turbulent airplane landing. She remembered a many-voiced crowd at the flight center, remembered the flashing lights of tarmac vehicles and ambulances, got one glimpse of what seemed like hundreds of cameras. She looked for Hellmund in the crowd, but she was spirited away in an ambulance almost before she could say his name to the woman pushing her gurney.

She bobbed up into a dull, achy consciousness some time

later. Her blood-soaked pressure suit had been taken off her; she felt the hospital gown's binding at her collarbone. Her right hand, sheathed in a cast, swam in a low, insistent rumble of pain. Hellmund was sitting in a low chair at the foot of the bed. His elbows rested on his knees; his shoulders were hunched and rounded as though they had been chastened by circumstances.

Chloe thought it wise merely to observe him.

Eventually he looked over at her, inhaling a long, slow breath. "Hey, beautiful."

Chloe drew up a smile.

"I've been worried about you."

"Is Kassie Ng alive?"

"Kassie? Yes, she's going to be okay."

Under the covers, Chloe felt for the ring she had moved to her left hand. She ran her thumb over the shield of her father's tiny lapel badge.

"Are you doing okay, babe?"

Chloe gave a slow nod. "I think I just need a little more rest," she said.

"Do you need me to come back a little later?"

That sounded about right. Chloe nodded and let herself drift back.

When she awoke later, Sir Alexander Dunne was sitting in the same low chair.

Something was strange about him, Chloe felt. It took her a moment to put her finger on it: his hair was finally combed. It was still wiry and sun-damaged—all the wealth in the world would not give Sir Alexander an attractive head of hair—but he no longer had the unruly fright wig that he had sported every time she had seen him on *Imperium* and that had seemed a natural part of his mad wizard outfit. The wizard robes were long gone: he seemed an ordinary old man now in khakis and a golf shirt.

"Good morning, sunshine," he said.

"How is Kassie?"

"Kassie's going to be all right. She lost a lot of blood, but she's stable."

"And the others?"

"Some of us are a good deal poorer," he said. She noticed the breast of his golf shirt sported a tiny, tasteful OrbitalVentures teardrop. "However, all but four of us survived. Thanks to you, I think."

"Four?"

"Erik Rasmussen was flushed out of the airlock; Roger and Jessica Van Cleave died in the explosion; Viv Volterra is presumed drowned in the South Pacific."

Chloe's expression must have seemed nonplussed to him, because he continued a few seconds later: "When the hostages were being taken up to the *Sphinx*, Viv slipped away from the group and launched herself in the medevac capsule. The splashdown coordinates would have put her somewhere near Villings, one of the Ellice Islands. But the capsule was never found; she almost certainly sank to the bottom in it."

She stared back at him a long moment. As though he were unable to bear her silence, he added at last, "The rest of us, though, owe you our lives."

Chloe had enough gentility not to say that except for Kassie, she had given the hostages barely any thought during the entire ordeal: certainly not Viv Volterra, not the Van Cleaves, and not even Erik Rasmussen, except in that moment when she saw him expelled from the airlock and she wondered who he was. She had lived through those hours with no more rationale than what a prey animal would need: that survival is an absolute good.

"The rescue team managed to recover your laptop," Sir Alexander said with a tenderness that brought her back to herself.

"And they pulled out your planting units before *Imperium* was destroyed."

That part of her research was ruined, she knew. Even if the seedlings had been able to survive inside the BRIC-X units during decompression, and even if someone had thought to reconnect their lighting, the seedlings would not emulate a gravitropic response now that they had been brought back to Earth's gravity. Now they would simply express the gravitropism that came naturally to them. Still, she thought, it wasn't impossible to imagine that the BRIC-X units had been well sealed enough that they remained pressurized after the hull breach. Perhaps if the little plants survived, or even if they died, there was something more she could learn from them.

Later, after Sir Alexander left and she was alone again in the hospital room, a disorienting, bottomless moment opened up before her. Her memory colored the events in a stranger, starker light; she saw her last day on *Imperium* as she might see an optical illusion, with a new perspective snapping into clarity for her. It was a vision that she could not readily unsee, where words like *prey* and *predator* grew slippery, uprooted from any meaningful biological reality: Who had been predator? Who had been prey?

Chloe was released from the hospital a couple of days later, found herself in a boutique hotel room in Palmdale, thirty miles or so from OrbitalVentures headquarters. Sir Alexander had put her up there while she arranged to have her belongings shipped back to Oregon. *Are you ok?* Hellmund texted her. *I wanted to bring you home from the hospital.*

I'm ok, she texted back. *I just need another day to rest first.*

From her window she watched the families splashing in the pool and wondered what kind of person would visit Palmdale in July. It was still 102 degrees at seven o'clock in the evening.

Perhaps, she thought, these were all families passing through on their way to some other place.

Her belongings—what was left of them, anyway—formed a tidy pile at the foot of the hotel bed: three BRIC-X units, bulky as dorm fridges; her laptop; both her own cell phone and Erik Rasmussen's; inexplicably, the pistol in the duct tape holster she had fashioned. And, she realized, whoever had pulled her BRIC-X units from the lab must have known her, or perhaps had simply had an uncanny intuition: her weathered Oregon State Beavers cap sat atop the middle BRIC-X.

She was surprised that the gun had not been confiscated by law enforcement. She supposed that it wasn't clear what police department would have had jurisdiction over *Imperium*. At any rate, for all she knew, the company had handled the ordeal in-house. Handled it up to this point, anyway—she knew that someone would be knocking on her door sooner or later with a bunch of questions. There were two rounds left in the magazine.

All her personal effects—her clothes, her toiletries, her journal, the photos and magnets and knickknacks from her cabin—had been destroyed with *Imperium*. There was a new pair of shorts, a peasant blouse, a pair of sandals, all very Southern California, all in her size, that Sir Alexander had given her to leave LA General with; someone at OrbitalVentures had bought her another change of clothes, which hung by the door. The company knew all her measurements.

She took a little walk. Nothing strenuous—once outside, she could feel her wrist under her cast growing swampy with sweat. She stopped in at a drugstore, bought a phone charger, toiletries, a spray bottle to mist her seedlings.

She received a text that evening: *Hey, it's Kassie. I hope it's ok that Sir Alexander gave me your number.*

Where are you? Chloe texted back.

They just let me out. I'm staying with a friend in Whittier for a few days until I can fly home.

The two texted, then spoke, late into the night, talking about what they had seen.

It was a couple more days before Chloe felt up to taking an Uber out to Hellmund's place. He lived way out in Tehachapi, nearer to the OrbitalVentures launch center. The ride had cost nearly a hundred dollars one way, an expense she would have blanched at in another life. But she had had no rent to pay, no groceries to buy, during her months on *Imperium*, all while her checks from the university had been stacking up in her bank account Earthside. A hundred-dollar Uber ride felt like nothing.

Hellmund wrapped her up in a long hug as soon as she stepped up his front walk. Her head swam a little, either from the heat or from the vigor of the embrace, or perhaps just from seeing him again.

"I'm worried about you, Chlo," he said.

They walked together into his house, a sprawling Spanish colonial revival surrounded by an expanse of California juniper and creosote that threatened to stretch to the horizon. The crushing heat of the day was drifting toward a stifling blue evening.

"Can you stay?" he asked.

"Not long," she said. "But I definitely wanted to see you."

He was leading her through the house toward the back, talking now, chattering, about what had gone through his mind during the crisis, as he led her through the tiled living room. She followed him down the hallway that gave on to his study, the hallway she had seen in the background of the Skype call she and Kassie had made from *Imperium*'s fitness center. The clay masks were arrayed there on hooks, like a wall of portraits, each face frozen in grim ferocity.

As she followed behind, she plucked one of the masks from its hook on the wall. Hellmund, still talking, took no notice.

They came out on the patio, where they had once watched the stars at a party out by the pool, just before her launch. Now the place was quiet: there were two pool chairs, his cell phone lying on the seat of one, an ice bucket of beers like a mirage in the heat. "On second thought, I'm not so sure about the patio," Hellmund said absently, looking out at the pool. "We may need to wait inside until it cools off a little more."

The last time she had stood in this spot, the night before the launch, she had wondered whether she would ever look at the sky the same way when she came back. She had been wise to be skeptical. She saw Hellmund's phone light up on the pool chair as someone texted him. "Whatever you say, Tsadok," she said.

Hellmund snapped around to look at her then. His expression, startled at first, migrated slowly into something warier—perhaps skepticism, perhaps sarcasm. He seemed aware for the first time of the mask she had taken down and cradled in the crook of her cast. It was the pale, narrow-eyed face that had been Tsadok's avatar on the Crypsis app.

"That's my property," he said quietly, his voice riding over a dark undertow of emotion.

"I think there are some investigators who will want to have a look at it."

Hellmund remained frozen, staring at the mask. Chloe felt as though she could see a current of his thoughts making a bleak circuit behind his eyes. His hand shot out for his waistband. But Chloe had her pistol out and pointed at him before he could finish reaching for his own gun.

"Careful, Ron. I'm pretty jittery lately."

Hellmund seemed to regard his situation with disbelief. His mouth was a rigid line, unreadable in a way totally at odds with what she remembered of him, as alien to her prior vision of him as his hologram had been during the opening gala in the Fortuna Ballroom. Now he seemed a brittle, prematurely old man, rootless and drifting. The ice in the beer bucket collapsed into a new metastable configuration with a liquid rattling sound.

"You wouldn't shoot me, Chlo," he whispered.

"No, I wouldn't," she said. "But I wouldn't do a lot of things that I did."

He sat down on his pool chair, his shoulders rounded like a sandstone column subjected to an age of erosion. He stared at the muzzle of her gun, or perhaps beyond that at the mask in the crook of her arm. "Things got out of hand. I'm sorry."

"Ron, what happened up there?" Chloe knew as soon as she asked the question that she was hoping for an answer that he wouldn't be able to give. After all, he had not been there.

"You were never meant to be harmed. Those idiots had strict instructions."

"Instructions for what? To steal eight billion dollars for you?"

"It wasn't like that. The money wasn't for me."

"For the Reckoners, then?"

"What they do with the money is their business now. I was just a backer who gave them a tip about the operation."

"A backer. Awesome. The Reckoners are just another start-up for you."

"Believe it or not, I agree with their aims, Chloe. What they are doing is just wealth redistribution by other means."

Chloe took in Hellmund's explanation, delivered in that lecturing tone of his that made any pronouncement, no matter how ridiculous, sound like a self-evident truth. She felt the ten thousand square feet of Hellmund's house stretching off in every direction behind her. "And so you destroyed your own station to squeeze a few billionaires out of a tiny fraction of their money."

"*Imperium* was never supposed to be destroyed." His voice took on a pained whine that she had never heard from him in all the time they had dated. He looked down from the gun at the stillness of the swimming pool. "And it wasn't my station anymore."

Chloe regarded this last statement as some melodramatic bullshit about how he had lost creative control of the project. Only slowly did it begin to dawn on her that he was speaking literally.

"Alexander Dunne was going to have me forced out of the company," he said.

"Lots of people get forced out of their own companies, Ron. You take the payout and move on. Start another company. You don't shoot a bunch of people and blow up your life's work."

"It was supposed to be a simple hostage taking, Chloe—nobody was to be hurt. If it had gone the way it was supposed to, the stock value of Dunne's new company would have cratered, and a handful of choice assholes would be somewhat less rich. That's all."

She noticed that he had said nothing about the deaths of Konrad and Pasquale and Noelle. Had their killing also been some deviation from the plan? The sense grew in her that she had never really known Ronald Hellmund.

But looking down at him now as he sat with his head in his hands, Chloe knew that she wasn't going to shoot him. "I'm going, Ron." She backed away toward the patio door to the house, her weapon still trained on him.

Hellmund watched her leave.

Chloe backed through the house, went out the front door, walked up the road a long way before she holstered her pistol again. She walked one more block to where the Uber waited for her, running its engine wastefully into the night.

She climbed into the front passenger seat. "Let's go," she said to the driver.

She looked over her shoulder into the back seats as the car began its winding descent to the highway. Kassie Ng reclined there, her leg stretched across the seat in a full cast. "Did you get it?" she asked.

Chloe pulled off her old OSU cap. The tiny camera they had affixed to one of the eyelets was still running, sending its feed to a phone in her pocket: Kassie Ng's phone. She switched off the camera, pulled out Kassie's phone, handed both over the back seat to Kassie.

Kassie replayed a few seconds of the video. Chloe listened to Hellmund's plaintive explanation again from where she sat; he sounded both like and totally unlike himself. "The sound quality isn't great," Kassie said, "but we can definitely post this."

"You know, I never took you for a muckraker—all your new fans must be going to your head."

"You have to capitalize on your exposure," Kassie answered, tapping out something on the phone. "Thirty million followers aren't going to want to see another hedgehog video."

Kassie held the screen of her phone up for Chloe. "Do you want to do the honors?"

Chloe tapped the blue *Share* link.

Chloe wondered, as she looked back at Kassie, what had been accomplished beyond their survival, beyond sending Hellmund to jail. Already the likes, shares, and saves began tallying at the bottom of the video, before anyone could possibly have even finished watching it. Kassie looked back at her with the vague, amoral smile of a supremely self-possessed businessperson.

Ronald Hellmund sat where Chloe had left him, contemplating the patio and the silent pool. He had enjoyed living here. He would miss it.

Only much later did he remember his phone lying behind him on the pool chair. He picked it up, read the text he had just received. It was from his inside person—the one who, like him, was due a share of the money.

Better lie low for a while, he texted. He knew that investigators sooner or later would get their mitts on his phone records. But she was also a long way away by now.

EPILOGUE

Viv Volterra reached over to the other pool chair, where her phone had chirped in the blazing azure morning. *Better lie low for a while*, the text read.

Her mind drifted in a lazy swirl of feelings as she stared off, beyond the pool, beyond the chapel, sweeping her eyes up the hill to the silent, museum-like hotel above. Part of what she felt—if she were the type to analyze her emotions with any delicacy—was a wistfulness for Ron. Not a lot of people had been giving her the time of day when he'd shown up. Her company had imploded; the banks were treating her like some kind of homeless person who had come in to beg for change. The late-night talk show circuit, those people who had been fawning and creaming their pants over her a year before, decided all at once that she was nothing more than a punch line for the opening monologue. Ron didn't have to be nice to her then, but he was.

Had he wanted something from her? Sure. But he was a good lay. And he had needed someone, someone like her, that didn't mind suiting up for some dirty work. She knew how to use her powers of persuasion, keep the hostages—the rich ones, anyway—from doing anything stupid, keep them interested in paying up. And for playing her part, $50 million worth of crypto and a one-way trip beyond the reach of the SEC and the DOJ.

She was sorry not to be seeing him again. Yet wistfulness was only part of what she felt. Even she was not so cool as to be unmoved by her change of fortune. No matter how lonely, this was better by far than her raft of indictments. Most places without an extradition treaty to the United States were shithole countries; here, though, here wasn't so bad. Fifty million dollars would buy a lot of margaritas in Villings.

ACKNOWLEDGMENTS

More people helped me with *Exit Black* than I can say here. Over many lonely days when I stared at the wall and tried to string words together—or wandered around trying to understand Chloe and Dion's predicament—I received words of encouragement and gestures of support from so many people that I know I will fail to remember all the ways that they helped me. But you helped me. Thank you.

The following people had special roles in this book. First, to Brendan Deneen and Scott Veltri: Thank you for selling me on the idea of revisiting *Die Hard* on a luxury orbital hotel; also, thank you both for your willingness to have me approach the story in my own way, as a meditation on the limits of violence. I am grateful to both of you for your generous reading of my work and for your invaluable feedback and cheerleading throughout the process.

Thank you to readers of early chapters and drafts for your advice and encouragement: Jim Finley, Toby Peterson, Ann Eames, Phil Ekstrom, and Sandy Sanderson. Special thanks to my brother Paul Pitkin for insight into the vagaries of large money transfers. I tried to make good use of the advice I was given; any unrealistic elements in the book are either my mistake or sleight of hand in service of the story, the equivalent of *Star Trek*'s dilithium crystals.

Many, many thanks to the whole team at Blackstone Publishing: managing editor Ananda Finwall, editorial director Josie Woodbridge, publicist Sarah Bonamino, compositor Joe Garcia, line editor Riam Griswold, and interior and cover-art designer Alex Cruz. You have taken a scuffed-up manuscript and polished it into a beautiful book—it's an honor to work with you.

Thank you to my daughters for listening while I blathered and pontificated about this story during the drafting process. I got the idea for Chloe—and for her mental toughness—from you.

Finally, and most importantly, thank you to my wife, Carlyn, for your patience and your forbearance, and for being my first and most generous reader of the early drafts. You figured out how the characters are connected to one another better than I was able to.